Peril in PALM BEACH

a Beach House Mystery

Seth Sjostrom

Beach House
Mysteries

wolfprintMedia, LLC
Hernando Beach, FL 34607

For information, contact wolfprintMedia, LLC.

Trade Paperback
ISBN-13: 978-1-960501-26-4

1. Kate Harper (Fictitious character)-Fiction. 2. Nick Mason (Fictitious character)-Fiction. 3. Mystery-Thriller- Fiction. 3. Beach House Mysteries Series-Fiction 4. Peril in Palm Beach-Title.

First wolfprintMedia edition 2025.

wolfprintMedia is a trademark of wolfprint, LLC.

For information regarding bulk purchases, please contact wolfprintMedia, LLC at wolfprint@hotmail.com.

United States of America

Peril in PALM BEACH

Kathi, my eternal partner in crime (fighting).

Editor and word aficionado Hilary Turner.

My team at wolfprintMedia and Beach House Mysteries.

Cassie VanLangen for being a willing participant.

Michelle Goss for playing. I did as I was instructed.

My Hallmark, Christmas Con and Great American Family friends.

My reader friends that I have been blessed to meet over the years. You keep reading and enjoying, I'll keep writing!

Peril in PALM BEACH

One

The coastal breeze brought scents of hibiscus and orange blossoms as it swept through the lush estate grounds. The air had been heavy and dull until the wind blew in without warning. Shards of moonlight playing on the incoming tide were slowly veiled as a shelf cloud rolled in overhead. The crashing waves gaining in intensity were overmatched by the earth-shaking rumble of thunder.

The figure perched on the wall didn't mind the storm. The diminishing light and cover noise was certainly helpful, though the figure leaping off the wall and stealing across the opulent lawn didn't need that extra help.

Moving with great stealth and without hesitation, the figure moved between flashes of lightning. Skillfully avoiding the security cameras as had been rehearsed so many times in their head, they reached the sidewall of the beachfront mansion. Overconfidence in the front-facing cameras left this portion of the estate exposed, affording luxurious time to navigate the ascent up the side of the house.

From the welcoming garden trellis, the leap to the raised air conditioning compressor balcony, a staple on Florida homes, was easy. The next leap, a twelve-foot expanse to the guest room veranda was a more challenging traverse. Removing a telescoping fishing gaff, from its holder on the tactical backpack and extending it its full 15 feet, the figure then wedged it under one of the compressors while the other end was carefully laid on the target balcony.

With one reassuring breath, the figure knelt and grasped the pole with both hands before swinging over the edge. Legs dangling in the air, one hand preceded the other. Large raindrops began pelting down, coating the surface of the pole, making it precariously slick.

Each grasp required a fervent grip to avoid a lengthy fall and subsequent capture. Relieved to reach the balcony, the figure hoisted themselves onto the deck. The lock on the overlooked second-story balcony was effortless to dispose of.

As the door slowly swung open, a flash of light from the incoming storm revealed an empty room. A quick scan showed little of interest. Wiping wet shoes on what was likely an incredibly expensive rug, the figure stepped quietly to the bedroom door. Opening it slowly, they peered down the hall, ensuring the lights in the house were off.

Taking careful steps, the figure moved through the house. Finding the stairs that would lead them to payday, they used the rumble of thunder to move quickly. Reaching the master suite, snores echoed through the room in between claps of thunder. The person snoring wasn't much of a concern. The unfortunate wife with disturbed sleep lying next to her husband's cacophony was a risk.

With a calming breath, the figure proceeded. Reaching the massive master closet, the door was quietly closed. The soft blue LEDs from the pearlescent safe in the back of the closet was all the light the figure needed.

Moving to the safe, the figure removed the fascia of the digital lock. Inserting a probe until perceiving the subtle feel of a needle pressing into a wire, they connected the probe to an auto dialer that ran through thousands of combinations in a matter of seconds. Pressing an ear against the enamel-coated steel, the figure was rewarded with the sound of gears moving and locking rods pulling free from their holds.

Swinging the heavy door open, the figure found that the soft LEDs allowed for easy inspection. Ignoring the top items, gloved hands searched deep into the safe and along the bottom. Setting aside several watches and boxes of jewelry, a simple, leather-covered box was removed.

The box was placed into the backpack and the safe was politely relocked with the probe removed. The thunderstorm, seemingly directly overhead, made exit from the closet easy.

As thunder cracked, a seizing snore momentarily woke the man in the bed before a tap from his wife urged him to roll over, clearly a long-engrained response. Pressing deep into the shadows, the figure watched as the pair quickly melted back to sleep.

Not waiting for a second disturbance, the burglar wrapped their body around the door frame and into the hall. Quickly moving to the stairs toward the guest room used for entry, the thief froze. A light on the second floor had been turned on.

Peering carefully over the rail, the burglar saw a man in a robe climbing the steps from the ground floor, a box of crackers and glass of water cradled in his hands. The man seemed to have forgot something and spun on the stairs, retreating toward the first floor.

Leaping at the opportunity and in the shroud of a house-shaking thunderclap, the thief raced down the steps with scarcely a sound and slipped into the guest bedroom. Closing the door behind them, they moved quickly to the window and reversed the process from their entry.

The storm in full fury made for a well-concealed but also slippery traverse of the extended pole connecting the guest room veranda to the air-conditioning platform. Resting the guest room portion of the pole on the lower rung of the veranda handrail made for a slight angle. Aided by the torrential rain Florida storms were well known for, the thief was able to quickly slide to the platform. Without taking the time to climb up, they removed the from under the compressor and with one hand, the thief scrambled down the garden trellis.

Once more, timing their movement in between lightning strikes and avoiding the security camera angles, the thief disappeared into the night, their prize in hand.

Two

Kate Harper followed the GPS map on her dash along Florida's A1A Highway. Splitting the lushly appointed fairways of the Ocean Course at the Breakers and past the iconic luxury hotel's gated entrance, she slowed. The marker on her map showed that she was close to her destination.

Turning east toward the ocean a short drive led her to a massive, ornate gate.

Kate double-checked the address on her screen with the address on the column that supported the ornate gate her navigation system placed her in front of.

"This is the place… right next to the Breakers. Wow!" Kate whistled.

Before she could press the call button, the gate swung open.

Kate put her SUV in drive and accelerated softly down the palm-lined driveway. Lush green lawns flashed between the tropical trees. The drive curved gently to reveal an enormous stucco mansion flanked by jaw-dropping views of the Atlantic Ocean. Winding around a gurgling fountain with playful dolphins cast in a wave, she parked at the base of the steps leading to the front door.

Stepping out, Kate paused to take in the spectacle of the grand house. The two-story, sprawling home was encased in stone and coral. Majestic palms lined the exterior while vines crawled their way up and around pillars.

The large, double doors of the house opened wide. A sunny, well-dressed woman descended the steps, "You made it!"

"I did," Kate nodded. Her eyes scanned the estate, "Merilu, this place is… *amazing.*"

"Wait until you see inside, it's not to be outdone by the magnificent views out back," Kate's boss said. "Come on, I'll give you the tour."

Merilu escorted Kate through the massive doors of the mansion. Stone and coral floors and walls gave the space a substantial, yet cool feel. A curving staircase led to the upper floors while alcoves provided space for miniature indoor palm trees. Stepping farther inside, Kate appreciated that the grand staircase did little to hide the sweeping views of the Atlantic.

Hints of aqua blue in the furnishings and drapery matched the water, which was deservedly the primary focal point of the entry, and the effect spilled throughout much of the mansion.

Kate's eyes swept through the house as Merilu led her along. She found the décor tasteful yet, somehow, out of place. The house felt more European castle than Mediterranean-style beach house.

As they passed a room to the left of the entry, Merilu said, "This is the office. You are welcome to use it as your command center if you like."

Opposite the office was a sitting room. All of the furniture was placed in a conversational arrangement, each piece facing inward toward the others. Kate couldn't imagine the room being used when the rest of the house had sweeping ocean views.

Merilu slowed her pace as they entered the main living area.

Kate gazed around as she found herself in a massive living space. A wall of windows and French doors led to a sprawling patio overlooking the ocean. A long, curving sofa took up the center of the room.

"That has to be the largest piece of furniture I have ever seen," Kate said.

"It was assembled in place by an Italian designer," Merilu said.

"I see. I can't wait to see what budget I get to play with," Kate said.

Merilu laughed.

On one side of the living area was a magnificent fireplace that took up a large portion of the wall and yet somehow managed to not take over the room. All eyes were held by the bank of windows and the glistening afternoon sun shining off of the Atlantic.

The other side of the living space was a large bar that opened up into a kitchen large enough to operate a restaurant. A massive white slab of marble sat upon matching white cabinetry. The kitchen, too, was cast all in white. Save for the stainless-steel range and hood, the only color came from a basket of tropical fruit and trimming from one of the estate's many palm trees.

"This is quite the spread," Kate said, her hands fanned out along the back of one of the white, leather bar stools.

"It's kind of a blank canvas, isn't it?" Merilu asked.

"It isn't exactly offensive, but there is so much more potential to be brought to life," Kate said.

Merilu grinned, "That is why I brought you here."

Kate nodded as her eyes swept the room.

"The estate is known to be the home of Palm Beach's most exclusive soirees," Merilu said.

"I hope red wine is off the menu," Kate said, her hands sliding along the white furniture.

Merilu laughed. With a wave of her hand, she said, "Come on, I'll show you upstairs."

With a nod, Kate followed Merilu up one of the curving banks of stairs. Poking their heads inside several rooms along the way, each large enough to be a master in any other home, Merilu paused with Kate outside of a pair of doors, "This is the master suite. You are welcome to make yourself home in it until it's turn for renovation. If you time it right, you can just hop to one of the other rooms."

Kate moved in tight little steps, making a sweeping pirouette. Her eyes danced around the room and she gasped, "This room is larger than my last condo."

Flowing through the suite and its massive canopy bed, chaise lounge, sofa and private balcony, Kate peered out as waves splashed against the rocks and spilled onto the beach below.

Her head spun.

"You up for the challenge?" Merilu asked.

"It's a little overwhelming. Everything is already exquisite," Kate said.

"The owner is hoping with your touch, the house will feel lighter. More beach vacation, less stuffy chateau," Merilu said.

"Owner…" Kate pondered. A series of clues from her tour bounced through her head. The large bouquet of hibiscus flowers reminded Kate of a particular fragrance. The subtle appliques carved into the fireplace and the large bar area. Kate knew she had seen them before. They weren't random designs. Suddenly her eyes burst wide, "This house belongs to Cassie VanLangen."

"Your keen sleuthing skills never disappoint," Merilu smiled. "Cassie is a friend of mine. When she decided to work on this project, she asked if I knew someone. I instantly thought of you."

"Thank you, it… it is an honor," Kate said.

"I don't know if honor is the right word, but I hope you find my home hospitable," a voice called from the doorway. Cassie VanLangen stood just inside the master bedroom. A pair of sunglasses were sandwiched between two fingers. Her flawless skin gleamed in the deep vee of her sundress. To Kate, she looked like a model ready for a photo shoot.

"Cassie, meet Kate Harper. Kate has an amazing eye for making homes feel elegant, playful, and comfortable all at the same time. Kate, Cassie VanLangen," Merilu introduced the pair.

"Your home is lovely," Kate said.

Cassie eyed Kate for a moment and cocked her head, "Honeysuckle with just a hint of warm amber."

Kate flushed, "Had I known, I would have worn *Eau de Palmier*. It's one of my favorites, I uh, kind of save it for special occasions."

Cassie laughed, "It's all right. I happen to be sporting a lovely fragrance of coconut and UV protectants, myself."

"Your home is already so lovely," Kate gushed.

"It looks like it belongs to a cosmetics mogul. I would rather it looks more like…. Well, a cosmetics mogul on vacation," Cassie laughed.

Kate smiled, "I think I can help you out with that."

"I am having some extensive renovations done. I was hoping you could follow the construction crews and tackle rooms as they were completed. I am hoping the house can be the site of an upcoming fragrance launch party, so we are just a little bit on the clock," Cassie said.

"Absolutely," Kate nodded.

Cassie glanced at her watch, "Speaking of vacation time, I think it is time for chilled beverages by the pool. I hope you two will join me."

Kate started to speak but Merilu stepped in, "We'd love to. I'll help Kate get settled. I'll help her find something more suitable for the patio and we'll be right out."

"I'll have Gustavo put something on ice," Cassie said.

"Gustavo?" Kate asked.

"Cassie's steward," Merilu said. "Kind of a right hand, chef, sommelier, barista…"

Kate laughed, "Of course. Don't we all have a Gustavo?"

"Speaking of housemen, it's too bad Nick couldn't make it," Merilu said, a wary brow raised.

Kate stiffened and blushed, "He is helping a friend restore a sailboat up in Cape May, New Jersey."

Merilu eyed Kate, "It's okay. I am as much your friend as I am your boss. I want you happy. I see a sparkle when you talk about him. Your cheeks are flushed."

Kate's cheeks only grew a deeper hue of crimson.

"Well, let's get you settled and meet Cassie out by the pool. She takes her poolside cocktail hour very serious," Merilu said.

Three

Kate pulled her luggage in from the car and hurriedly slipped into a flowy sundress. Hurrying out to the patio, she met Merilu and Cassie by the pool.

Cassie looked over the rim of her large, amber-tinted sunglasses, "Now you look much more Palm Beach ready."

The whir of a blender sounded from a corner of the patio. A middle-aged man with olive skin worked behind a small bar.

"I hope you like mango. Gustavo makes the most delicious, fresh-pressed mango mojitos," Cassie said.

"That sounds marvelous," Kate said, her eyes taking a visual tour of the estate's back yard. The moment she stepped out onto the back patio, she was overwhelmed by the commanding views of the ocean and the gleaming pool that seemed to melt into the Atlantic. In a corner of the property, a large gazebo stood sentry with views of the ocean.

Gustavo brought a tray of mojitos over to the women. He offered a friendly nod and smile toward Kate, "And who is this lovely lady?"

"Gustavo, meet Kate Harper. She'll be putting the finishing touches on the redesign while I'm gone. Please treat her as a guest during her stay," Cassie said.

"I shall ensure she is well cared for," Gustavo assured.

"You are in for a treat. Gustavo is a world-class cook and knows his way around a cocktail, too," Cassie said.

"No complaints here," Merilu said, taking a sip of her mojito.

The three melted into their chase lounges as the cool drinks made their way past their lips.

"Ms. VanLangen, your house is gorgeous," Kate said.

"It's Cassie, and thank you. After the way Merilu raves about you, I can't wait to see what fresh spin you put on things," Cassie said.

"I'm excited to get started," Kate said. Craning her head toward the house, she asked, "What sort of renovations do you have planned? I'd like to work them into my ideas."

Cassie shrugged, "New flooring throughout. The flooring here was laid during a time when dark woods were all the rage. I want something lighter. I want to feel at the beach even when I am inside."

"I like that," Kate said.

Merilu smiled, "I knew you would."

"I would like new hardware and fixtures as well. I was hoping you could have a hand in their selection?"

"Of course," Kate nodded. She squinted over her mojito as the late-afternoon sun managed to find a line between the roof of the house and the slats of the pergola.

"Would you like a hat?" Cassie asked, her fingers tapping the brim of her own wide-brim sun hat.

"No, thank you. I should have grabbed my sunglasses. If you'll excuse me, I'll run up and grab them really quick," Kate said.

"Of course. I'll have Gustavo rustle up some caprese and perhaps a second round," Cassie swirled the ice in her otherwise empty glass.

Kate headed upstairs, jogging down the hall toward the master bedroom. Her eyes fought to adjust from the bright sunshine outdoors to the muted light of the tinted windows.

Pushing into the master bedroom, Kate leapt back as a figure was stooped over her bed rifling through her bag.

Easing forward, she observed as the figure quickly move on from the bag and turned their attention to Cassie's dresser drawer. Disappointed to find they were cleaned out for the renovation, the figure stood up.

"Can I help you?" Kate asked. She readied herself for confrontation.

The figure stiffened before slowly turning to face Kate.

Instinctively, Kate took a half step toward the doorway.

As the figure completed their turn, Kate found a man wearing a surprisingly pleasant smile, "Well, this is embarrassing."

"That is one possible word for it. Might I ask what you are doing rifling through my things?" Kate demanded.

"I… I didn't realize they were yours," the man defended himself, a distinct British accent in his voice.

"Okay. Mind telling me what you are doing rifling through *Cassie's* things?" Kate pressed.

The man took a step forward. Kate took another half of a step back.

Holding his hands in front of him, the man waved, "I am a friend of Cassie's. I lost something here at… at her last get-together. I was hoping to find it."

"In a bag on a bed? Clearly, you knew it wasn't *your* bag," Kate asked.

"I thought it was Cassie's, right or wrong," the man shrugged.

"This seems like something you should talk to Cassie about," Kate said with scrutinizing eyes.

The man flushed, "It is of a rather… personal nature. I was hoping to collect it without a fuss. I'm sorry, who are you?"

Kate bristled, "You are going through my things in someone else's house of which I am guest, I think I'd rather know who *you* are first."

"I suppose that is fair. My name is Henrique Despereaux. I am a friend of Cassie's. And at one point, quite more than that," His jovial face fell melancholy as he spoke. "That is what brings me here, as you say, rifling through her things. Or your things, as it were. It seems I am late once again."

"Again?" Kate frowned.

"Never mind. I don't suppose you know what happened to her things?" Despereaux asked.

"No. The house is about to go through some renovations. I believe everything was packed up. As I said, whatever it is you need, you'll have to get it from Cassie," Kate said.

The man's face fell even lower, "I see."

Henrique Desperaux eyed Kate for a moment as if there were more that she was going to concede in the conversation. When it was clear Kate had nothing or would reveal nothing further, he gave a polite nod and started to walk out of the room.

"Hold on. Where, exactly, do you think you are going?" Kate asked.

The man offered a look that was a mischievous as it was contrite.
"I, uh, I was hoping to make a quiet exit?"

"Oh no. You can't waltz into someone's home and…"

"Technically, I was afforded access," Despereaux said.

Kate cocked her head. Despereaux held out a key, dangling it from his fingers, "And my gate code apparently still works. De facto permission, really."

Kate's glare bespoke her steadfast position.

"Henrique! What are you doing here?" a voice called from the top of the stairs.

Kate turned to find Merilu striding toward them. She called out, "I came up to see what has kept you. Now I know."

"Merilu. What a divine pleasure," Despereaux smiled a wickedly pleasant smile.

"For you, perhaps. Does Cassie know you are here?" Merilu asked, her voice sharp.

"I was just explaining to… I'm sorry, I never did your name," Despereaux smiled at Kate.

"I'll give it when I find you the slightest bit credible," Kate snapped.

Merilu chuckled, "At least our resident sleuth is on to you before your charms were able to muddy her mind."

"Sleuth, huh? Perhaps I can solicit your services?" the man asked.

Kate looked at Merilu who shook her head.

"Perhaps you should come at a time when you are announced and ring the doorbell. Then we can talk about any proposed services," Kate said. With an arm held out, she motioned for Despereaux to leave the master bedroom.

Snatching her glasses from the top of the bureau, Kate joined Merilu in marching Desperaux down the stairs.

"All the way out, Henrique," Merilu said as Despereaux paused at the front door.

His shoulders slumped, "Adieu, ladies."

Kate and Merilu stood at the doorway, watching the man climb into his red Jaguar convertible and drive down the long palm treelined driveway.

Kate looked at Merilu.

"Oh, Henrique is a third or fourth cocktail conversation," Merilu said. "I will speak with Cassie about her gate code and misappropriated house keys."

"What was he doing here? He said he was looking for something," Kate said.

"Henrique has a long, silver-tongued history with Cassie. And a longer list of swooned conquests in his wake," Merilu said. "Come on, I think I need Gustavo to pour a bit heavier if we are to have this conversation."

Four

Cassie laughed off the tale of Desperaux's intrusion.

"I have to give it to Henrique," she said. "He doesn't give up easily. I will have Gustavo change the gate code and ensure lock changes are part of the remodel plans."

Despite twisting ever so slightly in her seat, the cosmetics mogul yielded no further insight into the strange, if charming, man that Kate had caught rummaging through the master bedroom.

When afternoon cocktails melted into dinner at sunset, the conversation about Henrique Desperaux had been completely put to rest.

Kate's curiosity was left unsatisfied but deemed it not her business to continue to pry. She found it difficult to stay fixated on her questions given the remarkable location anyway. Instead, she soaked up the evening with Merilu and Cassie.

Gustavo had set out an array of appetizers for them. Toast points with crab dip, homemade hummus and avocado fries.

"You eat like this every day?" Kate asked. "Gustavo is an amazing chef."

"No, though he'd like to cook like this for me all the time. Many days the menu is made up green smoothies and salads," Cassie admitted. "But, sharing the evening with friends is a special occasion. Speaking of special occasions, I am hosting one final party before the renovation begins. You must join us."

Kate winced, "I don't think I packed for a gala."

"We'll go shopping tomorrow. My treat. It will be fun!" Merilu interjected.

"Splendid!" Cassie raised her glass. "To strong women and strong drinks. I think Gustavo is showing off a bit with his creations."

"All the fresh squeezed fruit comes straight from estate trees and my favorite rum," Gustavo said.

"Oh, I wasn't complaining, Gustavo. It is a merry evening," Cassie giggled.

Gustavo seemed satisfied with the response as he sat down plates of miso-glazed butterfish. Long strands of gently seared broccolini lined the edge of the tender fish.

"This looks delicious," Kate said. "Was it caught locally?"

"I grabbed the butterfish straight from the docks in West Palm," Gustavo affirmed. "Please, enjoy."

As Gustavo disappeared, the ladies dove into their plates.

"This is like a permanent vacation," Merilu said.

Cassie nodded toward a building on the far corner of the property that looked like a mini version of the main house, "I have offered you the guest house many times. It doesn't get used often, outside of storing my things during the renovation."

"I am enjoying staying there for this visit," Merilu said. "The waves crashing right outside my balcony is heaven."

"I love the private beach. You two should be sure to enjoy that while you're here. Just check in with Gustavo before you go. He can tell you about the surf conditions and anything else you might need to be aware of. Plus, he'll check up on you and make sure you stay hydrated," Cassie said.

"He is such a catch," Merilu said.

"He was a good find. Great at his job and pleasant to have around," Cassie agreed. Sliding her half-eaten meal and empty cocktail glass forward, she said, "Well, ladies, I am going to head to bed. I need to get my beauty sleep."

"Well, you are the queen of beauty," Merilu quipped.

"Now you know my secret," Cassie smiled. "Help yourself. The run of the estate is yours."

"Goodnight, Cassie," Kate said.

Merilu shot a glance at Kate, "Evening swim?"

"I think the day in the sun has tuckered me out. I am going to stare at the waves for a while," Kate said.

"If you change your mind, the water is fabulous," Merilu said, excusing herself from the table.

Kate nodded and watched Merilu walk away. Pivoting, her eyes locked onto the incoming surf as it pounded the shoreline. The short jetty that created the private beach for Cassie's estate provided a source for large waves that were enjoyable to watch shoot high into the air.

The evening moon provided plenty of light to allow nighttime watching. Its glow glistened off the water creating a beam that stretched out from the beach and disappeared as it reached for the horizon.

Kate settled into a blissful state. Letting her arms fall heavy on the armrests of her chair, her hand glanced off her phone. The flashing light of a missed message caught her eye. Sliding the phone open with her thumb, she saw that Nick had texted her hours ago.

Instinctively readying to prepare a reply, her finger hovered over the keys. She eyed the time. It had gotten late. Electing not to disturb Nick, she closed her phone.

Fingers tapping, she argued with herself, wanting to reach back out to him.

Sticking to her decision, she stood up and decided to call it a night herself. She would call Nick in the morning.

Heading into the house, Kate made her way to the enormous master suite. Tossing open the doors to the balcony, she let the rhythmic pounding of the surf fill the room like music. The soft Atlantic breeze played with the sheer curtains making them dance lightly in the air.

Plopping arms spread wide on the king-size bed, Kate felt like she was in a spa.

"No," she said to herself. "I've never been this relaxed in a spa."

Staring at the slow-moving blades of the ceiling fan Kate listened to the waves. The curtains occasionally licked their way into her peripheral vision.

Shaking off the oceanic lullaby, she forced herself to roll off the bed and reluctantly run through her nighttime routine. Brushing her teeth and smoothing lotion over her sun kissed skin, Kate was satisfied enough to allow her weary legs to wander back to the bed and let the lavish coastal escape lull her to sleep.

Five

Kate awoke in nearly the same wide, flailed limb shape she had fallen fell into bed with.

Sun streamed through her east-facing windows, teasing another warm Florida day. A morning breeze helped to moderate the heat and temper the humidity.

With a yawn and a stretch, Kate climbed out of bed. Hearing the tinkling of dishware, she cocked her head and made her way to the bedroom door.

Cracking it open, she found a tray of croissants, fruit, fresh squeezed Florida orange juice and, much to Kate's delight, a carafe of coffee. Scanning down the hall, she could scarcely understand how its deliverer had disappeared so quickly.

Kicking the door the rest of the way open, Kate lifted the tray and transported it do the balcony through the doors she had left open all night long.

Setting the tray next to a small table by the balcony, Kate settled in for breakfast alongside the sweeping views of Cassie VanLangen's estate.

Pouring herself a cup of coffee, she peered over the edge of the balcony rail. Cassie and Merilu raised their mimosa glasses in the air as good morning to Kate.

Enjoying her perch, Kate hesitated to relocate, but felt awkward eating while looking over them. Taking several quick bites of her croissant, she refilled her coffee cup and abandoned her breakfast spot.

Heading downstairs and out on the patio, Kate joined Cassie and Merilu with a meek smile.

Cassie took a sip of her mimosa and smiled, "I trust you slept well. I instructed Gustavo to bring you breakfast, it looks like he was right on time."

"It was delicious. Thank you," Kate said.

"The architect will be here in an hour. He would like to go over the plans with you and get your thoughts," Merilu said.

"Yes, I would love your opinion before we launch fully into the renovation," Cassie said. Her eyes brightened, "But first, one final celebration. I'll be here in the guest house for two more days and then I am off to Paris. You are welcome to bedroom hop in the main house for the renovation or take up residence in the guest house. You stay wherever you are more comfortable."

"Thank you," Kate said. "I appreciate the flexibility. I'll play off the needs of the construction crew and ensure I am out of the way."

"I take off the same day as Cassie, so you will have the grounds to yourself. Along with Gustavo and the renovation crew during the day," Merilu said.

Kate swallowed a little hard as her eyes swept the sprawling estate, "I'll take good care of the property."

"I know you will. I am looking forward to the debut gala when it is all finished," Cassie said. She nodded toward the pitcher of orange juice and champagne, "Shall we pour you a glass?"

"I think I should get ready for the day," Kate said, excusing herself.

"When you are done with the contractor, we'll head out dress shopping," Merilu called.

Kate nodded, "It sounds fun."

She felt both excited and awkward about the idea of her boss take her dress shopping. Kate shook off a flashback from a good many years prior of shopping with her mother. The thought only made Kate feel even less comfortable but she managed to squeeze out a smile just the same.

Walking briskly away, Kate disappeared inside the sanctuary of the main house.

Showered and slipped into a flowy sundress, Kate headed back toward the gazebo. Her phone buzzed in her hand. Looking down at the caller, she pressed the accept button.

"Nick, it is so good to hear your voice. Sorry I didn't get a chance to call you back yesterday. By the time I noticed your text, it was late. I didn't want to disturb you," Kate said.

"No worries. Working on the sailboat all day, we turned in pretty early," Nick said. "How is Palm Beach?"

"Oh, my goodness, Nick. This place is an oceanfront palace. I had no idea that Merilu's friend was Cassie VanLangen," Kate said.

"Cassie VanLangen…" Nick's voice trailed as he tried to process where he had heard that name before.

"As in cosmetics. As in one of the biggest names in the cosmetics industry around the world," Kate said.

"Wow. The place must be nice, tell me about it," Nick requested.

"For one, the place is huge. It sits right on the water, with its own private beach, I might add," Kate said. "The house is enormous and elegant. And there is a guest house larger than any home I have ever lived in."

"You had me at private beach," Nick said.

"You would love it," Kate said.

"Tell me about the job. What are you signed up to do?" Nick asked.

"Cassie… Ms. VanLangen… wants me to redecorate from top to bottom on the heels of an extensive remodel," Kate said.

"It sounds amazing," Nick said.

"It is. It is just missing one thing…" Kate started.

"Ms. Harper?" a dignified voice cut into Kate's conversation. She looked up to see a debonair man standing before her, a set of blueprints tucked under one arm, a laptop in his other. A broad smile spread across his face until he lost grip on the laptop.

Kate rushed to help, managing to sandwich the laptop between her hip and his thigh, preventing it from crashing to the patio floor.

"Uh, Nick. I've got to go. I'll call you later," Kate said quickly into her phone.

"Kate…" she could hear Nick's voice fading as she lunged to capture the laptop with her hands. Click the "end call button", Kate looked up slowly as she and the man peeled their bodies away from each other.

Holding the laptop out for the man, she said, "I'm... I'm Kate Harper."

The man flashed a smile that Kate was sure would have melted all the gelato in Milan.

"I am Marco DiNova. Ms. VanLangen's architect on this little project of hers. You, Ms. Harper, are a lifesaver. I can't tell you what a miracle you have made by saving my laptop. I am in your debt," the man smiled as he gave a slight bow to Kate.

Kate flushed. "It seems as though we will be working together. You can call me Kate."

"Well, Kate. Please, call me Marco." The man spoke with a luxurious Italian accent.

Kate glanced at the papers still tucked under his arm and asked, "Those the plans?"

"Yes. Let's show you what we are doing for Cassie," Marco said, nudging with his shoulder toward the cover of the gazebo.

"That would be great. I have been struggling to imagine since this place is already so lovely," Kate said.

"It is. It reminds me a bit of a French museum instead of a coastal getaway. More equipped to fundraisers for a stuffy art crowd, less airy vacation spot," Marco said.

Rolling out the plans he had drawn out, the architect ran through an overview. "This is all mostly cosmetic stuff but requires removing all the trim work and flooring along with all of the fixtures in the house. Each section will require a day or two of demo with four to five days to complete the floors and new trim, not including painting. We'll have the electrical and plumbing work done all at the same time. We'll schedule some finishing work after that is completed. It is extensive, but as they say, she has some good bones, this estate."

Kate shuddered slightly at the chosen phrase but pressed out a smile, "It looks great. I am excited to get to work on it."

"Cassie says she would like your eye on the fixtures. Perhaps we can make a day of it. Plan a trip to Boca and dine in the wine cellar at Arturo's or al fresco at Renato's in Palm Beach. Either is authentic with desserts you will never forget," Marco said.

Kate wasn't sure if it was his accent or if the man she had just met was outright flirting with her.

"Sure," she stammered. "We'll see what we can fit into the schedule."

Kate felt her temperature rise despite the shade of the gazebo and cooling onshore breeze. She was glad to hear Merilu's heels against the hard surface of the patio.

Willing her cheeks to return to their normal color, Kate took a step away from the plans and away from Marco, "Merilu. You should see the plans. I think Cassie will be very happy with them."

"I'm sure she will in yours and Marco's capable hands," Merilu smiled at Kate and offered head tilt toward Marco.

Marco splashed a sly smile at Merilu.

Merilu turned her attention to Kate, "Ready to shop?"

"Yes!" Kate exclaimed a bit more exuberantly than she had intended.

"Great! I know this wonderful gelato shop along Worth Avenue," Merilu said.

"Gelato…" Kate melted, nodding absently.

Six

Kate was glad to have Merilu drive. Her keen knowledge of where to go made the trip less stressful. Her gleaming pearlescent Mercedes G-wagon fit in well with the rest of the high-dollar European vehicles that rolled up to the Worth Avenue Shops valet.

Stepping out of the car, Kate's head spun 360 degrees. Amidst the towering palms was a string of shops that she pictured at home on Rodeo Drive. The shoppers, donned wide-brim sun hats and their arms laden with packages with labels Kate had never dreamed of owning.

Merilu cast Kate a glance as if sensing her trepidation, "Ready to have some fun?"

Kate forced a smile, "Let's do it."

Shedding her reluctance, Kate fell into step with her friend and boss.

Merilu's eyes swept Kate up and down. Chewing her lip for a second, she mulled, "Chanel… Versace… No! St. Barth or Lily Pulitzer. We'll let your beach lifestyle spirit shine!"

"Sounds good to me," Kate said, willing to be led.

Strolling down the immaculate sidewalks, they made their way to their first stop. A concierge met them immediately as the heavy wooden doors were held open for them. Wafts of tropical and floral scents filled the air.

"It even *smells* expensive," Kate whispered to herself.

Kate's eyes swept the racks, not knowing where to even start. Flipping a tag, she spied the price of a dress, and her face turned pale.

"Don't even worry about that," Merilu said in a sing-song voice as she raced over to a rack and began quickly sliding hangers around so that she could assess the wares.

An attendant stepped up, "May I help you find something?"

"My gorgeous friend needs a dress for a Palm Beach gala," Merilu said.

The attendant gave Kate once over. Studying her sundress and quickly dismissing it as decidedly not from a rack on Worth Avenue, the attendant said, "Will the event be indoors or outdoors?"

"A little of both," Merilu said.

"At a restaurant or hotel?" the attendant continued.

"Cassie VanLangen's estate," Merilu said.

The attendant's eyes went wide, and she was suddenly far more invested in her guest's, "Ms. VanLangen, well, right this way. We have some of the most beautiful dresses."

Merilu shot Kate a look.

Begrudgingly, Kate followed.

The attendant displayed her hands toward racks of exclusive designer dresses.

Merilu danced among the racks, picking out options for Kate to consider. The attendant took turns presenting offerings. One by one, Kate studied the choices, her lips pursing as she looked them over.

"They are nice," Kate said. "But I don't think any of them are me."

Merilu's eyes grew wide. Racing to the back of the store, she pulled a dress of the rack.

"That is an excellent selection," the attendant approved, her eyes twinkled with the potential commission.

Kate allowed Merilu to hold the dress up to her neck. She was silent as her friend gave her a once over.

"You don't like it…" Merilu winced.

"It's nice, I just don't know," Kate said. Snatching a much simpler, flowy dress off a neighboring rack, Kate asked, "How about this one?"

Studying Kate as she held the dress tight to her chest and swirled, Merilu cupped her chin in her hand. Considering her friend's option, she said, "Hmm. I like it. I do. It screams Kate Harper, but I'm not sure it is gala worthy."

Kate frowned.

"It's okay, we have other shops to visit," Merilu said. "I think it is time for gelato!"

Kate's eyes danced a little at the proposition, "*That* screams Kate Harper."

Merilu laughed, "Come on, let's take a break."

Thanking the attendant, they left the store and entered the palm-lined streets of Worth Avenue. Walking with a greater bounce in her step, Kate followed along with Merilu.
Piccolo Gelato was tucked down one of Worth Avenue's many alleys.

Navigating through the corridors amongst the shops and eateries felt like walking through a quaint Italian neighborhood.

The shop was busy with families pouring over their many flavor options. Gelato Al pistachio, stracciatella with its chocolate and for di latte base, and limoncello were labeled as their fan favorites.

When Merilu and Kate got to the front of the line, neither had made up her mind.

"This is so difficult," Kate said, feeling pressure as another family walked in behind them.

"Our fan favorites are always great selections. Our flavor of the month is a wonderful taste of tropics in the summer," the bubbly girl behind the counter suggested.

"I'll have that," Kate nodded.

"I'm sticking with… stracciatella. Why fight the classics?" Merilu said.

Both ladies seemed relieved to have their weighty decisions off their shoulders. Waiting for their scoops, a couple ducked into the shop and out the Florida heat and humidity.

With their gelato in hand, Kate and Merilu made their way to a little wrought iron table. demi-spoons stuck in the creamy, Italian treats, they took seats across from one another.

"This is nice," Kate said.

"It's good to catch up on something other than work," Merilu said.

As they prepared to take their first bites, Kate's phone buzzed. Merilu waved the back of her fingers toward Kate, "You can get that."

Giving her phone a quick glance, she silenced the call and brushed Merilu's suggestion off. "No, it's girl's day out. How often do we get the chance to have moments like this?"

"It might be Nick," Merilu suggested, her voice drawing out like a song lyric.

Kate brushed off the idea for a second time.

Merilu cast a scrutinizing look across the table at Kate who seemed intent on enjoying her gelato. "So… what is the deal between you two?"

Nearly choking on her bite, Kate set her spoon down. Sitting across from her boss and friend, she flashbacked to sitting on a porch swing with her mother admitting her first crush.

"Nick is… wonderful. He's charming, kind, caring…" Kate's eyes wandered to a random focal point somewhere past Merilu's gaze.

"Sounds horrible," Merilu quipped.

"*He* is wonderful. I… I have my own hills to climb before I can fully commit to a serious relationship," Kate said.

"Hills as in the reason you responded to my ad for a beach house stager that wasn't afraid to move around. A *lot*," Merilu said, her eyes prying slits above her spoonful of gelato.

Kate's face reddened.

"Some wounds take longer to heal," Merilu admitted. "But you can't let life, or a good man, slip away because of it."

"This is *really* good gelato," Kate bobbed her spoon over her cup.

"Unless he's not the one," Merilu pressed, undaunted by Kate's deflection.

"I don't know," Kate said, her voice breathy. Her eyes locked on Merilu, "How would I know if I don't let him all the way in."

Merilu nodded in silence, her raised brows letting Kate know her unspoken thoughts.

Kate was relieved when Merilu dove in with her spoon to focus on her gelato. Kate looked down at her own bowl where she was making little abstract loops in her coconut mango frozen treat. She was surprised how much the conversation challenged her.

With a sigh, she filed the thoughts away to focus on her day. "Good gelato," she mumbled, her eyes landing on the blur of shoppers laden with bags along the rows of shops.

Undaunted by their initial attempt at dress shopping, Merilu led Kate through more luxurious stores. As they entered a shop with a distinct, but elegant tropical vibe, they both took a breath. The mannequins adorned with flowy tropical dresses almost looked like Kate at a glance.

Merilu grinned, "I think we found the right place."

Like a little girl in a toy store, Merilu rushed ahead, her fingers running along at least one dress in each rack that they passed. Stopping in front of a display, Merilu snatched a dress off the rack. Whirling, she wore a broad smile and gasped, "Kate! This! I have to see this on you."

To Kate's surprise, she liked the dress as well. Giving a nod, Kate accepted the dress and held it up to her shoulders. Kicking her leg out, she gave the dress a little movement. "This is lovely," Kate said.

"Try it on!" Merilu nearly squealed in her excitement.

"Okay," Kate agreed, spinning to find the dressing rooms. As she did her eye caught the tag and she swallowed hard, "Um, Merilu… it's a bit expensive."

"We are going to a Cassie VanLangen party. It is time to splurge," Merilu said, unaware of the eyes that swiveled as she said so.

"Yeah, but…" Kate started.

"It is an order from your boss. Now, march!" Merilu said.

In a reluctant huff, Kate walked away with the expensive dress in hand.

An attendant led her to a dressing room. Sliding the dress off the hanger and slipping it on, Kate gasped, unable to suppress a smile. "This is a lovely dress," she muttered to herself.

From out in the store, she could hear Merilu calling impatiently, "Let me see, let me see!"

Ignoring another childhood flashback of school clothes shopping with her mother, Kate complied. In her bare feet, she stepped out of the dressing room.

Merilu stood outside the dressing room corridor, her eyes lit up. "Kate!" she gasped. "You look beautiful!"

Kate blushed, "It *is* a nice dress."

"Come on, give it a twirl," Merilu said, moving her fingers in a tight little circle.

Once more, Kate complied and did a tidy pirouette.

"How do you feel?" Merilu asked.

"Like I'd be horrified to be within ten feet of a glass of red wine," Kate said.

Merilu scowled.

Kate conceded, "I feel… great. I am quite sure this is the nicest dress I have ever worn."

"Well, I love it," Merilu said. With a hand to her chin, she looked thoughtful, "Now we need shoes!"

Kate's chin fell.

Merilu swished her away with the back of her hand, "I know a great place."

Grabbing Kate's hand, Merilu guided her down the sidewalk. Dodging a Rolls Royce and gleaming Ferrari, they crossed the street and ducked into Via Amore, one of Worth Avenue's many side alleys.

Flowering vines created an archway for them to enter that was dotted with whimsical sculptures. Merilu led Kate into a shop through the European garden-like atrium.

"The owner is a sweetheart and a couple of her designers are close friends of Cassie's," Merilu said.

"Sweetheart, eh?" a cheerful voice greeted them.

"Hi Stephanie, it's great to see you again," Merilu said. Turning to Kate, she said, "Stephanie travels the fashion shows and has an eye for finding smaller designers who are great at their craft."

"Everyone needs a shot at sharing their work," Stephanie said. "What can I help you two with?"

"My friend Kate needs a pair of shoes to match this gorgeous dress," Merilu said.

Kate revealed the dress by unzipping the garment bag she was carrying.

"It is lovely," Stephanie said. Eying Kate, she guessed, "Eight and a half?"

"Nine," Kate said.

"I will be right back," Stephanie said, a finger drawn in the air.

In moments, the proprietor returned with a box under her arm. Sliding open the cover, she revealed a pair of shoes.

At first, Kate hesitated. The leather shoes were beautiful but had a look of lethality to them.

Stephanie smiled, "Try them on."

Kate took the shoes. Finding a chair to plop into, she kicked out of her sandals and reluctantly slid her foot into one of the shoes. "Hmm," she murmured. Placing on the second shoe, Kate stood up.

Taking a step or two, she looked at Stephanie and Merilu, "These are remarkably comfortable. They are beautiful, but I am shocked with how comfortable they are."

"We'll take them. They are perfect for the dress," Merilu said.

Shoes in hand and her new dress cradled in her arm, Kate waited alongside Merilu for valet to bring her car alongside.

The valet took Kate's items for her and stowed them carefully in the back seat of Merilu's car.

Settled into the luxury car's leather seats, Kate tried to understand why she felt so exhausted. She could see Merilu still grinning from the driver's seat.

"You really like this," Kate said.

"I do," Merilu's eyes danced. "There's one final thing to put a stamp on our shopping spree and refuel a bit."

"What's that?"

"Lunch! One of my favorite places is not far from here," Merilu said.

"Okay, as long as…" Kate started before Merilu cut her off.

"My treat! Trust me, the food and the setting are fabulous. The bill can be a bit tough to swallow… but it's worth it!" Merilu said.

Realizing she was along for the ride, Kate nodded, accepting her boss' whims. Smiling quietly, she realized much Merilu was thoroughly enjoying the day.

Merilu's favorite lunch spot perfectly met the mood for the day. After a short coastal drive south of Worth Avenue, Merilu guided her gleaming SUV down the long drive of Eau Palm Beach Resort and Spa.

Perched right alongside the Atlantic Ocean, its blue waters lapping against the sugary sand, Breeze Ocean Kitchen deposited diners in front of breath-taking views.

"This is fabulous," Kate said.

"It's vacation in a lunch spot," Merilu said.

"My kind of place," Kate's eye swept the colorful, yellow-striped umbrellas standing sentry in the center of each immaculately white table.

Merilu grinned, "I thought you would like it."

"I may have to borrow a few design cues," Kate said as they were escorted to a table right along the beach. "It reminds me of what I picture early 1900s ocean side boardwalks would be like."

"Just missing the blue striped full-body jumpers," Merilu said.

"While there is something to be said for their modesty, I'll take today's choices and options," Kate said.

Pulling open her menu, Kate reviewed her options.

"The crab cakes are delicious. Smoked tomato butter…" Merilu said.

"That sounds interesting. Is that what you're having?" Kate asked.

"Today is treat day. I am going with the lobster cobb salad," Merilu said.

Kate's eyes flitted on the salad portion of the menu and set it down.

Merilu eyed her with curiosity.

"Ahi citrus. Sounds light and refreshing," Kate said.

"Perfect for al fresco dining oceanside," Merilu said.

As the waiter came to retrieve their orders and their menus, Merilu asked for two jam cocktails, a Breeze Open Kitchen favorite.

Kate settled back into her seat. She didn't need a cocktail to feel fully relaxed with the Florida sun muted by the bright-colored umbrellas and the breeze off the Atlantic dancing along her skin.

As their blueberry-tinged beverages arrived, Kate raised her glass, "Thank you for a surprisingly fun day."

"My pleasure. You make my properties so successful, this is a long overdue gesture," Merilu smiled back.

"Well, thank you, just the same," Kate said.

"Not everyone can live out of a suitcase," Merilu said.

"Are you kidding me? Treasure Island, Carolina Beach… Cassie VanLangen's estate in Palm Beach? It's like I'm on permanent vacation, other than the fact that I am working most of the time. But I'm working in little slices of paradise. No complaints here," Kate said.

"Can't be easy on your personal life," Merilu said. A sly smile pursing through her lips, "Unless you found someone with a similar affinity to travel and all things beach like you."

Kate twisted in her seat.

Her phone buzzed. Reaching to swipe *ignore call*, Merilu waved her off. Glancing at the screen, she saw *Nick Mason* scroll across.

"Take it. I'm going to the ladies' room to freshen up before our food arrives," Merilu said, excusing herself from the table.

Kate nodded. Picking up the phone, she rose from her seat to lean over a quiet part of the veranda.

Realizing she had missed several texts from him, she flushed.

"Nick, I am so sorry. I have been spending time with Merilu," Kate said.

"It's fine. I was just checking in. Did you see the photo of the dolphin checking my buddy and I out while we were working on his boat?" Nick asked, his voice cheery.

"No, I, uh," Kate stammered. She couldn't understand why her cheeks grew warm. "I honestly haven't checked my phone much. Merilu has been taking me on sort of a tour to her favorite Palm Beach hot spots. We're at lunch now."

"Oh, I didn't mean to cut into your day. We can talk later," Nick said.

"It's all right. I have a moment. How's your project going?" Kate asked, her eyes seeking out the calming water of the waves splashing onto shore.

"It's… a lot of work. Good to catch up with my buddy though. You know, work is always better when you're near the water. In this case, on the water," Nick said.

"I was just saying that to Merilu," Kate said.

"How about you? Enjoying Palm Beach?" Nick asked.

Kate's eyes danced around the oceanside restaurant, "You would love our lunch spot. Right on the beach. Plenty of fresh seafood, not as fresh as if we caught it… I mean if caught from the shore."

"Sounds nice. Send me a photo. Speaking of fresh caught, my buddy and I have challenged ourselves that we must catch our dinner each night. A nice respite from working all day, anyway," Nick said.

Merilu appeared with a waiter shadowing not far behind.

"Merilu is back and lunch looks like it's about to be served," Kate said.

"Well, I should let you go. It was good to hear your voice, Kate," Nick said.

"Yours too," Kate nearly choked the words.

"Have fun with Merilu. Let me know if you need any handyman help down there," Nick said.

"I will. Have fun with your friend, Nick," Kate said.

Ending the call, she sat back down at their table just as Merilu slid back into her chair.

Merilu looked at Kate, "You are positively crimson. How was your call with Nick?"

Kate felt as though her cheeks were on fire, "Fine. He sent me a picture of a dolphin swimming near the sailboat he is working on."

The waiter set their lunch plates down.

"I want to see," Merilu said just as Kate was putting her phone away.

Pausing, looking at their food and then up at an expectant Merilu, Kate yielded. Opening her phone, she slid her thumb to the text and clicked on the photo. Holding it across the table, she watched as Merilu studied the photo.

"Handsome man. You sure we don't need him and his tool belt for this remodel?" Merilu asked as she situated the napkin on her lap and settled into the table.

Kate swooped her phone away and stuffed it back in her handbag.

"This lunch looks great!" she said, eager to turn the topic of conversation.

Merilu eyed her employee and friend for a moment. Conceding that was all she was going to get out of Kate, she too, turned her attention to the plate of food before her.

"So, how'd you and Cassie VanLangen come to be friends?" Kate asked.

"We met at the University of Milan…" Merilu started.

"I didn't know you went to Milan," Kate said.

Merilu shrugged, "For a semester. Part of an exchange program. I met Cassie there. Encouraged her to make the return trip with me to attend a semester at Saint Leo University in Florida."

"Quite the change," Kate noted.

"It was fun. She got to show me northern Italy and I got to show her Florida and our notorious beach life," Merilu said. "Her parents were so mad at her. They thought it was a foolish escape and a speed bump in her education. It powered her to become one of the most successful women in cosmetics and fragrance."

"I always assumed it was a family thing," Kate said.

"Nope. All Cassie's. Her name no doubt helped, but it was all her," Merilu said.

"Two very successful women," Kate said.

Merilu laughed, "I like that in real estate I can disappear. Cassie is tabloid fodder. I wouldn't enjoy that."

"She is kind of a celebrity," Kate said.

"It's a surprisingly cutthroat industry. She is always looking over her shoulder fending off a backstabbing," Merilu said.

"That sounds awful," Kate said.

"Then again, she does have people all around the world paying top dollar for bags and sunglasses with her monogram on it," Merilu said.

Kate frowned, "CVL. I've seen those. A departure from cosmetics and fragrance."

"A nod to her family's business. It was part of them making up, I suppose," Merilu said. "Fashion was her family's claim to fame. The extension was an olive branch. At least at first. Until Cassie's items became the most profitable line they ever had."

"She has the Midas touch. And it makes sense. She is vibrant in almost every way. And yet, remarkably down to earth," Kate said.

"She is. She's been a great friend. I am glad I was able to get you two together," Merilu said.

"Me too. I mean, it is an honor to work on her beach house," Kate said.

"You're the best. I can't wait to see the coastal retreat you make out of it," Merilu said.

Kate nodded, looking off at the incoming waves, "No pressure."

"You'll do fine," Merilu said. As the waiter came by, she nodded for the check and asked for her SUV to be brought out front by the valet.

"Thank you, again, for a fabulous lunch," Kate said as they slid out of their seats. Standing up, they took in the ocean view and the breeze gently tussled their hair one more time.

"It was fun," Merilu said standing in front of the resort foyer looking for her Mercedes.

Kate noticed Merilu freeze. Her friend's body pivoted as though she were about to retreat back into the resort. Before she could complete her turn, they were greeted by a call and wave from an elegantly dressed woman standing by the curb. A valet held a parasol over her head as her car was brought alongside.

"Merilu!", the woman called, waving her hand at the wrist like a princess in a Disney parade.

Kate watched as Merilu bit her lip before breaking into a broad smile and striding toward the woman.

"Teresa! How lovely to run into you here," Merilu called.

Kate followed in her wake.

"Teresa, have you met Kate Harper? She is one of the most respected interior designers in Florida," Merilu said.

Kate flinched at the introduction but extended a hand.

The woman grasped Kate's hand with both of hers and looked Kate in the eye, "Teresa Lilley. How wonderful to meet you. Any friend of Merilu's is a friend of mine."

Merilu choked in a manner that caused both Teresa and Kate to swing their heads. "Sorry, Florida pollen. So heavy this time of year."

"Yes," Teresa said as she let go of Kate's hand.

"It's nice to meet you too. Teresa Lilley of Lilley cosmetics?" Kate asked.

The woman beamed, "That's me!"

Stepping back, the woman quickly gave a Kate a once over.

Kate shrunk back as she tried to interpret the woman's eyes that scanned her from head to toe.

"Interior designers…" Teresa considered. Her eyes widened, "Have you been brought in to work on Cassie's little bungalow? How charming. I just had had my mansion touched up by a designer from Naples. Carlito Bacco… do you know him?"

Kate frowned, "No. I don't believe I do."

"Well, I'm sure you'll make Cassie's place *adorable*," Teresa beamed.

"I have an idea, why don't you join me for dinner? Tomorrow night? I can show you Carlito's handywork. Maybe give you some inspiration," Teresa said.

Kate's eyes shot to Merilu who, for the first time since Kate had known her, stumbled for words.

Merilu shook herself and offered a warm smile, "I… we'd love to. But Cassie is hosting a dinner before she takes off for Milan."

Teresa's head dropped an inch as she eyed Merilu with a twinkle of mischievousness, "Is she? Well, perhaps I'll stop by. Wish her well. I am also heading to Milan. I imagine for the same reason."

"You are also up for fashion week's exclusive fragrance," Merilu said.

Teresa brightened, "I am! I have… a good feeling about my chances this year. Though I am sure Cassie has something brewed up as well."

"I have no doubt you both have a wonderful chances," Merilu said.

"Well, I must be off. Perhaps I will see you tomorrow. Kate, it was a pleasure," Teresa smiled at Kate and Merilu before standing by her driver's door. A valet sprinted around the car to open the door for her.

The roof of Teresa's long convertible Rolls Royce lowered revealing custom salmon hyacinth leather seats with the Lilley logo embossed on each head rest. As the cosmetics magnate started her car a light waft of hyacinth fragrance filled the air.

Teresa beamed and fluttered her fingers at the ladies standing on the curb, "Ta ta!"

Kate and Merilu watched as the Rolls Royce roared away and Merilu's Mercedes was brought alongside the curb.

"Cassie is going to kill me," Merilu muttered.

"Not friends?" Kate asked.

"Bitter rivals. They mostly play nice when everyone is looking. But when they're not... not so much," Merilu said, her eyes focused on the road ahead.

Kate nodded in silence.

Seven

After their day of shopping and treating themselves, Kate could have easily slipped away to her balcony to stare at the rolling Atlantic waves crashing to shore.

As Kate and Merilu walked into the Palm Beach estate, Kate realized her respite would have to wait.

"You're back! I hope you girls had fun," Cassie called out to them before they could disappear into their respective rooms. "Please, you must join us for dinner!"

Kate forced out a congenial smile as she cocked her head at the word 'us'. Her eyes glanced at Merilu who also seemed to be contemplating a response.

"Of course. Let me put my things away," Kate said. She paused as she sniffed the air, "Gustavo hard at work?"

"He is indeed," Cassie smiled. "Hurry, hurry. I'll have him whip up some mojitos for you."

Obligingly, Kate hurried up the stairs to stow her bounty from shopping.

When she found her way to the back patio, Gustavo stood at an open French door with a cocktail glass in hand. "Passionfruit mojito, nice and light," he said.

"Thank you, Gustavo. You are amazing," Kate said.

Gustavo smiled as Kate walked by. He disappeared back toward the kitchen to return to his meal preparations.

Kate followed the voices to the dining table under the gazebo. Merilu was already seated next to Cassie while Marco DiNova stood up and pulled out a chair for Kate.

Offering a gracious smile, Kate accepted the seat next to him.

Kate's eyes fell on the man sitting next to Cassie opposite of Merilu. The file folders in her mind fought to align the face with a name. She suddenly brightened, "You are…"

"Kate, meet Donovan Drake. Donovan, Kate Harper, a friend of Merilu's and now mine," Cassie said introducing Kate to a handsome man.

Kate studied him for a moment likening him to a living, breathing Ken doll.

"You were on *Heart's Cove*," Kate said, mentioning a long-running soap opera.

Donovan smiled, "You're a fan."

Kate shook her head, her eyes dipping into a frown, "No… my college roommate was and had it on quite a bit. I did see you in the Christmas movie, though. It was a sweet."

"*'Twas the Night Before a Kiss*. My first Romance Channel gig," Donavan said.

"Well, it is nice to meet you," Kate said.

"Nice to meet you, too. Cassie has the most amazing friends," Donovan said, his eyes lighting on Marco in almost a twitch.

The quick glance was not missed by Marco.

"I have the best friends, old and new," Cassie said, raising her glass.

While the others joined her in raising their glasses, Kate watched the silent drama between Donovan and Marco.

She didn't have much time to observe before Gustavo returned with a pitcher of sangria for the table and five fresh glasses.

"Gustavo, you're too good to us. Remember, tomorrow is a day off. Your job is to relax and enjoy the day with the rest of us," Cassie said.

"At least after breakfast," Gustavo said. "I had planned lilikoi mimosas with Florida stone crab benedict over conch fritter biscuits."

Every jaw at the table dropped.

"Right. Your day off begins *after* breakfast!" Cassie laughed.

The table let out a collective sigh as Gustavo hurried back to the kitchen.

"To Gustavo," Merilu chuckled and raised her glass.

"To Gustavo!" the table cheered.

"In other news," Cassie began. "Marco has officially moved into one of the guest suites. So, you will have company while you stay here. I will tell you, the downside of a big house nestled into an estate built for privacy, it feels eerily lonely at times."

Kate glanced up from her mojito. Her eyes darted from Cassie to Merilu to Marco. The Italian architect offered a warm smile.

"Yes, that is very comforting," Kate said, swallowing her sarcastic tone.

"We will have great fun, in between our work on the house, of course," Marco said.

Kate smiled back, "Big house, lots of work. I am sure we'll stay plenty busy."

"Oh, there are always moments to carve out for a little frivolity. Besides, taking time to relax helps spur creativity. It will ensure we give Cassie our absolute best," Marco said.

Kate nodded quietly and focused deep on the crushed mint and mango at the bottom of her glass.

Gustavo's Michelin star-worthy meal couldn't come fast enough for Kate. The break in the conversation allowed her to shift attention from her working alongside Marco to Cassie's new beau.

"So, how'd you get your big break, Donovan?" Kate asked.

The muscular blond flashed a dazzling Hollywood smile, "I was doing an ad for shaving cream. It was weird, since it was outside at a beach shower, like where you wash the sand off your feet. The casting director for *Heart's Cove* was there with her children. She told me to pop in for a reading and the rest was history. Lucky, I guess."

"My family always says 'you make your own luck'," Cassie interjected.

"I suppose so," Donovan nodded. Stirring the food on his plate he seemed momentarily lost in his thoughts.

"I like your family's motto. I think circumstances happen. The question is how we respond to them," Kate said. "Congratulations on your success, Donovan. Is that what is bringing you to Italy?"

Donovan shrugged, "There is an opportunity my agent set up for me. We'll see how it goes."

Kate noticed the actor squirm slightly, his eyes flashing at Cassie.

"Besides, we're hoping it will allow us to spend some time together in between work," Cassie said.

"What about you, Merilu? What is your next venture?" Marco asked.

"I am bidding on a big project. It is very competitive, and I don't want to jinx it, but it could be a game changer," the real estate developer said, her voice more nervous than confident.

"It sounds like opportunities abound for all of us," Marco grinned. Raising his glass, he toasted, "To opportunities!"

"To opportunities!" the table chorused.

When the meal had been cleaned up and bottles of wine emptied, Cassie led the dinner party in excusing herself, "We have a long day tomorrow and I refuse to have puffy eyes. Goodnight, everyone."

Donovan nodded and allowed her to escort him out to his car.

"When the beauty queen leaves the party, it is good to follow suit," Merilu said, slipping away from the table herself.

Marco's eyes locked on Kate's.

Kate blushed, "I think I should head in, myself. I am not sure what to expect from a gala like the one we about to partake in tomorrow."

Marco waved her off. "A bunch of people shoved into expensive clothing trying to one up each other with grandiose stories."

Kate frowned, "Not your scene?"

"Oh, it is," Marco laughed. "It can be quite the spectacle."

"Sounds better to observe than participate," Kate said.

"Ah, but you miss out on the sport of it. Parties like Cassie's take it on such grand scale. It should be good fun," Marco said.

"Well, just the same, I think I will try and get my rest as well," Kate said.

"Pleasant dreams," Marco said, searching the table for a bottle of Sangiovese that had not been entirely drained.

As he wandered off, Kate took the opportunity to sneak over to the rail that separated the lawn from the beach below.

Leaning against the ornate steel, she stared out at the ocean. Sprays of white flew into the air catching the slivers of moonlight that spilled out of the wispy clouds.

Kate's thoughts surprised her as her mind drifted to staring at the same ocean a little over seven hundred miles north. Nick Mason stood next to her. His presence was reassuring. At times it was electrifying. She curved her shoulders almost expecting his hand to drape over them and pull her closer.

She could almost hear the clinking of wine glasses as Nick offered her a night cap against the backdrop of crashing waves.

"Perhaps sleep will come a bit easier after a final glass," a voice called.

Kate jumped. Pulled out of her brief daydream, she turned to find Marco standing in the shaft of moonlight, a freshly opened bottle of red wine in hand, a pair of wine glasses dangling from his fingers. His Italian accent somehow seemed thicker and lusher under the veil of the night sky.

Kate's mind whirred with reasons to decline.

As if sensing her hesitation, Marco spoke softly, "One glass to take in this exquisite evening. Tomorrow night will not be near as calm."

Kate nodded despite herself as though his words carried immense logic.

Pouring a glass, Marco handed it to her. Pouring his own, his eyes never leaving Kate's he managed to stop before reaching the lip of the glass.

Thanking him, Kate turned abruptly to face the ocean.

Marco stepped next to her, his gaze following hers. He was so close, she could smell his cologne.

"What a view, eh? It will be a pleasure to work on this exquisite property," Marco said.

His breath danced alarmingly close to the side of Kate's neck.

"Mmm," she pulled a step away. "Yes. A great property."

Pulling the glass to her lips, Kate drained it in one large gulp. Handing the glass back to Marco, she said, "Thank you for the wine, Marco. I'll see you in the morning."

Kate spun and made steady steps toward the house. Her skin felt as though it glowed from inexplicable heat. She relished the cool night breeze as it soothed her skin. As she reached the door to the house and she slipped inside, she shook her head.

Scowling to herself, she struggled to understand the palpations of unexplainable guilt that washed over her. She didn't do anything wrong. She wasn't even in an official relationship. Yet, feelings swirled within her that twisted her heart.

Closing the door to her room, she leaned against it. Clutching her chest, she tried to make sense of her emotions.

"Too much wine. And Italian cologne. *Way* too much Italian cologne," Kate reconciled and prepared for bed.

Eight

Kate had barely taken a sip of her morning coffee when she heard a raucous commotion in the front of the house. Peering around the corner, she was alarmed when the front doors burst open.

A well put-together woman pushed past Gustavo who had answered the door. "All right… lose that bouquet, our new one goes there. The one with the birds of paradise peeking through the giant banana plant leaves!" the woman called out as she marched.

Glancing at her clipboard, she motioned with a pen. "Candle stanchions go there. Come, come. We have lots to do!" she called out.

To Kate the woman sounded part drill sergeant and part Disney villain as she almost sang her orders.

Peeling back behind the relative safety of the kitchen pillar, she waited for the entourage to pass before tip toeing her way toward the stairs.

At the tail end of the procession, Gustavo leaned over and whispered, "Smart choice. Best to stay well out of the fray."

"Sound advice," Kate said.

"Oh, breakfast is still on. We'll have it out in the gazebo. The party planner won't get there until the interior is completed," Gustavo said.

"Any ideas where to hide after that?" Kate asked.

"The beach. This is a great day to down to the beach and read a good book," Gustavo said.

"Hmm," Kate looked thoughtful. "I have been carrying around this mystery I've been meaning to get to."

"I may just join you. I have a thriller that I stopped on a cliff hanger when Cassie got back to town. Might just be the day to finally find out what happened," Gustavo said.

Kate smiled, "Then I'll see you out there!"

Gustavo nodded and headed toward the kitchen.

Kate's eyes swept from the amiable chef to the wisp of party decorators. They flowed through the house in a way that reminded Kate of flock of sparrows making shapes in the sky with their tight formations.

Shaking her head, Kate jogged up the steps toward her room. Mindlessly making the turn toward the master bedroom, she jumped back when a figure stood before her.

"Marco?" she snapped.

"Sorry to startle you. I… I was going to see if you were ready for breakfast," Marco said.

Kate's eyes gazed at the open bedroom door behind him.

"I just spoke with Gustavo, it will be in a bit," Kate said, her suspicion raised.

"Right. Just thought maybe you'd like help with the espresso machine…" Marco continued.

"I'm a quick study, but thank you," Kate said.

"Right. Well, see you at breakfast," Marco called and shuffled away a hand raised over his head.

Kate cocked her head as she watched the man walk away. Turning back toward the master suite, she pushed the door open. Her eyes swept the room. Looking for anything amiss, she took an uneasy step inside and closed the door behind her.

Moving carefully throughout the space, she grunted as she found nothing out of place.

Casting a final wary glance toward the closed bedroom door, Kate finished her coffee and got ready for breakfast.

When she made her way to the gazebo, Kate found a full contingent eagerly awaiting Gustavo's promised breakfast.

Flanking Cassie, almost indecipherable as to whom was dating her, were Donovan and Marco. Opposite of Cassie was Merilu. Kate's eyes bounced though the seating options and elected to sit in the chair next to Merilu opposite Donovan.

Marco rose from his seat and Cassie elbowed Donovan to rise and offer Kate a flute of lilikoi mimosa. Kate thanked him as both he and Marco took their seats. Marco looked unsettled by Donovan beating him to the punch.

Not pleased with the focused attention, Kate was glad when Gustavo wheeled around the corner with a tray of crab benedicts balanced on his arm. Placing the last plate at his own seat, he welcomed a mimosa pour from Marco and joined the group.

"Please, enjoy!" Gustavo said as he settled in.

Kate bobbed her head for a quick prayer and stuck her fork into Gustavo's brunch masterpiece. Taking a bite, she swooned. The entire table swooned.

"Gustavo, this may be the best thing you have ever served at this estate," Cassie said.

Gustavo blushed.

"I have been to some of the finest brunches in Palm Beach, this tops them all," Marco said. "This may be the best benedict I have had outside of the Waldorf Astoria."

"It is of debate whether eggs benedict was designed for the pope at the Vatican or for wealthy couple in New York," Kate said.

"Either way, these are delicious!" Merilu said.

"Absolutely," Kate echoed.

Merilu's eyes flicked from Kate to Marco and back to Kate again. She seemed to sense some tension between the two.

"Cassie, the party prep is nothing short of impressive," Kate said.

"For Palm Beach, it is par for the course," Cassie said, her voice waving off the perspective of austerity.

As the team of party preparers closed in, Kate asked, "What can we do to help?"

Cassie laughed, "Stay out of their way. I've learned just sit back and let them do their thing."

The table laughed.

"Seriously, today is a day to relax and have fun," Cassie said. "The beach forecast is fantastic. There are chairs, I'll send down a cooler filled with iced beverages. But protect your skin."

"Aren't you coming with us?" Kate asked.

"I have some work to do before tonight and my upcoming trip. But I will see you at the party," Cassie said.

"I have some work to catch up on myself, I'll try and join you down there in a little bit," Merilu said.

"Cassie said it is a day off. There is some decent surf, I'm heading down there," Gustavo said.

"If you're not opposed to bouncing ideas off each other, I think I'll slip down to the beach for a bit," Marco said.

"I've got extra boards," Gustavo said.

Marco waved his hand, "I'll keep my feet on land and leave you to fend with the sea creatures."

"I might give it a run if the conditions aren't too rough," Kate said.

Marco looked surprised.

Gustavo grinned and nodded with appreciation, "Great! I've got a great mid-board that should be just right."

By the time Kate reached Cassie's private beach, a set of chairs with a large umbrella was set up for them. As promised, a cooler filled to the brim with icy beverages sat between the chairs.

Holding the sun bonnet that Merilu had gotten for her on Worth Avenue against her head as the breeze threatened to take it, Kate made her way to one of the chairs. Her full-length cover up flowed gently as she stood staring at the waves. Her large, amber-tinted sunglasses shielded her eyes from the brilliant beam of the late morning sun.

She watched as the horizon was dotted with yachts steaming up the coast. The largest carried a helicopter on its stern deck. The trailing yachts, each large enough to live very comfortably on, looked nearly as magnificent.

"It's a different life out here, isn't it?" Marco's Italian tinted voiced asked.

"It is definitely different from how I live," Kate said.

"Merilu tells me you are quite the traveler," Marco said.

"Domestically, yes. Working for her, I get to visit a number of different beach spots around the country," Kate said.

"Perhaps when the project is completed, you can come to Italy. I can show you the country from an authentic lens," Marco said.

"Perhaps," Kate nodded. "You said you wanted to review some ideas?"

Marco's eyes flinched ever so slightly as the dismissive tone and refocus on house plans, "You mentioned the front sitting room was wasted space. I spoke with Cassie and she admitted, that parlor is almost never used. What were you thinking?"

"Well, if it is just wasted space, open it up. Take down the wall," Kate said. As the words came out, she let off a little shiver.

Marco cocked his head and raised a brow.

Kate squirmed and said, "I had a demo take a very weird turn once. But I think it is a good idea. Removing that wall adds even more space to enjoy the stunning views. It adds friendly conversation space that is part of Cassie's parties instead of being partitioned and quarantined off on its own."

"Hmm," Marco rubbed his chin. "We can put in a large pillar that matches the others symmetry and make the moment you walk into the house feel like you are embraced by the ocean."

"Sure, as long as it is not load bearing," Kate said.

Marco snapped his head at the wall and frowned. "Yes, of course. You *do* have an excellent eye, Kate."

Kate shrugged, "The secret to working on a beach house is all about appreciating the gift that is right in front of you. Our job is to not get in its way."

Marco laughed, "I shall have to remember that."

Their eyes shifted to the water where a pelican splashed down with an alarming lack of grace. A pair of seagulls glided in near it with a great deal more elegance.

Kate could feel Marco's eyes move back toward her.

"Beverage? Let's see what Cassie sent our way," Marco suggested.

"Surf's up!" Gustavo called, descending the steps to the beach with a surfboard under each arm.

Kate was glad for the intrusion.

"What do you think? You ready to go?" Gustavo asked.

"I've been eyeing the sets. Looks like the third wave is the best ride," Kate said.

"You know your stuff," Gustavo said. "I'm impressed."

"I had a great teacher," Kate blushed.

Accepting the surfboard Gustavo presented her, Kate looked back at Marco.

"You, know. I am inspired. You enjoy your day at the beach, I am going to work on plans to open that front room," Marco said, excusing himself from the sandy beach.

"All right, nothing left to do but conquer the waves," Gustavo said, darting over the breakwater and landing on his board. With smooth strokes, he quickly propelled himself to the swells.

Kate cast off her bonnet and swimsuit cover-up. Following behind, she had to tuck her board once to get past the breakwater. Straddling the board as she bobbed up and down on the rolling waves, Kate took a deep breath.

"Yeah, it's one of my favorite parts, too. There are days that's all I do, come out to the swells and watch the world rotate around," Gustavo said.

"So, I have to ask. How does an amazing chef become a personal chef and all-around assistant to a cosmetics mogul?" Kate asked.

Gustavo laughed and used his hands to display the beach and magnificent estate behind it, "Well, the room and board is unbeatable."

"That's true," Kate nodded.

"The real story is, I was working in one of Cassie's uncle's kitchens. He owns a Michelin-star restaurant in South Beach. He came in one day and asked what was wrong. I told him nothing but asked why he thought something was," Gustavo said. "He looked me in the eye and said, 'Gustavo, I hired you because of the passion for food that you have. I could see it in your eyes. Now, they look a bit hazy. You do good work, but your passion is missing'."

"I started to apologize but he waved me off. He said, 'Sometimes, a chef's passion is in creation. Sometimes a chef's passion is the delivery of highly crafted to food to guests. Your passion is in the creation.' He then scheduled a meeting with his niece and the rest is history," Gustavo said.

"Wow, Cassie's uncle sounds incredibly astute," Kate said.

"Yeah, he was a great guy," Gustavo nodded.

"Do you like it? Working for Cassie?"

"Yeah, I do. I really do. I can't imagine any place that I'd rather be. I get to create new dishes, experiment. The rest of the stuff, helping Cassie out, isn't part of the contract. I just like to help her. She's a great boss, a wonderful person," Gustavo said.

Kate could see the appreciation in Gustavo's eyes.

"All right, enough tongue wagging. There is a good-looking set coming, let's ride it!" Gustavo said, looking at the ocean behind them.

Kate righted herself, her eyes peering over her shoulder. Just before her board started to life, she was into her strokes, getting ahead of it. When the power of the wave pulled the board up, she leapt to her feet, her knees bent, fingers dragging along the waxed fiberglass.

Confident she was into the wave, Kate planted her rear heel and lifted out of her crouch. Arms stretched, she fought for balance as long as she could before the wave curled, dumping the board and rider. Landing on her feet, Kate bounced up, smoothed the saltwater hair out of her eyes and let out a grin.

Nine

Kate felt strangely nervous as she left the master bedroom to descend the steps to the main room below. While no guests had yet arrived, she was still met with an entourage.

Eyes swept up to greet as she paused uncomfortably.

"Kate, you look beautiful!" Merilu called.

"Exquisite," Marco added.

"You clean up well, surfer girl," Gustavo said.

With glowing red cheeks, Kate said, "Merilu is right, the right dress makes all the difference."

"That was just an excuse to go shopping!" Merilu said.

"May I get you a drink?" Marco asked.

"If it helps direct your eyes somewhere else... yes!" Kate said.

Marco quickly returned with a beverage from the closest of six bars that had been set up inside and outside of the house.

Brilliant display of tropical flowers were placed throughout the estate. Special lighting for the party had been strung from the high ceilings and stanchions of candles stood ready for the sun to set.

"Wow, they really did do a great job," Kate said.

"I can't wait to try the food. The menu sounded great!" Gustavo said.

"I bet you're happy to enjoy a meal that you don't have to cook yourself," Merilu said.

Gustavo laughed, "Actually, I had a hard time not poking my nose in there to give them a hand."

"Good thing the surf held up and kept you away from the kitchen," Kate said.

The doors to the patio swung wide and Cassie VanLangen strode into the house. All eyes landed on her. Nearly every jaw dropped in concert with each other.

"Cassie!" Kate called. "You look like a Greek goddess!"

Cassie walked up to the group. Her floor-length ivory dress hung over one shoulder in thick opulent folds. Around her neck, several strands of pearls hung in even intervals across her chest. Strings of diamonds cascading from her ears gleamed in the light sending out colorful shimmers of colorful light.

By the time she reached them, Gustavo had retrieved a beverage from the bar.

"Thank you, Gustavo," Cassie said. Watching everyone staring at her, she waved her hands, "It's a party, come on!"

As if on cue, a band started playing instrumental music. Kate cocked her head, finding the tune recognizable. With a nod of recognition, she realized the band was playing popular tunes in modern classical style. A flamboyant young woman with flaming red hair played violin in place of the vocals.

The house's elegant chimes called out that the first outside guest had arrived. The event staff dressed in crepe-colored, linen tuxedos and sun dresses opened both massive French doors at the front of the house.

Donovan strode through with a confident walk. Glancing at the catering staff for a moment, he seemed to realize that his tan linen suit and white shirt were not far from matching the gentlemen serving the party.

His flowy shirt unbuttoned to the cleft of his sternum served as enough of a differentiator to build a nod restoring his confident gait.

Cassie rushed up to greet Donovan. The actor dipped down to give her a kiss on the cheekbone.

"Hello, darling," Cassie said.

"Cassie, you look beautiful, as always," Donovan said.

The couple didn't have a chance to utter another word before the doors were once more cast wide.

Henrique Desperaux, dressed impeccably in a white tuxedo with azure trimmings, strode through the door.

"He's right, Cassie. You look divine!" Desperaux said.

Donovan bristled at Cassie's ex's appearance.

Cassie offered a poised smile, "Henrique, how good of you to show."

"Your personal invitation somehow missed me, but I did get a proper invite from one of your other guests," Desperaux said.

"You are welcome, as long as you mind yourself," Cassie said.

"Donovan," Desperaux nodded at the actor, his voice flat.

"Henrique, always entertaining to have you around," Donovan said.

Henrique's usually unflappable demeanor failed and his eyebrows creased.

Gustavo stepped purposefully in between the two rivals for Cassie's affection. Leading Desperaux by the elbow, he said, "Let me get you something from the bar."

Merilu leaned in toward Kate and hissed through grinning teeth, "Tonight is going to be so much fun!"

A stream of guests began making their way through the front door, Cassie, with Donovan by her side, greeted everyone as they walked in.

From a corner of the room, Merilu and Kate sipped their drinks. Merilu filled Kate in on who was joining the party.

A lovely woman clad in a shimmering dress walked into the house, arms flung open to hug Cassie and plant a kiss on each cheek.

"Who's that?" Kate asked.

"Michelle Goss, VanLangen Cosmetics spokesmodel."

After greeting the host, the spokesmodel took a step back and undressed Donovan with her eyes. She offered mischievous grin and poked a finger into his chest, "You better keep a close eye on this one, Cassie."

Cassie didn't have time to respond as a mousey man pushed into the house. Instead of greeting Cassie, the man took a wild pivot away from her and streaked toward the nearest bar.

"And that?" Kate asked.

"David Hammit. I'm not sure what he is doing here. He used to be Cassie's right hand at her company. They split rather abruptly when he left to work with Teresa Lilley," Merilu said.

"Her rival?" Kate asked.

"Yep. I wouldn't call it a friendly split, either. I can't believe he had the nerve to show up here," Merilu said.

"Based on the look on Cassie's face I think she can't believe it either," Kate said.

"We'll have to keep an eye on him, tonight," Merilu said.

"You think he could be up to something?" Kate asked.

Merilu pursed her lips, "There were suspicions of him engaging in a bit of corporate espionage before he left."

"I'm not sure how he could manage any of that at a party in a residence that is mostly packed up, but I'll help keep an eye out," Kate said.

"Uh, oh. This party is about to get a lot more entertaining!" Merilu said.

"I recognize her from the restaurant. Teresa Lilley herself," Kate said.

The cosmetics baroness walked up to Cassie as if they were old friends. Arms wide, the elegantly dressed woman wearing a jewelry store window's worth of diamonds gave her rival a hug.

A small entourage had followed Teresa Lilley into the party.

"Thank you, so much for having us. When Merilu told me about the event, I knew I just had to rearrange my schedule to stop by," Teresa said.

"Teresa, I am so glad that you did," Cassie said through an embellished smile.

"Maybe she and David are up to trouble together?" Kate asked.

Cassie's former employee dashed up to Teresa with a cocktail in hand.

"Most likely just making a show of it. Teresa will take any opportunity to find a way to try and upstage Cassie," Merilu said.

Kate's eyes followed Teresa as she made her rounds and soaked in any attention that she could. Marco, a willing subject, was lured into a loud, showy conversation about Lilley Cosmetics new offices and whether or not she could steal him away for a project.

Cassie didn't flinch. Her calm elegance greeted each guest who came to the party.

Merilu replaced Donovan at Cassie's side for a bit when it became evident the fidgety actor was getting board of greeting duties.

Kate took the opportunity to wander around the party, sampling hors d'oeuvres and exchanging critiques with Gustavo. Her eyes instinctively followed David Hammit and Teresa Lilley around the estate.

Locating the pair wasn't difficult, as Teresa acted as though the guests were at her party with grandiose gestures and vocal volume just shy of too loud. David Hammit, on the other hand, followed at Teresa's heels like a puppy. Anywhere she went, he was at her hip, overly conscious if her glass was dry and finding every word she uttered genius.

Michelle Goss, Van Langen Cosmetics' spokesmodel was in near competition with Teresa in demanding attention. She danced around the party engaging attention from whoever would pay it, especially from the handsome men in attendance.

The model even captured a bit of Donovan's time while Cassie was stationed in the foyer greeting guests.

When Michelle wasn't sharing playful banter with members of the opposite sex, she was cornered in a deep conversation with Teresa Lilley and David Hammit. At first, she didn't seem terribly interested in what they had to say, but something in the conversation struck a chord. Setting down her wine glass that she had scarcely allowed stay full, she leaned in close to Teresa, her eyes glancing over her shoulder.

For the first time in the evening, their voices were low enough not to be heard from across the room.

Kate began maneuvering through the crowd, trying to get within earshot. Pausing at a server with a tray of caprese bites, she listened.

"I'll tell my agent you'll be calling. Are sure this is a good idea?" Michelle asked.

"Darling, we'll make magic together!" Teresa sang.

David Hammit sneered, "You won't regret it, Michelle. Trust me!"

Noticing that other guests were in earshot, the group disbanded with the attention-seeking women resuming their gregarious patrol of the party.

Cassie had finally broken away from the front door. Her eyes swept the party to find Michelle laughing, leaning into Donovan.

"Cassie!" Michelle squealed. "Have you heard Donovan say lines from *Hope's Valley*? You know, the one where he professes his love under the moonlight to, uh, you know, that one girl? Well, of course, you have. What a riot!"

"Yeah, it's a riot," Cassie said. "Are you going to be good for your photo shoot? Plan on being at the rail fifteen minutes before sunset. I'll have someone notify you."

"I sure will," Michelle said. Abruptly stepping away, she flagged down a server lofting a tray of champagne flutes.

Cassie sighed and shook her head slightly, "It's a good thing the camera loves her."

Realizing her thoughts were spoken out loud, she apologized, "I'm sorry, I love Michelle, but she can be a handful."

"She seemed nice," Donovan shrugged.

Kate's eyes worked the room and then the back patio. By the pool, she found Teresa Lilley and her group of followers regaling Desperaux with some wild tale. Desperaux's eyes peeked over Teresa's shoulder as he watched Cassie walk by with Donovan in tow.

Dancing and squirming, he couldn't seem to find a way out of the conversation.

Another guest caught Kate's eye. A dapper man wandered by with a nearly full wine glass. He would offer a nod or thin smile as he passed other guests but didn't engage in much conversation.

"Who is that?" Kate asked Merilu.

"I, I don't know," Merilu said. "Cassie usually has a lengthy guest list. I don't think she even knows who's on it all the time."

"I can't imagine throwing a party where I didn't know the guests," Kate said.

"Look around. Among this mix you might have ambassadors, diamond brokers, real estate brokers… actors," Merilu said as Cassie seemed to have a curt word with Donovan.

The actor didn't seem especially moved by the words. Offering a shrug, he walked straight into the pouncing conversation of Michelle who corralled two fresh wine glasses from a server.

Cassie shook her head but pressed on, her confident smile never fading.

"You know, I think I'm good with my tidy little circle of friends," Kate said.

"In this world, you have competitors, people that want something from you, people who see you as a target or just want to be in the social page photos with you," Merilu said. As her eyes followed the stranger Kate had asked her about, she added, "Though sometimes, it can be rather entertaining. I think I shall solve the secret of your mystery man."

Striding off, Merilu approached the guest as he was leaning against the rail, close enough to a group of people that you might have thought he was in their conversation. As she closed in, it was clear he was staring at the ocean.

From her vantage, Kate could see that his eyes would occasionally scan the room before darting back to the waves crashing ashore. It seemed he was trying to avoid eye contact.

Seeing Merilu heading straight for him, his eyes moved left and right before locking on hers. As Kate watched, he offered a polite smile to Merilu. They nodded in conversation. Raising his glass in a friendly cheers, Merilu parted.

The man sipped at his nearly full glass and watched Merilu walk away. When she closed in on Kate, he took the opportunity to relocate.

Merilu beamed at Kate.

"Well?" Kate asked.

"His name is Neal Roth. He is in banking something or other, I don't know. His family is friends of Cassie's family and it was suggested he come to the party as he doesn't know many people in Palm Beach. He admitted he is a bit of a wall flower at these events," Merilu said.

"Very good sleuthing," Kate said. "But you just left him to skulk around by himself not knowing anyone?"

"I told him I would bring you over to say hello," Merilu smiled. Turning to where she had left the man, her face fell. "Where'd he go?"

"My guess is to be a more discrete wallflower somewhere else," Kate giggled.

"Huh, well I tried," Merilu shrugged.

The sun had hovered over the western peak of the house.

Michelle Goss, a bit tipsy, found Donovan's shoulder to lean on as she adjusted her shoe. She cast him a look and wry smile and asked if he would straighten the zipper on her gown.

She wandered over to where the photographer was set up. The setting suns golden rays blanketed the spot. The purple-blue sky faded into the azure blue sea with the crystal sand all under the natural golden hue.

As soon as the cameras began rolling, Michelle snapped into form. It became immediately apparent why she was a coveted spokesmodel. Sophistication and charm oozed from her performance as much of the party crowd gathered to watch.

Teresa wore a smile that looked a cat trying to swallow a feather. Leaning in she whispered to David Hammit who nodded and slipped away from the crowd.

Heading into the house, Hammit did a double-take before moving quickly for the foyer. Grasping the handle on the office door, he pulled something out of his pocket and unlocked the door. He looked surprised when it didn't immediately open.

Pushing his shoulder into it, it suddenly burst free and slipped inside closing the door behind him.

Kate quickened her pace. Reaching the office, she grasped the handle and flung it open. The slight man jumped at Kate's intrusion.

Immediately, his mouth began to sputter, "I, uh, I…"

"Are not supposed to be in here," Kate said.

The man's complexion paled, "Perhaps not. I left something behind from when I was employed, I had hoped to use this opportunity to retrieve it."

"There's a lot of that going around," Kate said. Noticing a piece of paper on the floor, she asked, "Were you searching for something?"

Picking the piece of paper off the floor, she saw that it was cover letter for a corresponding stack of papers on the desk.

"I haven't had the chance. You came in right behind me," Hammit said.

"Well, whatever it is you need from in here, you should do it with Cassie's knowledge," Kate said, her voice stern.

Hammit started to speak before stopping short. His shoulders slumped, "Yes, you're probably right."

"You have a key from when you were employed here?" Kate asked.

Hammit nodded.

"I'll hold it for safe keeping," Kate said, her hand thrust out with her palm up.

Reluctantly, Hammit pulled the key out of his pocket and slapped it down in Kate's hand.

"Thank you. Go enjoy the rest of the party. Teresa's glass might be empty by now," Kate said reaching for the door.

Before she could grab the handle, it turned. Taking a step back, she watched as the door swung open. A man slipped inside, his scanning behind him.

As he turned around, his face fell.

"Mr. Desperaux, and here we meet again. In another place you shouldn't be," Kate said.

"What are you doing here?" he snapped. His left Kate and glared at Hammit, "This little worm was snooping in here, wasn't he?"

"Which was what you were about to do?" Kate asked.

Desperaux shuffled his feet, "I'll save the conversation out of earshot from that turncoat."

"Turncoat?" Hammit snapped.

Desperaux squared up with Hammit, "Cassie was good to you. *Too* good and that is how you repay her?"

"Maybe we all have dreams of living in beachfront estates," Hammit said.

"Out!" Kate pointed. "Both of you!"

The men warily eyed each other as they slipped through the door Kate held open for them. As they disappeared to rejoin the party, Kate looked back in the office. Her eyes landed on the floor where the piece of paper had been. Hammit didn't have time to rummage before she followed him.

"Hmm," she shrugged.

Closing the office door and ensuring it was locked, she gripped the key in her hand. Spinning, she nearly collided with the front door opening.

Neal Roth slipped through, surveying the foyer. He tensed as he saw Kate standing there.

"Mr. Roth?" Kate cocked her head.

"You're the friend of Mary Ann," Roth said.

"Merilu," Kate corrected.

"Right, sorry," Roth said.

"Are you coming or going?" Kate asked.

"I, uh, I stepped out for a moment. I find crowds overwhelming. With all the attention of the photo shoot, my sanctuary by the seawall was suddenly overrun," Roth said.

"I see. I suppose I can understand that," Kate said. Seeing the party crowd once more mingling on the patio, she said, "You may be in luck. Your spot might have once more opened up."

"Thank you," Roth blushed. "I might just head there for a bit."

Kate nodded as the man made his way through the crowd. Picking up a full wine glass that had been stashed near a planter, he disappeared toward the back yard.

Kate held the key in her hand trying to decide what to do with it. Her dress did not have any pockets. Noting the planter where Roth retrieved the wine glass, she glanced around. With no one looking in her direction, she quickly pushed the key down into the dirt and smoothed it over with her hand.

Stepping away, her new shoes slipped slightly. Looking at the floor, she saw a small patch of dirt. Thinking her antics at the planter has spilled over, she paused. The planter dirt was black as dark roast coffee. The dirt on the floor was deep brown in color. Kate considered it for a moment before shrugging and enjoying the remainder of the party.

Ten

With the sun long having set, the party guests slowly began making their way to the front doors.

In a familiar fashion, Teresa Lilley had her driver pull around to pick her up in such a way that the other guests were blocked in. This allowed her and her entourage to flow through the remaining guests after Cassie had already said her goodbyes.

David Hammit lingered, his eyes constantly checking on Kate and her whereabouts. Seeing Kate shoot him a direct look, his head flopped and he moped his way toward the exit.

Henrique Desperaux offered Cassie a night cap which was denied as Donovan politely escorted him out of the house. Merilu leaned toward Kate, "I told you this would be fun."

"It was quite the evening. Elegant and sophisticated with a generous helping of snarky and ruthless," Kate said. "I didn't want to upset Cassie's evening, but I found David Hammit snooping in her office."

"That little rat. What was he doing in there?" Merilu's brows furrowed.

"He said he was looking for something of his that he had left behind when he worked with Cassie. I didn't give him any time to get very far," Kate said. "But speaking of snooping, Henrique slipped in right before I escort Hammit out."

"That double rat!" Merilu cursed. "It's a good thing you were here to foil whatever nonsense they were up to."

"Yeah," Kate nodded, her mind deep in thought. As she watched what appeared to be the last of the guests leave, she caught a reflection of someone behind them. By the time she turned around, the figure was gone.

Frowning she walked to the where she thought the person in the reflection had disappeared. Seeing no one there, she scanned the house.

"What is it?" Merilu asked.

"I swear I saw someone standing there. That Neal Roth guy," Kate said.

Merilu shrugged, "Of all the people staying to the end, he seems the least likely."

"Yeah," Kate nodded. "It's been a long night, maybe my eyes are looking for shadows."

"Maybe," Merilu chuckled. "Speaking of long nights, I am going to head to bed."

"Goodnight, Merilu," Kate said.

Cassie, holding Donovan's hand said goodnight and wandered off with two glasses of wine.

Marco, a slight hiccup in his step, wandered over toward Kate, "A nightcap?"

To Kate's relief, Marco was intercepted by Gustavo who offered Kate a polite nod, "You know, Marco, I have been waiting for the right moment to open a bottle of Whistle Pig Boss Hog X. Whattaya say, pal?"

"That sounds pretty good," Marco slurred, allowing Gustavo to steer him away from Kate.

The catering crew buzzed about, beginning their clean up.

Kate was content to retreat to her room. Glancing at her watch, she realized the night was still fairly young. Recalling a bottle of Opus One at the bar near the gazebo, she decided to have her own nightcap in the privacy of her own balcony.

She relished the relative calm after the storm of the party. Some time to herself to decompress after an evening over abundant in conversation sounded particularly good to her.

In the background, she could hear the clinking of glasses as the catering crew conducted the Easter egg hunt of empty and half-empty beverage glasses stashed throughout the estate.

Kate found the bottle and a fresh glass. Chewing her lip, she searched for a waiter's tool. Slipping behind the bar, she flipped on her phone's flashlight to find something to open the wine with. A gleam in the corner of her eye caught her attention. Past the bar, by the steps of the gazebo, something shone in her light.

Pivoting her phone to get a better look, the shiny object grew in brilliance. Kate stepped back, her hand to her chest. The shiny object was a bracelet wrapped around a delicate wrist.

Rushing over, Kate saw a splash of silken hair spilling over a shimmering dress. Sprawled on the steps of the gazebo was Michelle Goss, Cassie's spokesmodel.

"Michelle!" Kate gasped.

Bending down, she placed her hand on Michelle's shoulder. When there was no response, Kate looked for any signs of life. Desperate to see Michelle's chest move, her hand twitch or her mouth gasp. The spokesmodel's limp body failed to give Kate the reaction that she needed. Kneeling down, she placed her fingers against Michelle's throat searching for a pulse. Moving to her wrist, she hoped she'd find the faintest sputter. Nothing.

Kate reeled back, her heart sinking. Pulling out her phone, she dialed 911.

Calling for help, Gustavo was the first to join her at the gazebo. Merilu wasn't far behind. The commotion caught the attention of Cassie and Donovan. They all stood around the steps of the gazebo.

"Is she…?" Cassie gasped.

"She is," Kate nodded.

As more lights were turned on, Kate kneeled down. A pool of blood spilled over the edge of the steps, slowly making its way toward the step below it.

Bending so that she was looking sideways, Kate's phone light picked up the shine of a metal object. In the light's gleam, she could see the object has pieced the model's chest.

Kate whirled around, her face in horror, "She was stabbed!"

Palm Beach Police arrived quickly, within minutes of Kate's 911 call.

Ushering the horrified group away, the police cordoned off the area. Taking initial statements, jotting down names, the police men and women remained objective about the discovery. One by one, they separated the remaining people at the estate.

Kate's growing experience instantly identified the moment the detective arrived. The officers stood slightly more erect and took a wider stance around the victim, standing vigil over Cassie's guests to ensure no one left or interfered with the scene.

The detective scanned the patio and followed an officer to the gazebo. Kneeling down, he swept the model's body with his flashlight. It didn't take him long to see what he needed to see before barking out orders.

Soon the area was lined with crime scene tape and a forensics team along with a medical examiner's crew made their presence known at the scene.

Forensics did a thorough sweep placing placards and taking photos as they worked. When they were satisfied, the medical examiner's team swept in to take control of the body. After snapping their own photos of the slain woman and the immediate scene, they cast tarp over her body and brought in a gurney.

Cassie's guests had to sit quietly and observe the methodical study of the horrific scene before the detective finally came over.

"My name is Detective Dennis Castro, I am with the Palm Beach Police Department. First off, I am sorry for your loss. I can't begin to understand what you are going through right now. I can tell you, I will find out who did this and why they did this to your friend, colleague or relative. I am going to speak with each of you alone, one at a time. I am going to have to ask you some uncomfortable questions. It is part of the process and part of the resolution for Ms…?"

"Goss. Her name is Michelle Goss," Cassie choked out in a sob.

"I know this is hard for you. I am going to find out who did this to Michelle and bring her some justice. I am sorry there isn't more I can do," Detective Castro said.

"Whose house are we at?" the detective asked.

"Mine," Cassie said.

"All right. We'll start with you. Is there a good place we can talk in private?" Detective Castro asked.

"My office…" Cassie started.

Kate raised her hand, "You might want to use the sitting room."

Castro's head snapped to Kate, "Excuse me?"

"I found someone, a couple people, snooping in there this evening. I am sure it is not related but to be careful, I thought I should mention it just the same," Kate said, swallowing hard.

Detective Castro stared at Kate for longer than she would like. "I'm still going to start with Ms…"

"VanLangen," Cassie said.

"VanLangen. But I think I'm looking forward to my conversation with you, Ms…" the detective started.

"Harper. Kate Harper," Kate said.

"Well, Ms. Harper, sit tight. I'll be with you as soon as I'm done talking to Ms. VanLangen," Detective Castro said.

Kate offered a weak nod, not even realizing she was doing so.

As the detective left with Cassie, the rest of the group turned to each other with an avalanche of questions.

The officers stood between them to stop them from sharing information.

"The detective will be with you when he can be. Until then, we need you to not talk. We can move you further apart…" an officer said.

"No. We'll be quiet. I want to be close to my friends," Merilu said to a chorus of nods.

The officer crossed his arms and nodded.

Kate's eyes followed the path that the detective and Cassie had taken. She itched to be part of the conversation.

Resigning to waiting her turn, after she gave comforting glances to the rest of the group waiting to be deposed, her gaze shifted to the gazebo. The forensics team hovered around the medical examiners as they surveyed the scene.

Ultimately, they lifted the body of Michelle Goss and placed her on the gurney. The tarp shifted out of place; they quickly maneuvered it back to covering the body.

Most of Cassie's guests stared listlessly at the ground in disbelief or closed their eyes while shaking their heads. Kate craned her neck, trying with every ounce of her senses to pick up body language or to read the lips of the forensics team canvassing the gazebo area.

Bright lights were brought in to aid the team and to allow for detailed photography of the scene. Most of their attention was centered around the spot where Michelle's body was found. Slowly, their perimeter grew as they searched for clues throughout the estate's party area.

Hearing a sobbing Cassie, Kate looked up to see Detective Castro and an officer escort Cassie back to the group.

"I'm going to say this each time I meet with every one of you. When I am done with our initial questioning, you are free to go for the night. The entire estate is off limits. If you need something or if you are excusing yourself to your rooms or wherever you are staying, we will have an officer escort you. Until the forensics team is completed, the estate is on lock down. Ms. VanLangen says the guest house was off limits for the party as was the upper floor of the main house. Those areas are free for use once you have been escorted. I expect by the time you get up in the morning, the forensics team will have cleared most of the house and patio," the detective said.

With a nod toward Kate, Detective Castro motioned, "Ms."

"Harper. Kate Harper."

The officer next to the detective scribbled notes in a pad.

"Come with me, please," the detective spun and began walking without waiting for a response.

"Did you get a time of death? Did the stabbing kill her? How many times was she stabbed? How deep was it?" Kate asked in excited procession.

"Ma'am, we'll do the detective work, unless you would like to save us a lot of time and confess to something," Detective Castro said, casting a Kate an annoyed glance.

"Right. Sorry. I just don't understand how it could happen with everyone here," Kate said.

"Plenty of suspects, plenty of opportunity, and available means," the detective said.

"You just need motive and that will lead you to your suspect," Kate said.

As they slipped into Cassie's sitting room at the front of the house, the detective held out a hand for Kate to sit. Kate plopped on the edge of one of the sofas.

"You have any reason to wish Ms. Goss ill, Ms. Harper?" Detective Castro asked.

"Me? No. I really just met her this evening at the party," Kate said. Her wriggling in her seat and the emphasis on her first word piqued the detective's interest.

"Not you, but you are aware of others?" Castro pressed.

"Uhm…" Kate's squirming intensified. Clearing her throat, she said, "Well, she was a very gregarious person. I think it was just her nature, but…"

"But?" the detective asked, his voice steely calm.

"There wasn't a soul at the party that she didn't interact with," Kate said.

"And that is a problem?"

"It depends, I suppose. If you came with a date, if you did business with her, if you might consider doing business with her… she seemed to like playing the crowd," Kate said.

"Playing the crowd? How, exactly?"

"Cassie and Teresa Lilley are competitors. Michelle is currently contracted with Cassie, but she seemed to spend a lot of time with Teresa and one of Cassie's former employees David Hammit. He left Cassie's company on bad terms," Kate said.

"But he was at the party?" the detective asked, nodding to the officer to ensure he was jotting notes.

"Yes. It seemed to take people by a bit of surprise. He really wasn't welcome, but Cassie wasn't going to make a fuss," Kate said.

"And… Teresa Lilley?" the detective continued.

"I noticed them have a pretty serious talk. I meandered my way over…" Kate started.

"I'm sure you did," the detective said before retracting. "I'm sorry. Please, continue."

Kate nodded, ignoring his insinuation, "I heard them arguing about contracts and that Cassie wouldn't let it stand, especially on the eve of her launch. Teresa just laughed."

"Hmm," the detective looked up thoughtfully. "Dropping her contract before a product launch would provide Ms. VanLangen a motive."

Kate screwed up her face, "Maybe. The way Michelle was flirting with Cassie's boyfriend was likely a better reason."

Detective Castro cocked his head, "The deceased was flirting with the hostess' boyfriend?"

"Oh, I don't think that is motive for murder. Cassie is very sure of herself. Very poised. I am sure Donovan Drake is used to being flirted with. He is a fairly well-known actor," Kate said.

"Poised people can wait for a convenient time and manage themselves through dicey situations rather well," Detective Castro said.

"True. I still don't see that as driving Cassie to murder," Kate said. "It was odd that Donovan seemed to grow more anxious as the party went on. They seemed okay by the end. They disappeared together."

"I don't believe we have Donovan Drake on our list of possible witnesses," Detective Castro frowned.

"I guess he must have left between the time he disappeared with Cassie to when I found… when I found Michelle's body," Kate said.

The detective leaned back in his seat and sighed, "So, who *do* you see as being willing to kill Ms. Goss?"

"Well, this David Hammit guy, was sneaking into Cassie's office during the party. Everyone was focused on Michelle's photo shoot. So he thought he'd have a clear shot," Kate said.

"But you caught him?" Detective Castro asked.

"I did," Kate nodded.

"Why weren't you with everyone else at the photoshoot?" the detective asked.

"Something rubbed me wrong about him and the conversation he was involved in with Michelle and Teresa Lilley," Kate said.

"If Michelle was about to defect, it kind of shines the light in a different direction, doesn't it?" the detective asked.

Kate's eyes narrowed, "You mean back to Cassie. Maybe, but, Hammit was sneaking into her office. Henrique Desperaux was as well. It wasn't the first time I caught him snooping in Cassie's home."

"What do either of those events have to do with Ms. Goss' death?" Detective Castro asked.

"I don't know," Kate shook her head.

"Anything else we should know?" the detective asked.

"There is another man who was acting odd at the party," Kate said.

"Odd? Odd how?"

"He didn't seem to know anyone there. Kept to the shadows. Didn't speak to many people. When I caught Hammit and Desperaux sneaking into Cassie's office, he was sneaking back into the house," Kate said.

"Sneaking?"

"Okay, just walking in. But it was odd that he was out front at that time of the party," Kate said.

"Do you have a name?"

"Neal Roth. Supposed to be a friend of a friend, I guess," Kate said.

Detective Castro sighed, "Anything else?"

"Marco DiNova approached Michelle at one point in the evening. They seem to have had a heated discussion about something. Michelle flung her arms down to her side and walked away. Marco looked flustered and angry but then afraid people were watching. He shrugged, smiled and went the opposite direction," Kate said.

The detective cast an exhausted eye toward the officer taking notes. After hesitating, he turned back to Kate, "Anything else?"

"No. I think that's it," Kate said with an assured nod.

The detective studied Kate for a moment, "So, what is your connection with Ms. VanLangen?"

"I was referred by my boss, she's a friend of Cassie's, to help with her upcoming remodel," Kate said.

The detective's eyes wandered around the house, "It seems pretty nice as it is."

"It's lovely. She is looking for something a bit lighter and more coastal," Kate said.

"This friend that referred you, was she at the party?" the detective asked.

Kate nodded and cast a thumb over her shoulder, "She is staying in the guest house. She is one of the people who were still here when the party ended."

"I see. Does she have any relationship with Ms. Goss?" Detective Castro asked.

Kate shook her head and shrugged, "I don't think so."

"Well, you've certainly… shared a lot of information," Detective Castro said standing up from his seat. With an arm extended, he indicated that Kate should head back toward the group.

Kate paused as they passed the stairs. A part of her wanted to sneak away and use the vantage of the master bedroom to surveil the patio, but she sensed her friends might need her that night.

Eleven

Kate sat back with the rest of Cassie's guests waiting to be questioned by the detective. The group looked increasingly wary as the already horrific night wore on.

One by one, Cassie's guests were led into the house by the detective and unceremoniously deposited in the separated patio chairs with officers overseeing them like they were in high school detention.

When the last guest was allowed to return to the group, Detective Castro announced, "Thank you all for your time. I know it has been a difficult evening. All of you are restricted from leaving town. We may have further questions for you."

"Detective Castro!" an officer called, a serious note in his voice.

The detective spun to find two officers jostling a man forward, "We found this man hiding in the bushes along the side of the house when we were canvasing for prints."

"Henrique!" Cassie gasped.

Castro nodded, "Henrique Desperaux. Your name surfaced more than once. I have quite a few questions for you. For starters, what are you doing hiding in the bushes?"

"It's not what it looks like. I… I was looking for something when the commotion started. I knew it wouldn't look good if I was… here. When you came, I found myself kind of trapped," Desperaux said, looking more apologetic and embarrassed than guilty. Kate noted his accent seemed thicker than usual.

"Mr. Desperaux, I agree with you. It doesn't look good. I think I will ask you questions down at the station," Detective Castro said.

Turning back to the group, the detective added, "I will want to see all of you tomorrow. Follow the forensic team's instructions explicitly or they have orders to arrest you on the spot. Goodnight."

The detective ordered an officer to take Desperaux to the Palm Beach Police Station. Stopping to confer with the lead crime scene technician, Castro cast an over the shoulder glance at Cassie and her guests before slipping away.

Cassie, who had oscillated from horrified to embarrassed to frightened, dropped her head in her hands and began sobbing.

Merilu closed in and draped her arm around her. Gustavo and Marco scooted close.

"Michelle had a way about her that most people loved, but those that didn't… Why? Why tonight? Why here?" Cassie asked between tears. Turning her head, she stared out at the ocean as the evening breeze gently flowed through her hair.

"That is what the detective is going to figure out," Merilu said.

"Why question us?" Cassie asked.

"Just protocol," Kate said. "I noticed the officers had lined up the catering staff to see what they saw tonight as well."

Cassie looked at her friends gathered around her, "Surely none of us… It's unthinkable!"

Her head returned to hands as her body shook.

"Come on. I think our minds and emotions have had about all they can take tonight. Let's get you to bed," Merilu suggested, nudging Cassie's shoulder.

Cassie nodded. With a sniff, she asked, "Gustavo, would you bring a bottle of the Clase Azul?"

"Of course," Gustavo said, immediately getting up to head to the house bar.

"A night cap. If there was ever a night demanding one…" Marco said.

"Something to wash away those images," Kate said. Not intending for her words to bring action, Marco hurried off behind Gustavo. Turning her attention to Merilu and Cassie, she asked, "Are you two going to be okay?"

Merilu nodded, "We'll be okay. It has definitely not been the end to the evening any of us had imagined."

"Certainly not," Kate said. "If you two need anything…."

Kate walked over to the seawall, taking a wide berth around the gazebo. Even the power of the waves couldn't sooth her. With a big sigh, she leaned over the rail.

Her phone buzzed. Glancing at the screen, her heart did a flip.

"Nick!" Kate answered.

"Hey, is everything okay?" Nick asked.

"Yes. I'm sorry I haven't gotten back to you. It has been a trying day," Kate said.

"Not tripping over more dead bodies," Nick laughed into the phone.

The line went silent.

"Kate…" Nick pressed.

"Someone was murdered. Cassie's spokesmodel," Kate said, her voice soft.

"What happened?" Nick asked.

"I… we don't know. I just found her, lying in the gazebo. She had been stabbed," Kate said.

"You found her?" Nick asked. "Are you okay?"

"Physically, I am fine. Yes," Kate said.

"Kate, I'm coming down there," Nick said, ready to hang up the phone and find his car keys.

"No, you don't need to do that. Let's let things sort out. I'll keep you in the loop, I promise," Kate said.

"You're going to let the police handle it right? What am I saying, of course you aren't," Nick fumed into the phone.

"I think even this one might be too big and too close for me to get involved in," Kate said.

"I like that answer, but why am I having a hard time buying it?" Nick asked.

Kate laughed, "Because I tend to get… curious."

"Curious. That is one way to put it," Nick said. "So, what happened?"

"The party was ending. The guests had all gone home. I went to the gazebo, and I found her lying there. She was stabbed. With a letter opener, I think," Kate said.

"You think?" Nick asked.

"I didn't get a good look, and I didn't want to disturb the body. From what I could see, it had that sort of handle and blade shape. The police detective wouldn't confirm it for me," Kate said.

"Imagine that. You are already making friends with the detective," Nick said.

"I don't think he cares for me all too very much," Kate admitted.

Suddenly, a voice called out, "Kate! There you are. I wasn't sure if murder was a bourbon or red wine sort of occasion. So, I brought both!"

Kate turned to find Marco with two neatly poured glasses of bourbon cupped in one hand and a pair of wineglasses dangling between the fingers of his other. His Italian accent oozed with enough charm and overt volume that Nick could hear it through the phone.

"Kate?" Nick called, his voice almost a screech.

"I'm sorry, Nick. It's one of Cassie's house guests. The architect on the remodel," Kate said.

"Contractor on the remodel?" Nick repeated. Whispering to himself, he said, "*I'm* supposed to be Kate's contractor."

"What?" Kate asked.

"Oh, nothing. Just thinking I should really head down there," Nick said.

"No. I'm going to wind down and turn in for the night. Good night, Nick," Kate said.

"Good night… Kate," Nick said, the phone going dead.

"I hope I wasn't interrupting," Marco smiled. Even in the aftermath of murder, his teeth seemed to gleam in the moonlight. He held the drinks up for Kate.

Kate glanced at her phone and then at the gazebo. Taking one of the glasses of bourbon, she tilted it in Marco's direction. Taking the glass to her lips, she tossed it back in one unceremonious gulp. "Thank you, that hit the spot."

Marco stared open mouthed. Collecting himself, he said, "You… you handle yourself well under these… unusual circumstances."

"Sadly, not my first rodeo," Kate held her arms tight to her chest. Her eyes moved away from the Italian man and toward the Atlantic. She was begging for the waves to console her. She pulled her arms in close to create space.

"Not your first… rodeo?" Marco asked.

"Long story." Kate said, breaking from the ocean view. Facing Marco, she said, "I'm sorry. As you can imagine, it has been a long, trying day. I think I am going to turn in. And lock my bedroom door."

"Yes, I suppose I should do the same," Marco. "Um, what happens tomorrow?"

"Assuming forensics is done working the crime scene, I imagine they will focus on the gazebo, the main area of the party, valet interviews and security footage. Once we get the green light, assuming Cassie is in the mood to continue, we reno the house," Kate said. Her voice was flat and her response deadpan formulaic.

Marco was both surprised and impressed with her grounded response.

"Well, good night then. I am just down the hall if you… should need anything," Marco said, his voice dripping with suggestion.

"Lock your doors, Marco," Kate said and disappeared past the crime scene tape around gazebo.

Twelve

Kate woke as the first sliver of sunrise broke the horizon. A dazzling array of colors with bands of gold, deep indigo and pinks met the visual end of the Atlantic.

Sitting up, Kate took a moment to appreciate the view before she allowed the horror and questions of the previous evening to seep back into her thoughts.

Glancing at the clock, she was surprised she had awakened. The late night and activities of the crime scene investigation unit scouring the estate had gone on through the night, making sleep difficult. It was the tug of unanswered questions that got her out of bed. The same lure drew her to the balcony.

Peering at the patio below, Kate saw an officer posted at the scene. He seemed to be attracted to the stunning daybreak view as well.

The gazebo was strung with crime scene tape. Little yellow markers dotted the patio marking potential clues to the spokesmodel's death. Kate's eyes tried to identify each point of the CSI team's interest.

Pulling out her phone, Kate took a wide view photo of the scene while the officer's attention was drawn to the sea.

Chewing her lips, she decided she would review the photo and retrace what she could remember over a cup of coffee. The trip to the kitchen would give her a chance to see what CSI flagged inside the house as well.

Opening the master bedroom door, she tiptoed forward assuming the other guests were still asleep. Sitting in one of the chairs, an officer rose to their feet. "Good morning, ma'am," the officer said, her voice low.

"Good morning. Is it okay if I get myself some coffee? I can get some for you and the other officers as well," Kate said.

"Officers. We have one posted out front as well," the officer said. "But thank you. I'm sure they would appreciate it."

Kate made her way to the Italian espresso machine. Setting out four cups, she stared at the machine. Chewing her lip, she tried to figure out how to make it work.

She flipped a switch on the autogrinder, which fed directly into the espresso portafilter. Nodding with approval that she had gotten that far, she inserted it in its hold. Flipping a switch, the machine warmed up, letting out a burst of steam, Kate jumped back.

She was shocked as a pair of hands clamped her shoulders, steadying her.

Turning slowly, she found Marco's ever-present smile looking back at her.

"Easy, Kate. Here, let me help you. I have one of these at home," Marco said.

A raspy morning voice from across the room called out, "I've got it, you two. Why don't you have a seat on the veranda? I'll make the coffees and whip up a breakfast. Get them right out to you."

"Gustavo. Good morning. Breakfast on the veranda is a fine idea. It would be good to have all of us together," Marco said.

"Good morning, Gustavo and Marco. If it's all the same, I would like to have coffee in my room. I'm still a little shaken up over last night's events," Kate requested.

"Of course," Gustavo nodded.

"Well, when you are settled, we should meet up with Cassie and see how she would like us to proceed," Marco suggested.

Kate pressed a smile, "That's a good idea. Just give me a bit to… collect myself."

As she started to walk away, she turned to Gustavo, "If it's not too much trouble, I offered coffee to the police officers. While I would have eventually figured it out, they might prefer a cup from you anyway."

"No trouble at all," Gustavo said.

Kate hurried up the steps to her room. Instinctively, she locked the door behind her. Walking out to the veranda, she pressed against the rail. Normally, her eyes would have been locked on the ocean and its soothing waves. This morning, her eyes swept a crime scene.

Before reviewing the image she'd taken on the phone, she surveyed the scene once more. Her mind working through the night as she recalled it playing out below her.

Her chest tightened as she recalled the image of Michelle Goss lying awkwardly on the gazebo floor.

Working backwards she tried to recall anything that stood out.

In her mind's eye, she saw a spilled drink just over the model's shoulder. Ice, clear liquid and a lime.

"Ice!" Kate gasped. "She had just been killed!"

Though she was whispering to herself, her outburst caught the attention of the officer on the patio. Kate offered a sheepish wave. Receiving a nod back, Kate continued her mental journey.

With a note pad on the veranda table and the vantage from the balcony, Kate did her best to recreate everything she had seen the night before, especially in the snapshot of time right before she found the body of Michelle Goss.

Cassie had worked the crowd with aplomb as any socialite would. Even with the less-than-welcome guests at the party- Teresa Lilley, David Hammit and Henrique Desperaux, she maneuvered through the party with grace.

Kate recalled Michelle being the center of attention in multiple conversations. Each had the participants looking over their shoulders as if to ensure only their circle was within earshot. Kate didn't notice it at the time, but she specifically recalled the conversation shift when Cassie was nearby.

Merilu was the perfect ambassador. Whether by Cassie's side or on her own, Merilu worked the party with elegance, yet in a manner that never deferred the attention from Cassie. Kate appreciated her boss and friend's deft presence. The one moment in the evening where Merilu seemed to lose her poise, was in the brief but noticeable conversation she'd had with Michelle.

As Kate's memory wandered around the party, it was impossible to miss Marco circulating. He flashed his smile to everyone wearing a dress. Cordial, attentive, yet, very Marco. Most seemed used to his antics. Some played along with it or politely, yet, curtly moved the conversation along. The model fell into the played-along-with category.

An attendee who had garnered a lot of attention was Donovan Drake. There wasn't a camera or social media post that he didn't find a way to be a part of. While he started the evening by

Cassie's side, he had frequently wandered into conversations with attractive women. Michelle was no exception. From Kate's perspective, the conversation seemed friendly, until it wasn't, and the model moved abruptly away from the actor.

David Hammit seemed to be a cloudy presence from the moment he stepped into the party. From bypassing the hostess's greeting to inciting discussions of Cassie's spokesmodel to having some role at Teresa Lilley's company, he seemed to be in the thick of negative energy all night. Kate could almost suggest he was a sinister presence in his attendance at the party.

Then, there was Teresa Lilley herself. While her overt actions and words were bubbly and generally kind, there was a subversiveness to her interactions as well. She tried to absorb as much spotlight from Cassie as she possibly could. She was definitely disingenuous, but Kate couldn't quite think of her as having murderous intentions. Besides, she *wanted* the model to defect. It clearly would have been a big win, at least to her already impressive ego.

Kate couldn't believe Henrique Desperaux was caught by the police hiding in Cassie's bushes *after* the murder. She couldn't determine whether it was foolishness, rotten luck or the man had a much worse hidden agenda than snooping. He certainly was determined to find something at Cassie's house. Him being caught where he shouldn't have been continued to rack up the points. The police finding him hiding in the bushes at a murder scene elevated the qualitative score.

Finally, Kate's eyes swept the back patio. She traced a mystery man to the front entrance where he had come through at the same time David Hammit and Desperaux were intent on searching Cassie's office. Rarely making eye contact or speaking with anyone at the party, the man identified as Neal Roth was lurking in the shadows throughout the event.

Kate tapped her notes, searching her head for any other piece of last night's puzzle she could think of.

Her thoughts were broken as she heard a mild commotion. Thinking it might be Gustavo delivering breakfast, Kate peered over the edge of the balcony.

A defiant Cassie VanLangen strolled from the guest house toward the main house tugging a fine set of white and brown Italian luggage behind her. The small wheels rumbled across the stone patio announcing her intent. An anxious frown creased her typically composed face.

Turning, Cassie said something to Merilu with animated gestures before handing her luggage off to a driver who wheeled them away.

Merilu trailed behind. Glancing up, she spied Kate watching the scene unfold. A hasty wave and grim smile beckoned for help.

Thirteen

Kate hurried down the steps to greet Cassie and Merilu as they entered the house. The driver whisked past with the luggage and out the front door.

"Good morning, ladies," Kate said, stepping in front of her friends. Hands clasped in front of her, she put a subtle barrier between them and the door.

"Good morning, Kate," Merilu said.

"Hi, Kate," Cassie managed. Her vibrant eyes were distant and vacant.

"How is everyone this morning?" Kate asked.

"A little shaken up," Merilu admitted.

"Shaken up? I think I might turn this renovation into a prep to sell," Cassie snapped.

"This is tough to go through, for sure," Kate said.

"A woman. A… friend… was murdered on my patio!" Cassie said, her voice in a shaky crescendo.

"It is going to take some time to process all of our thoughts and feelings, for sure," Kate said. "Where… where are you off to?"

"I can't stay here. Not with… I just figured I'd go ahead and get started on my travel. Let you and Marco have the run of the house. I have encouraged Merilu to go home as well," Cassie said.

"I see," Kate said slowly. "The police generally have a 'don't leave town' philosophy."

Cassie's head snapped to Kate and she blinked, "They said something like that. I'll let my lawyer handle it."

Merilu gave a little shrug, her eyes locking on Kate's.

"Donovan is waiting for me and my driver. We are going to ride to the airport together and I am going to escape to my flat in Milan. He is off to shoot scenes for his next film," Cassie said.

"Escape is probably the apropos term for the actor best known for a shampoo commercial," Henrique Desperaux's distinctive voice said.

All eyes swept to the front door.

"What are *you* doing here? Returning to the scene of the crime?" Cassie spat.

"The police let me go. Not before a very long night in their inhospitable accommodation. I came to collect my missing item before it disappears for good," Henrique said.

"Your what? Why would it be here?" Cassie said before her eyes changed and she nodded quietly, "I see. Fine. I will get it for you and then maybe you won't be hanging around my home quite so much anymore. Certainly not hurling accusations of murder at me while you trespass."

"*You* certainly have a reason to have been angry at Michelle," Henrique said.

"I have… had many reasons to be upset with Michelle, but murder?" Cassie retorted. "To be frank, I thought maybe it was you."

"Me?" Desperaux looked wounded.

"She lured you into a destroying a relationship while snapping your precious little heart into teeny little pieces," Cassie said.

Desperaux looked at Merilu and Kate, "I hardly think this is the time…"

"Don't you?" Cassie sneered as she led them to her office.

In his most British accent, Desperaux said, "It wasn't Michelle who broke my heart."

"It wasn't her who broke mine either," Cassie snapped. "That was your responsibility."

Continuing in a huff, she pushed into her office. Sliding what appeared to be a panel in the wainscotting out of the way, she revealed a small, pearlescent safe roughly the size of a dormitory refrigerator. Holding her finger to the sensor, the tumblers spun into position and the door sprung open.

Cassie stumbled back, her hand on her chest. Her cheeks paled as she gasped, "It's gone!"

"What is gone?" Desperaux leaned forward to peer over her shoulder.

"Everything," Cassie sighed.

Kate stepped closer, "What did you keep in there, may I ask?"

"My passport, my black card, my banking information…" Cassie replied.

"And jewelry!" Desperaux said.

"Well, yes, I put some jewelry in there. Most of that is in…" Cassie's eyes grew in horror.

Racing past the group, she sprinted up the steps to the master bedroom. Entering the closet, she reached under a shelf holding neatly folded sweaters and pressed another fingerprint reader.

To her relief and surprise, the jewelry in the safe was where she had left it. Her hand on her heart, she let out a sigh.

Desperaux's head bounced back and forth as he tried to catalogue the safe's contents.

"We need to call the detective," Kate said. "I'll let one of the officers know what we've found. Make sure your office is locked up tight."

Desperaux looked visibly stressed and agitated, "I should probably go."

"Oh, no, Henrique. You are staying right here," Cassie growled.

Desperaux's head bobbed to his chest.

Cassie slapped herself on the forehead, "I can't go to Milan without my passport!"

"*That* is what you're concerned about?" Desperaux scoffed. "Michelle was killed in your backyard last night."

"I know. That is why I want to leave. I can't get that image out of my mind," Cassie said.

"Yeah," Henrique nodded. "I imagine it is hardest on you. I'm sorry."

The two seemed to share a sentiment of mutual support for a moment.

Marco and Gustavo appeared at the foot of the steps to see what the fuss was about.

Kate carefully noted everyone's responses to each other and the safe being broken into as she walked over the office assigned to the interior of the house.

"Excuse me, Officer. Ms. VanLangen has just realized that her safe was broken into. I believe Detective Castro needs to know about that," Kate said.

"Thank you, ma'am," the officer nodded and pulled out her cellphone to immediately dial the police detective.

Gustavo put his arm around Cassie and steered her toward the patio, "Come. Let's have coffee and breakfast."

Cassie froze, "No. Not out there."

"Fine," Gustavo nodded. "That's okay. We'll have breakfast in here."

"Thank you, Gustavo," Cassie said in a breathy voice.

The group followed Gustavo as he escorted Cassie to the dining table. Pulling out a chair, he sat her down in it and shuffled off to bring in their breakfast items.

Marco went to retrieve two more coffees for Cassie and Merilu.

Kate paced in the foyer for word on Detective Castro. Her mind played on how the theft of the safe contents, all the attention on the office and the spokesmodel's murder all tied together.

She eyed the office and cocked her head. In Cassie's state, she didn't latch the door closed. Striding over, she played the handle. Cassie locked it, but didn't close the door all the way. Pushing into the office, Kate's eyes scanned the room. She recalled the paper that had fallen on the floor. Her eyes moved to the pile on the desk where she replaced the paper.

If David Hammit was telling the truth and he didn't touch the papers, it had to end up there somehow. Giving the room a quick survey, Kate moved to the office window behind the desk. The frame of one of the windows was a fraction higher than the other. Investigating, Kate brushed the sheer fabric aside. One of the window latches was perpendicular to the frame while the other was in line with it.

"Someone opened the window of the office," Kate said. Shooting a look over her shoulder, she eyed the stack of papers directly in the path of the window's breeze if there was one. "That's how the paper ended up on the floor."

A voice made Kate jump, "Being in the location of the reported crime makes you look like a suspect. Talking to yourself makes you sound like a candidate for our local mental wellness initiative."

Kate pushed her lips together in discomfiture at seeing the police detective standing in the doorway.

"Detective Castro," Kate blushed.

Waving his hands in front of him, Detective Castro said, "That was unfair. Detectives talk to themselves all the time. We just have the badge to imply we are sane while we do it. Then again, we usually aren't suspects in a murder and an apparent burglary."

"I'm a suspect?" Kate gasped.

"Everyone is a suspect," the detective said. "Especially those attending the party of the deceased, staying at the home of the murder scene and incidentally standing in the precise location of a reported crime."

Kate nodded, "Yeah, that's fair."

"Care to tell me what you are doing in here?" the detective asked.

"I was waiting for you in the foyer. I realized Cassie hadn't closed the office door all the way. When I came to check it, I thought of the paper from her desk I saw on the floor last night when I caught David Hammit sneaking in. Seeing the windows, I had a hunch. One of them is unlatched," Kate pointed toward the windows behind the desk.

The detective followed her fingers and studied the windows. Turning back, he nodded, "Yep. This one is unlatched. You didn't touch it?"

"It is how I found it. I merely peeled the curtains back. Note how the window is right in-line with the stack of papers," Kate pointed out.

"So it is," Detective Castro said. Standing upright, he swelled his chest, "I think you should probably join the others. The officer out front said something about coffee?"

"I'll be sure one is made for you," Kate said.

"Thank you," the detective said, returning his attention to the unlatched window.

Kate paused in the doorway before leaving the detective to his work.

Fourteen

Kate watched as Detective Castro led his forensics team in a thorough scouring of Cassie's office. As she tried to peer into the room, the detective had an officer stretch crime scene tape with a wide berth around the office and out in front where the office windows were.

With a disapproving look at Kate, the detective closed the door.

Kate spun with a pout to find Gustavo holding a tray of espresso drinks.

"You want a peek at what they're doing?" Gustavo asked, a grin spread wide across his face.

Kate nodded, accepting the tray held out of her.

"I'll knock on the door," Gustavo said. "When you are done, breakfast is ready."

"Thank you, Gustavo," Kate said.

Lifting the police tape high enough for Kate to duck under, Gustavo rapped on the door with his knuckles and stepped away leaving a smiling Kate at the door with a tray full of coffee drinks.

A crime scene tech opened the door, "We are processing the room."

"Yes, of course. Detective Castro requested a coffee?" Kate said.

Craning her head around, she could see the detective stand up from his squat position by the safe and sigh.

"I'll come get it. You stay there, Ms. Harper," Detective Castro said.

Kate watched as the detective gingerly made his way to the door. It gave Kate enough time to catalogue what the forensics team found important. She found techs hovering over the safe with powders, sprays and shining lights, the window frames and the desk. All areas that Kate assumed would be of note.

What she found interesting was a tech scouring the lock, "They didn't use a key?"

"Excuse me?" Detective Castro screwed up his face.

"Here's your coffee," Kate said. "Seemed like most of the interested parties had a key."

Detective Castro looked at Kate for a long minute, a sour expression on his face. Finally, he answered, "Well, if your story is correct, there were two people with keys who had them taken away in the course of the evening."

"True," Kate said. Her mind instantly returned to her catching David Hammit and taking the key from him. Her eyes went wide, "I put Hammit's key in the planter!"

Handing the coffee to the detective, she rushed to the planter. Poking her fingers in the dirt until they met resistance. With a pinch, she pulled the key from the soil. Holding it up, she called, "Here it is!"

Kate brought the key to the detective.

Castro looked at the key.

"What am I supposed to do with that?" he asked.

Kate beamed with pride, "It's evidence!"

"It technically wasn't used in a crime, and clearly not the crime we are currently investigating," the detective said.

Kate's face fell. With a frown, she asked, "You think the lock was picked?"

"I don't know. I think we need to determine how the room was accessed, who accessed it, why they accessed and what they took," the detective said.

"Well, yeah," Kate said.

"Ms. Harper," Detective Castro said, his voice even. "Leave the detective work to me and my team."

"Of course. Yes. Just wondering if I can provide you any of the necessary details to help you and your team out. As a witness," Kate said.

"Well, that is appreciated. Now go enjoy your breakfast and let us do our work. Oh, and tell your friends I would like to speak with them before they leave the estate. Thank you for the coffee," Detective Castro said, closing the door.

Kate remained holding the key in the air, "What am I supposed to do with this?"

"Give it back to its owner!" Castro's voice could be heard through the door.

Dusting soil off the key, Kate made her way toward breakfast.

The mood at the table was somber. It was the quietest the group had been since Kate's arrival. Marco tried to encourage conversation, but his attempts were met with little more than grunts.

"Hi guys," Kate said as she sat down.

"Anything new from the detective?" Merilu asked.

"They are tackling the office. They'll get to the bottom of it," Kate said. Looking at her plate, she found caprese avocado toast with a fried egg and bacon. "This looks fantastic, Gustavo."

Peering at Cassie's plate, Kate watched the cosmetics mogul playing with her food. A glance at Merilu elicited a shrug.

"Oh, and Detective Castro wants to speak with us before we go anywhere," Kate said.

Henrique stood up from the table, "I just remembered, I need to go…"

"Nowhere, Mr. Desperaux," Detective Castro said. "What are you doing here?"

"I, uh, I came to check on Cassie," Desperaux said.

"Given we found you prowling around in the bushes shortly after a murder had taken place, you might understand how that seems suspicious," the detective said.

"I was just leaving," Desperaux said.

"Sit down, Mr. Desperaux," Detective Castro demanded.

Henrique Desperaux melted back into his seat.

The detective studied the audience.

"As for the rest of you, I need to ask that you all remain in town. Ms. VanLangen, I had a quick word with your driver. I am sorry to tell you, your travel plans will need to be delayed," Castro said.

Directing his attention to Cassie, the detective asked, "Why don't you walk me through what you found?"

"It's what I didn't find, but, yes," Cassie said.

Holding his arm out, the detective asked, "Would you show me?"

Cassie got out of her seat and followed the detective to her office. Kate slipped away from the table and quietly followed what she felt was sufficient paces away.

"Ms. Harper, you are welcome to follow with Ms. VanLangen's permission, but I will not have you skulking behind us," Detective Castro said without even turning his head.

"I'd like for her to come," Cassie nodded.

Kate hastened her pace in a series of quick skips to catch up.

Arriving at the door, the detective led Kate and Cassie into the office.

Walking to the desk and looking over the safe, he asked, "What all did you keep in here?"

"My passport, a few legal documents, my black card, and occasional jewelry that I took off in my office that I didn't feel like running upstairs for," Cassie said.

"I'll need a complete list. We'll do what we can to recover the items," Castro said. "Was this office locked or unlocked during the party last night?"

Cassie looked flabbergasted, "I mean, the door was closed. I don't typically lock my office door in my own home, but with the party, I made sure it was locked. Of course, we all heard about Kate catching David Hammit, my former employee and Henrique attempting to gain entry."

"Oh, right. Here is Hammit's key," Kate held the key still stained with soil remnants from being shoved in the potted plant.

Cassie took the key.

"Given the safe was opened, I am not sure the office door lock would have made much of a difference," Kate said.

"True, an interior door lock would be child's play for anyone with the skills to break into a safe," Marco agreed, flashing Kate a smile as though they were somehow allied.

All eyes looked at Marco who had appeared in the doorway.

The detective looked even more disgruntled. He cast a glance at Cassie who shrugged at Marco's presence.

"Sorry for the intrusion. I am merely saying that interior doors are meant to be an inconvenient obstacle, not security," Marco said.

The detective grunted as he studied the Italian contractor. Kneeling, he inspected the safe, noting the model. "It's a good safe. Since the estate is part of a murder investigation and what appears to be a burglary after the murder, with police officers on the property, I'm going to have to lock the house down. I want forensics to sweep the entire house," Detective Castro announced.

"You don't look hopeful that you'll find anything new," Kate said.

The detective cocked his head toward Kate, "What makes you…"

"An average person can't crack a safe," Kate said. Eyeing Marco and nodding her head at where Gustavo and Henrique were finishing their breakfasts, "Unless they have inside information like someone close to Cassie. They might know codes or be able to guess combinations. A professional thief won't have likely left any clues behind."

"You're not wrong," Castro said. His eyes told he knew more, but he did not share his thoughts.

Kate looked thoughtful as though her own words had sparked an idea.

"Who all had access to this area?" the detective asked.

Cassie paled as she considered her somewhat lengthy list, "Apparently David Hammit and Henrique. Marco has access to the entire house. Gustavo. The cleaning staff."

"Cleaning staff?" Castro asked.

"Contract group. They take care of several houses along the A1A," Cassie said.

"I'll ask you to get me their information," the detective said.

Cassie nodded.

"Were these items present last night?" the detective asked.

Cassie looked confused, "I, I don't know. I didn't go into the safe last night."

Looking at his notes, Detective Castro tapped the list of people present, "I'm going to have to demand that none of you leave the area. We may have more questions for you."

"But I have a launch coming up in Milan," Cassie protested.

"Let's hope I work fast and get lucky, or you'll have to attend virtually," the detective said.

"I need to call Donovan… and my attorney," Cassie said.

"You do what you need to, Ms. VanLangen," Detective Castro said. "You clearly have a group of people around you. If you need anyone to talk to, we have a trauma specialist at the precinct."

"Thank you, detective," Cassie nodded.

Walking back to the group at breakfast, Henrique asked, "Anything new?"

Quizzical eyes fell on Henrique but no one responded.

"You never took anything out of the safe, a small box? Perhaps?" Henrique asked.

"No, at least I don't think so. Why?" Cassie asked.

"It has to be here. I need to find it," Henrique said.

"If it was in the safe…" Cassie warned.

"I know," Henrique said, his head bobbing down to his chest.

Fifteen

"Gustavo, a pitcher of sangria. It looks like plans have changed," Cassie said.

Gustavo quickly disappeared.

Desperaux stood, "I really should be going. Thank you for allowing me to stay for breakfast."

"The detective said everyone had to stay," Cassie said, her voice curt.

Desperaux's head dropped, he looked genuinely saddened.

Cassie sighed, holding her arms out, she said, "Come, my old friend."

Looking unsure for just a moment, Desperaux quickly accepted the offer and gave Cassie a hug. Kissing her on a cheek, he said, "I'm sorry you have to go through all this."

"Thank you, Henrique," Cassie said.

As Desperaux bid the table a good day, he made for the door.

"Behave!" Cassie called as he reached the door.

Desperaux turned on his heel and offered a salute before disappearing.

Returning to the table, Gustavo set glasses out in front of everyone and poured the fruit laden beverage into beautiful sea glass tumblers.

Realizing one person had left, Gustavo started to walk away with the extra glass.

"Oh, no. You are joining us, Gustavo," Cassie waved her hand across the back of an empty chair.

Gustavo hesitated before agreeing to sit. Pouring himself a glass he slipped into a chair.

"To Michelle, may her soul rest in peace," Cassie held the glass in the air for others to join her in the toast.

Uneasy eyes glanced out at the gazebo.

The table fell silent after the toast.

Shuffling uncomfortably in her seat, Cassie finally gave up. "That's it, I have to get out of here. Merilu, would you mind driving me? I will get a place at the Breakers until I am cleared to go to Milan. If you will all excuse me, being here is too much for me right now. I trust the three of you will make yourselves comfortable until you are cleared to proceed with the renovation? Marco, perhaps you can present some designs to replace the gazebo?"

Turning to Kate, Cassie said, "Forgive me, Kate. I would completely understand If you wanted to remove yourself from this assignment and go home yourself."

With a quick glance at Merilu, Kate flashed a comforting smile. "I would just as soon see this through. As Merilu's friend, I wouldn't feel right leaving when you need help the most. Besides, you're right. Once we are allowed to go to work, Marco and I will refresh the estate into something that feels like a home to erase bad memories and create wonderful new ones."

"That is a very positive spin on this… heart-wrenching situation," Cassie said.

Merilu's eyes thanked Kate.

Her driver long since dismissed, Cassie discovered her luggage sitting neatly by the front door. Merilu followed to drive Cassie in her SUV to the grand beach hotel nearby.

Kate could see that she was upset. The past forty-eight hours had taken its toll on Cassie. Merilu stood elegantly and dutifully by.

When the ladies had left and Gustavo returned to his duties, Kate found herself alone with Marco.

The Italian developer smiled, "Well, we might as well occupy our minds with things that are less terrible."

Armed with the house plans, his laptop and a bottle of Montepulciano di Abruzzo, he settled in next to where Kate was sitting, gazing over the beach in the shade of a mimosa tree. Seeing Kate's disagreeable look, he shrugged, "I figured we might as well make the best of it," Marco said.

His voice was oozing with the type of charm that set off Kate's alarm bells. Studying Marco for a moment, she acknowledged that the man was handsome. His olive skin, ocean matching eyes and gelato melting smile, Kate wriggled uncomfortably in her seat.

Focusing instead on the work spread out on the table, Kate shrugged. "I suppose I would rather stay focused on something."

She didn't want to admit that she was focused on solving the mystery of Michelle's murder and Cassie's missing items.

"I'd love your advice on the rework of the gazebo," Marco said, leaning into Kate as he poured two glasses of the Italian red wine.

"Yeah, absolutely," Kate nodded, scooting away for a breath's more space than Marco was affording.

Kate studied Marco's vision, and admitted, "Your designs are really good, Marco."

"I tried to look into Cassie's heart," Marco said. "And at the same time, offer a some sort of tribute to Michelle. Her favorite flower was the ghost orchid. Despite her… at times raucous exterior, she had a deep soft spot in her. She tended to have a heart for rare things that were endangered. The ghost orchid is one of those things."

"Marco, this is… inspiring," Kate said. "I love the design. I might change the layout as well. Placing new aesthetics on the gazebo is one thing. Making it something shaped entirely different would help avoid those heart-breaking memories every time she sees it, never mind spends time in it."

Marco nodded with a hand to his chin, "What do you have in mind?"

"What if you changed the layout so it wasn't just a place to escape the sun and look over the pool and lawn? What if you turned into something that Cassie could watch the ocean from?" Kate suggested.

Marco nodded, "I like it."

With a pencil, he started crafting lines. A spiral staircase wound to a tiered gazebo that would easily see beyond the lawn to the beach and crashing waves below. Transformed from the traditional octagonal design, the entire structure looked more like a maritime outpost.

"You worked it up that quickly? Marco, this is exceptional!" Kate said, standing over his shoulder. "You might add some additional support for the added height, but it looks amazing!"

"Your vision of beachfront spaces is inspiring," Marco said. "I would love to take some of your interior ideas and add them to the new gazebo area. Pillows, textures, counters, flourishes…"

"Yes, of course!" Kate said, pulling the laptop closer to her. "What if we take splashes of bright blue… almost like the desk chair cushions and incorporate it throughout the house?"

"Sort of like maintaining the theme," Marco nodded.

"Yes. Subtle, we don't have to go crazy with it, but it will tie everything in. It will be fun, definitely beachy, yet still have a sense of elegance," Kate said.

"I see why Merilu thinks so highly of you. We architects take design from schooling as well as a bit of imagination. You take inspiration from the environment and the emotions of your clients to create scenes that they get to live out," Marco said, pouring another glass of wine.

"I guess I've never quite heard it that way, but if that is how it comes about, I'm happy to give them or their guests, experiences that are memorable," Kate said.

Encouraged by the vision of Cassie's reimagined estate, Kate and Marco rolled up their sleeves for hours. Moving from room to room, they plotted the architectural details with the final decoration schemes.

To Kate's surprise, the pair worked very well together. When their momentum slowed down in the early afternoon, they took a step back.

"How about another bottle of liquid inspiration? I spied a lovely Nebbiolo from Barolo in the cellar…" Marco started.

"I don't think any more wine is a good idea. I was thinking about digging around in the kitchen for a snack," Kate said.

"A plunder expedition in the kitchen, that is a delightful idea. What do you say we see what culinary trouble we can get into?" Marco suggested.

"I'll check with Gustavo," Kate said.

"No need. I ran into him when you were reviewing color palates for the guest bedrooms. With Cassie staying at The Breakers, I encouraged him to take a day off. I believe he headed up the coast in search of more raucous surf conditions," Marco said.

The idea of being alone at the estate with Marco didn't sit incredibly well with her. Her senses urged her to proceed with caution.

With a feeble nod and a thin smile, she reluctantly agreed.

"Wonderful. My family has this amazing Cacciucco recipe. Let's see what is stocked in the kitchen!" Marco declared as though he were about to set siege.

"What goes with Cacciucco ?" Kate asked.

"How about garlic butter toast points?" Marco asked.

Kate laughed, "All right, I think that is within my culinary grasp."

Sixteen

Kate set the table while Marco finished the Italian seafood dish. Taking in the two place settings, she didn't like the look of the table or the situation. Retrieving another setting, the table for three looked and felt more innocent.

"Someone joining us?" Marco asked, using both hands to carefully bring out a soup tureen.

"If Gustavo comes back from surfing, I am sure he'll be famished," Kate said.

Marco looked thoughtfully at the settings and offered a feeble nod, "Yes."

Kate hurried to get her toast points while Marco grabbed a bottle of wine. Returning to the table, Kate set the platter of bread down as Marco readied the bottle over her glass.

"None for me, thanks. I think I am good with water and lemon this evening. It just sounds fresh and cleansing after everything," Kate said.

"Suit yourself," Marco said, pouring a tall glass for himself.

"This smells amazing," Kate said as she ladled soup into her bowl.

"It is usually made with octopus, squid and cuttlefish, but white fish and shrimp is an acceptable substitute," Marco said.

"Well, thank you for making it. I think we had a productive day," Kate said.

"I think we had a magnificent day," Marco said, over-accentuating the entire sentence.

Kate's phone buzzed. Seeing the call was from Nick, she hesitated before swiping it closed. She squirmed in her seat.

"So, Kate. You do not have a boyfriend?" Marco asked, his eyes intently locked onto Kate's.

"Um, no. I guess not in those exact words," Kate said.

"You've not met the one then?" Marco asked.

"I, I really don't know. I am just not in a place where a relationship is my top priority," Kate said.

"That can be okay. Two adult friends can enjoy each other's company without obligation," Marco said, playfully dipping bread into his soup.

"If you mean by sharing a meal or working on a project together, sure. But if you are implying anything else…" Kate started as her phone buzzed again.

Nick's name popped up again. Kate was concerned something might be wrong. Turning to Marco, she said, "I'm sorry, I really need to get this. Dinner was delicious. Thank you."

Kate scooted her chair out and took quick steps away from the table as she accepted the call. Making her way to the edge of the property overlooking the beach, Kate answered, "Hi, Nick. How's the sailboat coming along?"

"Unfortunately, we ran into some dry rot. Fixing that took us all day, knocking us a bit off track," Nick said.

"Oh, gosh. It's a good thing you are there for your friend," Kate said.

"I called. I was beginning to get concerned," Nick said.

"Well…" Kate hesitated. "On top of last night, Cassie's safe was broken into."

"I thought police officers were stationed there all night," Nick said.

"They were. We aren't sure when it was broken into, but it had to be in the middle of the night," Kate said.

"If the safe was broken into and the police were there, it had to be in inside job," Nick said. "It had to be one of the people staying there."

"I thought of that, I'm just not sure," Kate said.

"Are you at the estate alone? You need to be careful, Kate," Nick said.

"No, Marco is… here. Gustavo left for the afternoon, but he'll be back. Merilu got Cassie settled into the nearby hotel and decided to book a room at the hotel for herself," Kate said.

"And leave you there by yourself with a potential killer?" Nick gasped.

"Well, I guess of all the suspects, the ones here are lower on the list…" Kate attempted to explain.

"But they *are* on the list, Kate," Nick's voice shared his displeasure with the news.

"You shouldn't be there by yourself…"

"I'm fine," Kate said.

"You say that a lot," Nick said. "I don't like the idea of you being all alone where a murder had just taken place. Maybe they didn't find what they were after and come back?"

"I'm not on the estate alone," Kate said.

"Right… this Marco guy," Nick said.

"Cassie's architect. Gustavo, her chef, er bartender… is here as well," Kate said.

"I'm not sure that makes me feel any better," Nick said.

"Marco and…" Kate began.

"Right, Marco. The new Nick!" Nick fumed.

"There is only one Nick Mason," Kate said.

"Kate, I really don't think leaving you there without someone you can trust is a good idea," Nick said. "I can be there in… Well, I can be there tomorrow."

"I'll be okay," Kate laughed. "I do appreciate it. And I would like you here. But you are already behind schedule on your friend's boat."

"You take priority!" Nick said almost as surprised to say it as Kate was to hear it.

"Thank you, Nick," Kate said, her eyes locked on the waves washing onto the soft beige sand.

"I'm worried about you," Nick said.

"I'm fine. It is quiet here. The gates are locked down, even Cassie would have to be let in at this point," Kate said.

"I think you should stay at a hotel," Nick said.

"I might once we get going. It sounds like we'll be released to start work tomorrow. It will good to be able to get moving as fast as possible," Kate said.

"That, I don't disagree with…" Nick's voice went quiet for a moment. "Let me come down. I can help."

"Your friend needs you. We'll get together as soon as you are done," Kate said. Her voice was soothing.

"Something to look forward to," Nick said.

"Yeah," Kate said. "I should turn in."

"Hmm," Nick was clearly not happy with the results of their conversation.

"Goodnight, Nick," Kate said.

"Goodnight, Kate. Take care of yourself," Nick said.

"I will. I promise," Kate assured him.

Hanging up the phone, Kate leaned with her palms against the rail and watched the ocean waves crash to shore. At the barrier between Cassie's property and the neighboring resort, the seawall stretched several feet into the water. The jutting concrete caused for spectacular splashes as the sea thrust into the air.

The sound of the water was soothing. Mixed with the cool night air, Kate almost felt comfortable for the first time in nearly two days. With a resolute breath, she glanced over her shoulder before returning to watch the waves chase little dots of sand crabs up onto the sand.

Cocking her head, she realized something in her brief glance was off.

Turning completely to face the house, her heart skipped a beat. A flash of light splashed across the windows of the master bedroom.

Seventeen

Kate's chest tightened as her eyes locked on the patio windows of the master suite. Subconsciously, her feet slowly moved in the direction of the house. Never taking her eyes off the windows, she started to relax.

Pivoting her view, she looked out onto the water thinking maybe a passing boat played a trick on her eyes. Not seeing anything, she turned back, trained on the master bedroom.

A light, less bright than before, flashed against the windows. Someone was in her room!

In a full sprint, Kate raced toward the house. Flinging open the patio doors, she entered the house. Listening intently for footsteps or other sounds, she bounded up the steps to the second floor.

Placing her ear against the door, she grabbed the handle. With a deep breath, Kate gave it a twist. For split second, her head argued between slow and stealthy or bold and fast. Bold and fast won as Kate pushed the door open and burst into the room.

Panning the master suite with the aid of moonlight streaking into the room through the French doors, Kate found the room empty. Hearing the sound of a hanger being jostled on its rack, Kate spun her attention to the closet.

Repeating her process of grasping the handle and collecting herself, she didn't get the option to determine her approach. Instead, the closet door was thrust open, slamming into her shoulder and knocking her to the floor.

A blur of a dark shape bounded over her and darted to the balcony doors. In one smooth movement, the figure slipped through and disappeared.

Kate picked herself up and rushed to the veranda. Pausing for a moment, she spun in a 180 degree arc, prepared to meet up with her foe. Instead, she found herself on an empty balcony. Taking little steps in each direction, Kate tried to make sense of what had happened. Leaning over the balcony, she searched for signs of movement below.

Tracing the railing, Kate peered over the edge. She shook her head. Kate couldn't understand how the figure had just vanished.

Taking a deep breath, Kate walked back into the room. Flipping on the lights, she scanned the opulent bedroom suite. Everything seemed intact. Her things appeared untouched. A quick search of her purse revealed nothing had been taken.

Making her way to the closet, Kate's heart inexplicably did a flip as she peered inside. The area near the safe had been cleared. The safe itself was closed. Kate had no way of knowing whether the intruder had made their way inside it or not.

A chill ran up Kate's spine. She didn't feel comfortable standing inside the closet. With quick steps, she tiptoed her way out and shut the door behind her.

In the relative safety of the lighted bedroom, Kate assessed her situation. It was only then that her shoulder began to throb. Rubbing it gingerly, she murmured, "That's gonna bruise."

"Is everything alright?" a voice from the doorway said, making her jump.

Kate spun to see Marco DiNova standing just inside the master bedroom. A mostly drunk glass of wine in his hand.

"Uhm… yes," Kate said, her voice sounding more like a question than a statement.

"I thought I heard running," Marco said, poking his head further into the room and giving it a once over.

Kate nodded, "Yeah. That was me. I thought I saw something and I ran into to check it out. You didn't happen to see or hear anything, did you?"

"No," Marco shook his head. "Just you running on the stairs, I guess."

Kate studied the architect for a moment. Having no reason to not believe, for some reason, she didn't.

"Well, whatever it was, it must be gone now," Kate said. With a stretch, she yawned, "I better turn in."

"You're sure you okay? I mean, I could…" Marco started.

"I'm fine," Kate's response was so quick it must have sounded harsh.

Marco put his hands in front of him and waved. "Okay, okay. You have a good night, Kate."

"You, too, Marco," Kate said following him to the door. When he was in the hall, Kate softly closed the door and locked it. As much as she enjoyed the open air from the veranda, she made quick steps to cross the room and lock the patio doors, but not before taking a quick scan of the balcony and the estate grounds.

Standing in front of the windows with the bedroom lights on, Kate felt exposed to the world outside. She felt as if somewhere in that darkness, someone was staring up at her.

Shaking off the thought, she turned off all the lights, allowing the soft glow of the moon to light the room enough for her to get ready for bed.

Kate woke the next morning to the light sounds of porcelain dishes gently rattling. Pressing herself up from the bed, she opened heavy eyes. The east facing windows had already embraced the rising sun.

With a light groan, she flipped her legs over the side of the bed and stumbled toward the bedroom door.

Twisting the door handle, she found a tray of coffee, pastries and a yogurt parfait. Gustavo's head was bobbing down the steps.

"Gustavo?" Kate called.

The bobbing head paused. Gustavo turned and ascended a few steps, "Is there something else you need, Ms. Kate?"

Kate laughed, "No, Gustavo. Breakfast looks… perfect. I wanted to see if you would join me for breakfast this morning."

"Join you?" Gustavo asked as though the question was incredibly odd. Looking at the weary look in the usually strong woman's eyes, he nodded, "I'll come and sit with you."

"Good," Kate said. "Have you had breakfast?"

"Avocado toast and a sufficient supply of coffee," Gustavo said.

Kate grabbed the tray and avoided the houseman's attempts to wrestle it away from her. Defeated, Gustavo raced her to the patio door. Finding it locked, he turned the lever and pushed through the doors.

Setting the tray down on the patio table, Kate took her seat. Gustavo sat across from her.

Studying the contents of the tray more closely, Kate's hands dove for the latte. Pulling the caffeinated beverage to her lips, she took what felt like a life-invigorating sip. "Thank you, Gustavo. I needed this."

"Is everything okay, Ms. Kate?" Gustavo asked, a concerned expression creasing his brows.

"Not much sleep last night," Kate admitted. "You… you didn't happen to hear anything last night, did you?"

Gustavo shook his head, "No. Just Marco raiding the bar."

"I see," Kate said.

"Why, may I ask?"

Kate's eyes glanced toward the master suite. "Someone was in my room last night."

"What?" Gustavo leaned forward. "While you were sleeping?"

"Thankfully, no. Before I came up to bed, I saw a light in the bedroom. When I came up to check it out, someone in the closet pushed the door open and knocked me over," Kate said. "Somehow, they disappeared. They ran right out here and… vanished.

Gustavo's eyes scanned the veranda. He frowned as he couldn't imagine how someone might escape via the private terrace. "Ms. Kate, I think it is time you go somewhere safe like Ms. Cassie suggested," he said.

"I might," Kate nodded. "It was definitely running through my head last night."

"I'll call her and set it up," Gustavo said.

Kate shifted in her seat, "No, that's okay. I'll handle it. Thank you, though."

"Was, uh, was anything missing?" Gustavo asked.

"No. Not that I could tell. I was going to let Cassie know this morning. And phone Police Detective Castro," Kate said.

"That's a good idea," Gustavo suddenly stood up from his seat. "I think I am going to check the grounds."

"Another good idea. I'll come with you," Kate said.

"No, you enjoy your breakfast. I'll take a quick look around and let you know if I find anything," Gustavo said.

Without waiting for a reaction from Kate, Gustavo scurried away. Kate's eyes followed him as they peered over her coffee mug.

"Odd, but he does make a good latte," Kate said to herself.

Realizing she had landed at the frothy end of the cup, Kate was overjoyed to find that Gustavo had included a carafe of coffee with her breakfast. Adding to her cup, she swirled the ingredients together and took a sip. The caffeine did her good after a fitful night's sleep.

She wanted to do her own investigation, but she knew it would be best if the detective had the opportunity to sweep the estate first.

Her eyes widened. Slapping her hands on the table, she shot up from her chair, "Gustavo!"

Racing through the house, she scanned the back patio for the houseman. Not seeing him, she sprinted back through the house nearly colliding with Marco.

"Woah, woah," the Italian man fanned his hands out in front of him. "Is everything okay?"

"Yes. Gustavo, he is searching the grounds looking for signs of an intruder last night, but we should wait for Detective Castro. When you heard my footsteps… I saw someone," Kate said, her voice breathy.

"All right. Let's find Gustavo. I was going to inquire what was on the menu today anyway. Really craving saltimbocca," Marco said.

Kate shook off the unnecessary information. Spying the front doors, she ran and flung them open. She ran to the right while Marco, fresh on her heels, ran left.

"Gustavo!" Kate called. As she rounded the corner, the houseman appeared through the bushes.

"Yes, is everything okay?" Gustavo said, wiping bark dust off his hands.

"I was just thinking, we shouldn't disturb anything until the detective has a chance to check things out himself," Kate said.

"Oh, yeah. Right," Gustavo said. "I… I've made a circuit, but I haven't disturbed anything."

"Good," Kate said. "Come on, Marco is looking for you, too. He might accidentally muddle evidence while trying to find you."

"Right," Gustavo nodded.

Following him out onto the stone walkway, Kate noticed a little trail of soil left in each of his footsteps.

Marco stood at the corner of the house peering down the side yard. Hearing footfalls in his direction, he spun, looking initially startled. "Oh, there you are!"

"We should head inside. I'll call Cassie and Detective Castro," Kate said.

Receiving nods, she led the way into the house.

"You're sure there was an intruder last night?" Gustavo asked.

"He… or she, I guess, knocked me down. I have the bruise to prove it," Kate said. Tugging on her shirt sleeve, she revealed a sizable bruise on her shoulder.

"Kate, we should get you medical attention," Marco said.

"I'm fine. A good reminder to be careful, that's all," Kate said.

"Be careful? I will tell Cassie that you should be moved immediately," Gustavo said. Realizing his tone was a bit demanding, he softened, "For your safety."

"Thank you for your concern, Gustavo. We'll deal with all that after the detective has had a chance to inspect the property. I am keen to learn from Cassie whether… anything was taken," Kate said.

"Perhaps you startled the would-be thief," Gustavo said. "And they walked away with nothing."

"Or, there is something of at least perceived value here that Cassie hasn't had a chance to securely move yet and someone knows that," Kate said.

Both men appeared to stiffen with Kate's words.

Pulling out her phone, she dialed the police detective's number.

Eighteen

"Maybe we shouldn't tell the detective what happened last night," Marco said as he and Kate sat waiting for the police detective's arrival.

"What do you mean?" Kate asked.

"It will put a hold on the renovations and Cassie is on a timeline. Maybe… it was nothing," Marco shrugged.

"Nothing that put a bruise on Kate's shoulder?" Gustavo piped up as he busily spruced up the house.

"Remember, you aren't supposed to touch anything," Marco snapped.

"Oh. You're right," Gustavo said, shoving the cleaning towel into his belt loop.

A knock at the door halted their conversation.

All three heads swiveled.

Gustavo pushed up his sleeves and strode to open the door.

Detective Castro, flanked by a pair of uniformed officers stood in the foyer.

"Everything okay in here?" the detective asked.

"Seems to be a common question," Kate retorted.

"What?" Detective Castro asked.

"It was probably nothing," Marco said, almost to the surprise of Kate and Gustavo.

"Then why am I here?" the detective asked.

Kate strode forward, "I saw a light in the master bedroom last night…"

"From where?" the detective stepped into the house and whipped off his glasses.

"From out by the sea wall," Kate said.

The detective's eyes turned up toward the master bedroom, "A reflection on the window?"

Kate shook her head, "The light was from the inside. It wasn't a room light. More like a flashlight. It was brief, like someone trying to control the beam. I ran in to see what it was and…"

"Of course you did," Detective Castro snapped.

"I didn't find anyone at first. I reached the closet door, and it burst open knocking me down," Kate said.

The detective suddenly became interested in the story. "Someone was in there?"

Kate nodded, "They were. They pushed through the door, leapt over me and disappeared."

"Are you okay?" Detective Castro asked.

Kate paused. Her eyes glanced on Marco and Gustavo before tugging on her sleeve.

The detective's eyes widened as he saw the bruise on Kate's shoulder. "Okay. Tell me in careful detail what happened."

"I had just grabbed the door handle. I was ready to yank it open and the someone pushed through it. Hard. They knocked me over as they pushed through. They ran out of the room toward veranda. By the time I got out there, they were… gone!" Kate said.

The detective looked up the stairs, "Do you mind?"

"Not at all," Kate said.

Jogging up the steps, Detective Castro pushed into the room. He took a glance at the closet door and his eyes ran along the room to the French doors.

With both hands, the detective flung the doors opened and stepped outside. His eyes swept the length of the veranda. Peering over the rail, he moved along its expanse. Looking at Kate, he asked, "They ran out here and…?"

"And they just disappeared," Kate said. "They vanished into the night."

The detective frowned once more peering over the rail. "They have a ladder? A rope? A pole vault?"

"No," Kate shook her head.

"Well, I'll get forensics out here. Again. Anything out of sorts, anything taken?" Castro asked. With a sigh, he looked at the trio, "I was about to tell you had the all-clear to get going on your renovations…"

"I'm sure everything is okay," Marco said, his voice anxious.

The detective turned to face Marco directly, "All the same, Mr. Dinova, I think we'll give this a proper investigation."

"Of course," Marco said, his eyes darting to Kate's.

"You said the suspect was in the closet," Detective Castro said, pointing back inside the master suite.

Kate nodded, following the detective back inside the house.

"Nothing was touched?" the detective asked, scanning the room, eyeing Kate's purse.

"Nothing was taken, that I know of. I have no idea about the safe," Kate said.

Detective Castro looked at Kate, "Does Ms. VanLangen know?"

"I called her right after I called you. She should be on her way," Kate said.

As the detective walked into the massive closet and surveyed the scene, Gustavo's voice could be heard from downstairs joined by a woman's.

Their conversation moved its way up the stairs, "Kate, are you okay?"

"I'm fine, Cassie. Thank you," Kate said.

"My goodness, this whole affair is just so upsetting," Cassie declared. "What happened?"

Kate recounted her story from the previous evening.

"Why don't I get a suite for you at the Breakers," Cassie suggested.

"I don't think I'm in any real danger..." Kate started.

"Ms. VanLangen's right. We already have one victim and we don't know the motive. If they were deemed in the way..." Detective Castro began.

"Like Kate was last night!" Marco blurted.

"Like Kate was last night. Things could have been a lot worse for you," Detective Castro said.

"But, the intruder had time. If they wanted to kill me, it would have been a good opportunity," Kate said.

The detective cocked his head disapprovingly at Kate.

"Cassie, why don't you see if anything was taken from the safe?" Kate suggested.

"I really need to get everything moved. And beef up security around here," Cassie said.

The detective scratched his chin, "Where was everyone last night at the time of the intrusion?"

"I was out by the sea wall," Kate said.

"I was plundering the wine cellar," Marco admitted, a sheepish glance toward Cassie.

"I was in my room," Gustavo said.

"Was everything locked up?" Detective Castro asked.

"The front of the house was," Gustavo nodded. "I was in for the night. I always check the doors."

"The back patio was open, but I was there. I suppose someone could have slipped past me," Kate shrugged.

"How about the veranda?" the detective asked.

"The veranda?" Kate asked.

"Just covering all the bases. It sounds like whoever knocked you down was confident the veranda was an escape route. Maybe they got in that way," the detective said.

"It wasn't locked," Kate admitted.

The detective jotted something in his note pad.

Indicating the closet, Detective Castro urged, "Ms. VanLangen, the safe."

Cassie nodded and slipped into the closet. The detective, on her heels, spun toward the others, "I think we'll check this out on our own."

Kate, Marco and Gustavo froze in their tracks, hovering just outside the closet.

Before Cassie pressed the biometric pad, Detective Castro dusted the keypad and fingerprint reader. Shining a light, he scowled, "Clean. Not a single print. Not even yours, Ms. VanLangen. Go ahead."

Cassie pressed her finger to the pad releasing the steel rods that locked the door. Swinging it open, Cassie peered inside. "Looks like everything is still here," she declared.

"If you like, I'll send an officer to escort you and your valuables to a safe deposit until all of this is cleared up," Detective Castro said.

"I'd like that," Cassie nodded.

The detective led her back out of the closet, casting a furrowed brow at the eager eavesdroppers.

"I'll do a perimeter scan. I'll need forensics to come out again. They'll check for prints on all access points to the house. You have somewhere else you can stay, Ms. Harper?" the detective asked. "All of you?"

"I can set them up at the Breakers," Cassie said.

"I think it is a splendid idea for Kate. An unnecessary gesture for me," Marco said.

"I feel terrible. It is partly my job to watch the house," Gustavo said.

"You all do what you need to do. I will say I am a bit tired of coming out here. I am going to re-establish a small team to watch the house until we get to the bottom of this," Detective Castro said.

"Anything about the investigation you can share with us, Detective?" Kate asked.

The detective shot Kate a wary glance, "Nothing I'm at liberty to share at this point in the investigation."

Kate offered a mischievous smile, "You know, a little quid pro quo."

"Excuse me?" Castro snapped.

"I was just hoping you could share some information as to what you have found so far," Kate said, bouncing on her toes.

Castro folded his arms, "It is an on-going murder investigation. As far as I am concerned, you are all suspects."

Kate squirmed, "Then again, the Freedom of Information Act…"

"Exemption 7a. 'Could reasonably interfere with enforcement proceedings'," Castro snapped, his eyes declaring his irritation.

"Fine!" Kate flung her hand in the air.

"Kate Harper. Involved, unwittingly or otherwise, in two murder investigations… Now three. In each of the two prior cases, the police detectives noted warnings of incessant interference. I can tell you should you interfere in mine, Ms. Harper, you will be sitting in a jail cell until I am satisfied the investigation is closed. Are we clear?" Detective Castro said.

"You looked me up…" Kate said.

"I did background checks on all of the party attendees and a thorough peek into the sordid pasts of all of the named suspects," Detective Castro said. Squaring up with Kate, he repeated, "Are we clear, Ms. Harper?"

"Yes. We're clear," Kate said, dropping her chin to her chest.

"About the renovation…" Marco started.

"I was ready to give the all clear, but with last night's disturbance, I'd at least like to get forensics out here one last time," Detective Castro said. "Ms. VanLangen, would you be able to move the safe contents this afternoon?"

"I think so," Cassie nodded.

"I'll have an officer standing by to escort you," Detective Castro said. With a glance to Marco and Kate, he said, "Once forensics clears out, you can start the renovation."

Marco nodded.

"It sounds like we will have a busy day ahead of us," Kate said.

"I'll let the concierge at The Breakers know to be expecting you," Cassie said.

Kate hesitated, "Is the offer to stay in the guest house still open?"

"Well, yes, of course, but…" Cassie began.

"With the officers back on watch, I'm sure I'll be fine," Kate said.

Cassie huffed, "I'll have a room for you just the same."

"Thank you, Cassie," Kate said. With her hands gently clasped around her new friend's wrists, she added, "I'm sorry you're going through all this."

"I'm sorry *we're* going through this, my dear," Cassie said.

Nineteen

The forensics team worked with haste. Already having a solid lay of the land, they maneuvered quickly around the estate. Focusing their attention on the back and the side of the house as well as the master suite, they scoured for clues.

Kate found reasons to hover while the crime scene investigators did their work.

"Most of the soft earth along the house has been trampled. Multiple footprints, most of them scuffed," Kate heard a technician report.

"No prints on exterior or interior doors," another reported.

"Closet and safe are clean. There were minor scuff marks in the key override on the safe," a technician reported to the lead investigator.

The investigator shook her head as she studied the notes, "Castro is not going to like this. Come on, we *have* to find something!"

Kate shielded her eyes from the late morning sun, "Check the veranda rail and side of the house."

"Excuse me?" the investigator spun to find Kate move from hovering to stepping along side her.

"Whoever was in the house left via the veranda somehow. Maybe ladder marks, a retrievable climbing rope knot, somehow reached one of the pillars and slid down?" Kate suggested.

"We'll look into it. In the meantime, please let us work or I'll have an officer escort you off property until we are done," the investigator said.

"Understood," Kate said as she backed away.

When she was out of sight, she heard the investigator call out, "Check the veranda rail and columns for scuff marks!"

"It looks like we are going to get the all clear soon," Marco said as Kate slipped back into the house. "And you need something to keep you out of trouble."

"I suppose that is right," Kate said, still distracted by wondering what forensics did or didn't find.

"Let's get prepped. I have the contractors on their way, we're ready to finally get some work done," Marco said.

"All right," Kate said.

"Let's map out where we want to start and set the flow of work around the house," Marco said.

"Well, we know that Cassie and an officer need access to the master suite this afternoon," Kate said.

"Then we start on the opposite end of the hall with one of the guest rooms," Marco suggested.

"Sounds good," Kate said. With an eye cast out toward the back patio where the lead forensic investigator was receiving final findings, Kate watched as Gustavo came in from collecting herbs. "Ooh, leave the door open!"

Gustavo cocked his head at Kate. Turning to look over his shoulder at the investigator taking notes, he chuckled and nodded.

Kate wandered close to the door to listen.

"Hair fibers on the veranda rail. Probably belong to the house guest. No marks on the rail or the pillar except for one black scuff midspan on the column," the forensic tech reported.

"Good work. Try and get a scraping off the column and I'll request a hair sample from the estate's house guest," the investigator said.

Kate stepped out onto the patio. As her hair lifted in the Atlantic breeze, she spied a strand in the corner of her eye. With a pinch, she clamped it in her fingers and plucked it. Holding it out, she carried it to the investigator, "Here you go!"

The investigator pursed her lips. Pulling out a specimen bag, she said, "I was going to request to retrieve one from your hairbrush."

"Oh, that would have been better," Kate nodded. She brightened and said, "At least you can unequivocally know it is mine. A fresh sample."

"Hmph!" the investigator said. Turning to her team she gave the signal to wrap up. A tech finished scraping one of the tall pillars close to the veranda where a light mark had been left.

"Any idea if that was there before last night?" the investigator asked.

Kate shook her head disappointedly, "No. I really can't recall. I'm sorry."

"Well, we'll be out of your hair, if you'll excuse the pun, shortly," the investigator said.

"Thank you. And thank you for your work. I do really appreciate it," Kate said.

"That's fine. Just appreciate from... over there or something. Detective Castro really doesn't like outside interference in his cases," the investigator said.

Kate nodded.

As the forensic vans were replaced with work trucks, Kate and Marco led the construction foreman on a tour of Cassie's home. Leading them through the beachfront mansion, Marco was in his element. Holding out a set of blueprints, he navigated the house like an archeologist following a map to an ancient tomb.

Kate had to admit, she liked this version of Marco. He was vibrant as he shared his plans. His talent in design was evident yet he was open to ideas from the construction crew, especially in terms of structural changes. He also shared the spotlight with Kate, referencing her ideas as they flowed through the house.

The already excitable man was positively buzzing as the crew brought their tools into place and readied for work. Although Kate's role was largely relegated to the final phase of the project, Marco was keen to pull her into discussions with the foreman on her vision.

Kate grinned, "If it gets in the way of the ocean, you might want to rethink it."

"A beach house reno in a nutshell," Marco added.

"Got it. We'll get to work," the foreman said, hustling off to rally his crew.

Kate and Marco stood back and watched the work crew dig into their tasks.

"This is always the horrifying part," Kate said.

"There's nothing to be afraid of. It's just wood and plaster," Marco said.

"Not always," Kate said in a breathy tone.

"What?" Marco cocked his head toward Kate.

Kate chuckled to herself and said, "Nothing. I think I'm just better at the rebuild than the tear down."

"We'll certainly find what's lurking behind those walls," Marco said.

"What's that?" Kate gasped, her eyes wide.

"Plumbing, electrical, moisture, those are the things that really impact a project," Marco said.

"Right. Yes. That make's sense," Kate said suddenly wishing Nick was with her.

The front door opened.

"Knock, knock!" Merilu beamed as she side-stepped a hustling member of the contractor's crew.

"Merilu! What are you doing here?" Kate greeted her friend.

"I came to rescue my friend," Merilu said. Looking around the house at the bustling activity, she said, "It looks like you were greenlit to move forward with the reno."

"We were. We had a little excitement. Detective Castro and his team came. We are all fine," Kate said.

"A little excitement? You were attacked!" Merilu said.

Kate bristled, "I wasn't attacked. I was in the way."

"That is a charitable description," Merilu said. "Cassie says she has a place for you at The Breakers. It is a gorgeous property, you'll love it and be safe there."

"According to Detective Castro, I'll be safe here," Kate said, defiance clear in her voice.

"Kate…" Merilu sighed.

"I will make a judgment call. If I don't feel safe, I'll move to The Breakers," Kate said.

Merilu's hands fell to her hips, "You should make the move before *needing* to make the call, Kate."

"That can't be the only reason you came all the way here," Kate said.

"I'm worried about Cassie. She is an incredibly strong woman, but this whole escapade is breaking her down," Merilu said. "She said she was meeting an officer her to relocate her safe items to a safe deposit."

Kate nodded, "Detective Castro's idea. He is also posting officers to watch the property until the case is closed."

"Well, that is a small relief," Merilu said.

"I'll be fine. Look at all this activity," Kate said, displaying her hands toward the work crew.

"They aren't here in the middle of the night, Kate," Merilu said.

"No one is after *me*," Kate said.

"Not yet. Stick your nose in this and… and…" Merilu started.

Kate placed her arm around Merilu, "I know. I'll be careful. I am letting the detective handle this one. I swear."

"You had better," Merilu said.

"Come on, let's get you one of Gustavo's famous coffees," Kate said.

"I was thinking something stronger, but we can start there," Merilu laughed allowing her friend to tow her along toward the espresso machine.

By the time the whir of the espresso machine had died down, Cassie arrived with an officer following her close behind. Arms spread wide, she gave Kate and Merilu hugs.

"Have you talked sense into her yet?" Cassie asked.

"Not yet," Merilu admitted.

"Well, keep at it. I don't need the added stress," Cassie said.

"Cassie, I'll be fine. I promise," Kate said.

More to Merilu than Kate, Cassie said, "The dedication to the project is one thing, but I won't have another of my… my friends… be put in harm's way."

"Understood," Merilu smiled.

"Well, I am off to secure my things. What has this world come to?" Cassie huffed.

As Cassie walked up the stairs to the master suite shadowed by the police officer, Merilu pulled Kate aside.

Looking up at her friend, Merilu asked, "Is it dedication to the project or to the sleuthing?"

Kate shuffled and offered a weak smile, "A bit of both?"

"Kate! This has gotten too dangerous. You see something in your room, days after a murder has taken place, and you go *into* the room? What is wrong with you?" Merilu scolded.

"I wasn't sure. I certainly didn't want to cause a fuss if it was a trick of the light. The closet door thing took me by a bit of surprise.

To be fair, I think it took whoever was in there by surprise, too," Kate said.

"So, who do you suppose it was? How did they get up there? How did they get away… from the veranda? There are no stairs!" Merilu asked.

"I don't know. There isn't lattice. There are no vines. The closest palm trees would be a stretch," Kate shrugged.

Merilu looked all around Kate before whispering, "Or it is someone who knows the house. Has access to tools, ladders and the like. Able to stow them before being spied."

"I know. I thought of that. There have been a few… weird things," Kate said.

"Weird things? What kind of weird things?" Merilu asked.

"This morning, Gustavo went 'looking for clues' all the while trampling the likely path the intruder would have taken," Kate said.

"Obscuring footprints," Merilu said.

"Yes. The exact path would have been easy to avoid," Kate said. "There's more."

"More?" Merilu leaned in, her worried expression only deepening.

Kate shuffled and frowned before saying, "Marco was acting strange as well. For one, he's always around. Two, he was almost blowing off the incident in front of Detective Castro."

A slight grin slit Merilu's lips, "When Marco sees something he likes, he can be rather… persistent. As for the conversation with the detective, I don't know."

"It is possible that he just didn't want another incident to interfere with the start of the renovations, but it certainly made me question things a bit," Kate said.

"Well, keep your head on a swivel. After the other night, I don't know what to believe anymore," Merilu said.

"Always," Kate grinned.

"You! I don't know what to do with you," Merilu said in a frustrated groan.

"Know that I am going to help your friend in any manner that I can, *provided* it is safe to do so," Kate said.

"I'm going to hold you to that last part," Merilu said.

"What do you say we grab a bite to eat?" Kate asked.

"How about seafood? It's right around the corner and has a stunning view," Merilu offered.

"Sounds good," Kate said. "Let me tell Marco I'm leaving."

Seeing him on the terrace level just outside of the master suite, plans spread in front of the construction foreman, she met his eyes. Kate pointed at Merilu and then the door. Receiving a nod from Marco, Kate said to Merilu, "Lead the way."

Motioning for Kate to jump in the passenger seat, Merilu climbed behind the wheel of her luxury SUV. The blast of air conditioning was immediately refreshing as the Florida sun made its presence well known, since the doors of the house were open as the work crews moved in and out.

Twenty

In only a couple of turns, Merilu was waved by at a guarded gate. She drove down a long drive with well-manicured grounds. A large fountain framed in tall palm trees made a natural circle for traffic to flow through. Merilu stopped in front of a grand Italian Renaissance style resort hotel. Two towers with flags waving at their peaks welcomed guests.

"Welcome to the Breakers," Merilu said.

"Is this a sales pitch to get me to relocate?" Kate asked.

Merilu grinned, "It has a wonderful lunch spot. If that sways you to move in here during the investigation, never mind the renovations, so be it."

"You are good at your job," Kate laughed.

Merilu handed the valet her keys and joined Kate outside the foyer of the oceanfront hotel.

"This is lovely," Kate said.

They walked through automatic doors revealing stone covered walls with massive arches adorned with gilded artwork. Opposite the entrance was a Romanesque atrium.

The stone clad walls gave way to the white, Ionic swooping columns and oceanic blue accents of a long hallway. At the end of the hall, the showpiece of the hotel was clearly in view.

"That vista should look familiar," Merilu said.

"It is like being at Cassie's estate," Kate said. Admiring the light aqua blue waves splashing playfully ashore, she added, "The water is so beautiful. It almost looks unreal."

"Wait until you see the restaurant," Merilu said.

At the end of a long hall that seemed to empty right into the ocean, they hooked a right turn to be greeted by a hostess.

"Mind if we eat at the bar?" Merilu asked.

"Not at all," Kate shrugged. She eyed her friend suspiciously as she was typically a sit-at-the-table kind of diner.

Kate instantly saw Merilu's rationale. The entire bar top was a long, slender aquarium. Clown fish swam past coral outcroppings while little shrimp scurried along the sandy floor.

"This is amazing!" Kate exclaimed, studying the bar top and watching fish chase one another down the line of patrons. Moving her view from the bar top to the windows, she was greeted with another stunning view of the Atlantic Ocean. Framed by a palm tree, the panel-trimmed window looked like a picture frame hosting an almost too pretty to be real rendition of Florida's Atlantic Coast.

"Okay, this is double amazing," Kate said.

"I'm not sure if that is a thing. If it is, I whole-heartedly agree," Merilu said.

A smiling bartender, her back to paradise greeted the ladies, "Here for lunch?"

"We are," Merilu assented.

"Very good. Let me know if I can get you a drink to start," the bartender said.

Merilu grinned, "We don't have far to go. A short drive, walk or swim."

"We can even have a valet take you in a golf cart, depending on how far you have to go," the bartender said.

"How about you? Can you have a relaxing lunch?" Merilu asked.

"Sure. I'm not picking up any power tools today," Kate said.

"How about two flirtinis," Merilu suggested to the bartender.

Kate cast a sideways glance at her friend, "Forgive the name, they are pineapple infused cosmos with a splash of champagne."

"Okay, sounds good. Yes, two flirtinis," Kate giggled. "But I assure you, there will be no flirting here."

"Speaking of, how is life with Marco and Gustavo?" Merilu asked.

"A stronger rationale to relocate than fear of intruders," Kate said.

The bartender placed their drinks on top of the aquarium bar, "Sounds like you two have stories to tell."

"You have no idea. This one keeps me on my toes. She's a good designer and a better friend, so I keep her around," Merilu teased.

Kate peered at the menu, shrinking away from the conversation, "What's good here?"

"Everything. Just stick with seafood. Not that their other dishes aren't great, but come on, it's their specialty," Merilu said.

Kate looked down at a clown fish swimming by, "Won't they get offended?"

"No clown fish anywhere on the menu. It looks like their lives are pretty good and no bigger fish to make a meal out of them," Merilu said.

The bartender stopped by for their orders.

"I'll have the pecan crusted grouper with mango slaw and coconut lime sauce," Merilu said.

"Excellent. And for you?" the bartender looked at Kate.

"I can't resist the seafood club- lobster, crab, bacon and truffle fries!" Kate's face gleamed like a child in front of an ice cream stand.

"A favorite. I'll get you an extra napkin, though," the bartender said.

"Wow, another magnificent restaurant. You know how to pick them," Kate said to her friend.

"You must be pretty good, too. Our renters rave about the guides you put together for the guests," Merilu said. "A brilliant idea, by the way."

"I wish I could claim all the choices. Many of them are Nick's favorite spots. And when he doesn't know, he tends to know someone who knows," Kate admitted.

"Well, either way, it is a hit," Merilu said. "Say, why don't you have Nick come down? He could stay at the guest house. I'd feel a lot better. Or I'm sure Cassie would be happy to put him up here at the Breakers."

Kate appeared to ponder the idea for a moment, "No, he's busy helping his friend."

"And?" Merilu pressed.

"And what?" Kate asked.

"You are clearly smitten with him. What's the problem?" Merilu asked.

"There's no problem. We are just busy with our own lives, that's all," Kate said. She shot her friend with a side ways glaze.

"It's nothing to do with…" Merilu started.

Kate snapped, "It has nothing to do with *him*."

"Maybe not, directly. You are afraid to go down a similar path," Merilu said.

Kate pursed her lips, "The paths are nothing alike."

"They lead to the same place. The lovely heart of Kate Harper," Merilu said. "You have to realize Nick isn't *him*."

Kate's eyes shifted to stare out the window in effort to avoid the conversation. Her eyes locked on a sailboat, its tall sail sticking out above the horizon line as a endless ripple of waves danced toward shore.

"Ladies, your food is here," a young man announced, sliding plates along the top of the bar.

"This looks delicious," Kate said.

Merilu started to speak but Kate's eyes told her that the previous conversation was closed.

"I told you that you would like it," Merilu said, accepting the change in topics.

"Ooh," Kate gushed. "This is good, but I am happy for the additional napkins."

"Messy but good," the bartender chimed as she walked by.

Kate watched Merilu's eyes shift from her friend to her friend's plate.

"Would you like a truffle fry, Merilu?" Kate asked.

Merilu beamed, "Yes, please!"

Kate laughed as her elegant friend heartily grabbed several strings of truffle fries, dipped them in catsup and enjoyed a sumptuous bite.

"Who can resist a wonderful meal with an amazing view?" Kate asked.

"Stolen moments in paradise," Merilu said.

"It's why you do what you do, isn't it?" Kate said.

"I like to share moments like this with our guests. Couples and families that stay at our beach houses get to, if just for a moment, enjoy a bit of paradise," Merilu said.

Kate nodded, "I get it. Palm fronds whispering, waves splashing, the coastal breeze… It is peaceful and invigorating all at the same time."

"And that is why you are so good at what you do. You get it. You get every tiny aspect of beach life," Merilu said.

"I know more of it, now. I get the experience of interacting with it. Surfing, fishing, paddling out to private little islands… Your properties have so much to offer whether, guests want to sit on the balcony and enjoy the view or dive in and take part in it," Kate said.

"Sounds like Nick's influence to me," Merilu said.

Kate's blushing face told Merilu all that she needed to know.

As Kate turned away from her friend, her gaze down the bar caught something that made her freeze. Down the opposite end of the magnificent aquarium bar top, a man had just bellied up.

Kate recognized him from Cassie's party.

"Excuse me," Kate said, absently setting her sandwich down and wiping her hands on the napkin. Slipping out from her seat, she began making her way down the bar.

The man lifted his head, catching Kate in the corner of his eye. He had the same moment of recognition. Excusing himself from the bartender who had just walked up to take his order, he took large strides to slip around the pillar that separated the bar from the hostess stand.

Kate picked up the pace. She caught just a glimpse of the man before he disappeared into the hotel hallway. By the time Kate reached the hall herself, he was gone. Kate frowned. She should have been able to see him down the long hallway.

Doing a quick pirouette, Kate saw that one direction was outside, with the short stone walk and the beach below. The other, the hallway.

Pushing outside, Kate's head moved from left to right along the walkway. Leaning over the stone wall, she peered out onto the beach. The mysterious man from Cassie's party was not anywhere to be scene.

Cursing to herself, she said, "People around here somehow like to disappear on me."

With a sigh, Kate returned to the Seafood Bar.

"Where did you go?" Merilu asked.

"Remember that guy from the party the other night? The one no one seemed to really know?" Kate asked.

Merilu looked up and snapped her fingers, "Neal or something."

"Yes!" Kate said. "He was here."

Merilu looked around.

"He's gone. I tried to follow him out but somehow lost him," Kate said.

"Well, this is a big place. Lots of halls, lots of rooms," Merilu said.

"I suppose," Kate said. Her eyes stopped fruitlessly searching for his return to the bar and once more tried to settle on the breathtaking view outside.

Despite the beckoning of the Atlantic and the playful splash of waves launched off the rocks, she couldn't keep her peripheral vision from wandering and searching for Neal Roth.

Noticing Kate's distraction, Merilu offered, "It's probably nothing. I think he's like a major introvert or something. He kept pretty much to himself at the party."

Kate nodded, her eyes wandering toward where Neal Roth had slipped out of the aquarium bar. Her voice trailed as she muttered in a tone that failed to back up her words, "Yeah. It's probably nothing."

Twenty-One

The work on the estate had hit full steam. Demolition work on the guest rooms made a quick impact on the project. Massive dumpsters were piled high with flooring, old fixtures, and trim pieces that were slated to be replaced.

Kate looked up. Over the roof of the house, a large crane loomed high. The equipment piqued Kate's interest. Skirting along the side of the house seemed like a good idea anyway as work crews flowed through in a remarkably orderly fashion.

Several construction workers were removing the fasteners from the gazebo roof. When the trusses were free, the crane lifted the roof off the gazebo. Suspended by huge straps, the roof swung in the air until it was delicately laid on the ground.

Marco DiNova had sauntered out onto the sprawling patio to supervise the spectacle. Seeing Kate watching from the corner of the patio, he said, "Impressive work, isn't it?"

"It is," Kate nodded, watching the crews detach the straps lashed to the gazebo roof from the crane's hook.

"Figured we'd get all of the potential destruction out of the way right away," Marco said.

"Destruction? I thought we were going to preserve the gazebo with the new design?" Kate said.

"Oh, we are. I just meant getting that rig back here. How are you at exterior design?" Marco asked as his eyes cast across the lawn where the large tires of the crane created long tracks in the grass.

"Merilu likes my work," Kate said.

"Then you're hired," Marco said.

Kate put her hands on her hips and studied the estate's back lawn. Flowering bushes gave way to a variety of palm trees before opening up to the expansive beach and ocean views. "I'll work something up," she said. While attractive, none of the foliage and outside décor screamed beach to her, outside of the palm trees.

"I'm going to check in on the interior work. They should be wrapping up for the day soon," Marco said.

"I'm going to sketch out some ideas for the backyard," Kate said heading toward the house to gather her laptop and sketchpad.

Sitting poolside, Kate tried to imagine the ultimate resort-like backyard. On her laptop, she lined up plants native to Florida that would make a statement and complement the estate's stunning setting. Christmas Palms, white birds of paradise, Queen Emma lilies, hibiscus and palm-frond looking philodendron were her ingredients. Like a florist, she built foundation plants and sprinkled in accents.

Deleting some plants that Cassie had already had, Kate introduced a more tropical, thoughtful look for the backyard. While the additions were beautiful and reminiscent of a resort's grounds, they were all arranged to do one thing- draw the guests' eyes to the beach and the rolling waves of the Atlantic.

With a smile, Kate closed her laptop. With a deep, proud breath, she got up from her seat at the poolside table.

Turning toward the house, she saw Marco conferring with the construction foreman as his team was packing up for the day.

When he was finished, he smiled at Kate. "Do you have dinner plans this evening?" he asked.

"Was going to check in with Gustavo and see what he had in mind. Have you seen him?" Kate asked.

Marco frowned, "Now that you mention it, no. I don't think I've seen him all day."

"Hmm," Kate considered. "Is that unusual?"

"It is without him letting us know," Marco said. "Maybe with all the construction, he decided it was better to just slip out."

"Yeah, I bet that is the case," Kate said.

A broad smile spread across Marco's lips, "I guess that means we are on our own for dinner. Care to join me? I have an in at one of the most exclusive restaurants in Palm Beach."

Kate couldn't immediately come up with a reason why that wouldn't be a good idea and agreed, "Sure. With an opportunity like that, how could I say no?"

"Great!" Marco rubbed his hands together. "I'll get cleaned up. Meet in the foyer in half an hour?"

"Sounds good," Kate agreed. Still holding her laptop and sketchpad, she headed up the stairs to the master suite.

As she stepped into the bedroom, she cast a glance at the French doors leading to the patio. She developed a quick habit to ensure they remained locked. Walking up to them, she smoothed her hand over the a piece of clear tape she placed across where the two sides of the doors met together. If the tape was torn, she knew someone had made their way into the room.

Kate repeated the process with the closet door. Satisfied the room was as she had left it, she grabbed fresh clothes to get ready for dinner.

As she selected a sundress that she thought would be appropriate for an upscale Palm Beach locale, her phone rang.

Pulling the phone to her ear, she said through a subconscious smile, "Nick!"

"Hi, Kate!" Nick's friendly voice said through the phone.

"How's Operation Sailboat?" Kate asked.

"You should come up and see it for yourself one of these days. It would make an amazing bed and breakfast," Nick said.

"You know, we don't have any boats in our rental inventory. I'll have to bring that up with Merilu," Kate said. "That would be a lot of fun."

"How is the Palm Beach estate makeover?" Nick asked.

"Demo got underway today. Along with the interior decorating, I have been tasked with re-imagining the grounds as well," Kate said.

"You're going to turn that into a place the owner will never want to leave," Nick said. "What are your thoughts?"

"The place was already amazing. I am just reconfiguring the layout, nixing non-native plants for similar if not more stunning Florida varietals. All moving the eye to the water," Kate said.

"It will be spectacular," Nick said. He seemed to pause for an unnecessarily long moment. "What are you up to now?"

It was Kate's turn to pause before replying, "I'm going to go head out for… a quick bite."

"Oh, with the whole crew?" Nick asked.

"No…" Kate said. "It's just Marco and me here tonight. We aren't sure where Gustavo went to."

"Marco… right. Just the two of you…" Nick drawled.

"Yeah, just a quick dinner and then I'll probably get back to work. Now that I have figured out what I want to add, I need to come up with an order, quantities and all that stuff," Kate said.

"Oh," Nick said, his voice ringing with questions. "Well, don't let me keep you. Give me a call after dinner?"

"Yeah, I could do that," Kate said.

"All right, talk to you later, Kate," Nick said.

"Talk to you later, Nick," Kate hung up the call.

For some reason, she felt unsettled after the conversation. She looked out the French doors toward the water. The shimmer of the fading sun seemed somehow familiar and comforting and yet ominous. Shadows began to overtake the backyard. The gated estate felt somehow very open to the outside. As darkness fell, the possibilities of figures mixed in the shadows sent a chill down Kate's spine.

Tossing her phone on the bed, she realized her half an hour to get ready and join Marco in the foyer had nearly expired.

Hurrying, she put on fresh deodorant and slipped into her sun dress. Pausing to tease her hair, she stopped mid-fluff. With a shake of her head, she left to join Marco. Stopping at the bedroom door, she took a moment to refresh the piece of clear tape she had severed when she entered the closet.

Despite her trepidation about an evening out with the flirtatious Marco DiNova, Kate couldn't help but to begin to enjoy the setting. The swanky Café Boulud was a welcoming destination.

Led to their table, they found themselves scooting around a curved, cushy blue sofa. Tables were placed far enough so you could relax with a cocktail but close enough to easily scoot forward to enjoy your meal when it came.

As they were seated, Marco asked for a Masetto Toscano wine to be brought to the table. Kate noted the waitress's flutter of lashes at the selection- an indication the Italian architect was out to impress her.

Marco's intent only became more clear as he went on to order on her behalf for appetizers, "We'll have the Osetra Caviar and buckwheat blinis along with Florida Stone Crab, please."

Kate almost winced at the Italian's thickened accent and air of austerity.

"To the job getting started, finally," Marco raised his glass in the air.

Kate raised hers, a look of skepticism spread across her face, "This seems more like a celebration at the end of a job well done kind of meal."

Marco flashed a robust smile, "The Italian way is to enjoy every phase of the job."

"I suppose that methodology has merit," Kate admitted.

Marco leaned back on the plush sofa, his arm splayed out on the back of it. His hand danced within inches of Kate's shoulder.

Kate craned her neck around the restaurant, offering a reason to scoot an indiscrete bounce further away.

Marco continued to lean in. Taking a sip of his wine which he swirled in his glass, he said, "This wine is difficult to come upon. I haven't had the chance since Michelle…"

Kate's head swiveled and Marco stopped mid-sentence.

"Since Michelle. As in Michelle Goss?" Kate asked.

Marco flushed for a moment and then nodded slowly, "Yes. Michelle and I, we went out on a few dates. She was delightful. I miss her very much."

"How long did you two date?" Kate asked.

"For a few months. Nothing serious, but I thought maybe it could have been," Marco looked away, his eyes pensive.

"I'm sorry," Kate said, her voice soft.

"It is a shame life can be so fragile. This was such… a terrible tragedy," Marco said.

"It was," Kate's eyes searched his for insight. She found none.

Their appetizers arrived. Before Kate could pick up a menu, Marco instructed the waitress on their dinner choices, "Daniel's Bass en paupiette and lobster with ruby red shrimp ravioli. Graci!"

Kate boiled just a bit under the show of misplaced paternalism, "I am grateful for the experience, but I can order for myself or at least engage in a discussion on the meal."

"Of course, my apologies. I can call the waitress over and…" Marco started.

"No. It's all right. Just know that I take great pride in being able to stand on my own," Kate said.

"Understood. I did not mean to suggest anything to the contrary. I, I suppose I had wanted to impress you," Marco said.

Kate softened, "It has been an impressive evening. I don't think you need to try so hard. I mean, you did date a supermodel."

"Perhaps I try to be too clever for my own good. You have resisted me at every turn. I suppose I tried to up the ante, if you will," Marco said.

"Well, while I am flattered, but my heart and mind are elsewhere, Marco," Kate said.

Marco nodded, "I sensed as much. The… handyman."

Kate laughed, almost gushing in spite of herself, "Yes. The handyman."

"Well, he is a lucky man," Marco raised his glass.

Kate raised hers, "To a fun evening with no pretenses and preferably no murders or break ins or other nefarious activities."

"Cheers to that," Marco said.

As their meals arrived, Marco leaned in, "You must save room for the *migdarnises*, or petit fours. I'm sorry, I was doing it again."

"No, it is a wonderful suggestion, but I think after this, I will be stuffed," Kate said.

Suggestive Marco returned, "Perhaps a night cap back at the estate?"

Kate's face fell a bit, "I'll admit, I'm pretty wiped out. I think I'll be turning in early."

"If you change your mind…" Marco said.

"Of course," Kate offered a thin smile.

Twenty-Two

When Kate and Marco returned to Cassie Van Langen's estate, slivers of pink and the marmalade flamed skies of a brilliant sunset greeted them. So did a dark house.

"Hmm, Gustavo still isn't back," Kate noticed.

"Maybe Cassie gave him another day off. With everything that's gone on and the extra working getting the house ready for the remodel, he surely deserves it," Marco said.

"Yeah," Kate nodded, pushing her way into the house. Instinctively, she listened intently for sounds of movement within its massive corridors.

"Sure you don't want that night cap? We can hang out until Gustavo returns. It would be good to not be alone in this big house given the recent blight of shenanigans," Marco suggested with a nod toward the door.

For a moment, Kate hesitated. She had to admit, coming home to a dark house, even with a police officer parked out in front of the driveway gate, was a bit unsettling.

Before she could respond, her phone buzzed.

"I should get this," Kate said. Marco offered a defeated nod before pilfering the bar for himself.

Pushing through the patio doors, Kate walked outside. Pressing the Talk button, she said over the waves, "Hello, Nick."

"Hey, I know you said you were going to call me. Sorry if I'm overstepping," Nick said.

"Not at all. It's good to hear your voice," Kate said. "What's up?"

"Um, Marco DiNova," Nick started.

Kate cut him off. "Nick, we aren't going to do this, are we? I mean, relationships, whatever it is we have, they thrive on a foundation of trust."

"No, it's not that. I know you can handle yourself and I *do* trust you. Not that you're beholden to me or anything," Nick said. "I do worry about you, though."

"I'm fine. I'm back from dinner. Safe and sound. I'm going to head up to bed here shortly. Just waiting for Gustavo to come back," Kate said.

"The chef guys isn't back yet?" Nick asked. "Were you expecting him back?"

"Honestly, I don't know. He always seems to be around. And then there are times like now, where he just disappears," Kate said.

"Sounds kind of like that burglar of yours. You need to be careful Kate," Nick said. "And that's why I called. When we were done working on the sailboat, I had some down time. I looked up your friend Marco. This isn't the first time someone has met an unfortunate end with him in the picture. His wife vanished while they were on a sailing trip. She was never found."

"What? How did you… Why did you look him up?" Kate asked.

"Tell me that isn't something Kate Harper would do," Nick defended himself.

"Yeah. I suppose you're right. Did the report give an indication that foul play was suspected?" Kate asked.

"The news story kind of leaned that direction but it never outright accused Marco of any wrongdoing. There just wasn't evidence to support it. But the whole event sounded suspicious. Before they took off, witnesses in the marina heard them arguing. I guess it was pretty heated. His wife, Mariana, wanted to get off the boat, but Marco cast off anyway," Nick said. "A few hours later, Marco came back in the boat, minus one wife."

"That… that's terrible," Kate said. Her eyes glanced toward the house where Marco's silhouette could be seen in the French doors leading out to the patio. A shiver ran down her spine.

"She was loaded, too. Some old family money. A later article says he packed up soon after the funeral and moved to Palm Beach," Nick said.

"I don't… I don't know what to make of this," Kate said.

"There is more going on with your new friends than meets the eye. I didn't bring this up to give you a hard time. I just want you to be safe," Nick said.

"Yeah. I'll be safe," Kate said, her voice hollow.

"You should stay at a hotel. I know I'd sleep better. Or better yet, let me come down and…" Nick began.

"I don't need a chaperone, Nick," Kate said, a distinct edge to her words.

"I know that. I do. It is just two sets of eyes are better than one," Nick said.

"I'll be fine. Thank you, Nick," Kate said.

Recognizing a curtness to her voice, Nick sighed, "I went too far, I'm sorry."

Kate wanted to fume but she let her shoulders relax, "No, you're right. I would have done the same if murders and burglaries were happening where you were. Just, if you find out anything else, just call me."

"I will. Goodnight Kate. Be careful," Nick said.

"I will," Kate promised. "Goodnight, Nick."

Kate hung up the phone. Though her eyes were on the waves of the ocean splashing ashore, her ears begrudgingly ignored the soft rumble and instead were pegged to the estate house.

Turning, she jumped. Marco's silhouette had remained framed in the patio doors.

He pushed the door open and flashed a broad smile, "I poured a glass of Heaven's Door bourbon if you are so inclined. It'll help you sleep."

Kate studied Marco for a minute. Forcing a soft smile, she waved him off, "No, thank you. I think I'm developing a bit of a headache. I am just going to lie down."

"Yes, of course. Can I get you anything?" Marco asked.

"No, I have medicine if it gets worse. I'll grab a tall glass of water on my way up, though," Kate said.

"Allow me," Marco sat the bourbon glasses down and jogged behind the bar.

Kate began to object but realized it wasn't worth the words. She did find herself subconsciously watching him as he poured her glass of water to ensure no foreign substances were added to the drink.

"Thank you," Kate accepted the glass and turned to go up the stairs to the master bedroom. "Good night, Marco."

"Good night, Kate," Marco said.

His eyes followed her as she ascended. Kate could feel them as though they were reaching out toward her. She unconsciously hastened her gate. With her peripheral vision, she could see him watching her as she slipped inside the room.

Shutting and locking the door behind her, she set her water glass down. After checking her pieces of tape to ensure the veranda doors and closet had remained untouched, she sat on the bed. Her head swirled with the new information that Nick had shared. She wondered and worried about Gustavo and his absence.

She didn't lie to Marco. She was definitely getting a headache. Grabbing her water, she stepped out onto the veranda. Her eyes swept the grounds before landing on the ocean waves. The Atlantic was beautiful. It was graceful. It was powerful. She knew it could also be deadly. She wondered which of the seemingly charming, attractive people living the Palm Beach lifestyle she had met could also be a killer.

Pushing away from the rail, she retreated into the bedroom. Closing and locking the doors behind her, she got ready for bed. The idea of hot, cleansing shower was calling her.

Kate had drifted in and out of sleep. She tried pressing her head deep into the plush pillows but her senses cried to be on alert.

Every noise, clack of palm fronds in the wind, change in lighting with the moon playing peek-a-boo with the clouds woke her up until she could assess that everything was all right.

Deep into the witching hours of the night, Kate heard the slightest sound of a door closing. Sitting up, she thought she heard another sound she couldn't quite discern.

Tiptoeing across the room, she placed her ear to the door. Ever-so-faint sounds of footsteps echoed through the mansion. With a deep breath, Kate wrapped her fingers around the door handle. Disengaging the lock, she slowly depressed the lever until the door could to be cracked open.

Kate peered through the door, one eye fighting to spy the owner of the noises.

In the shaft of moonlight, a figured appeared. Gustavo tried to maneuver through the house as silent as he could. A glance over his shoulder to see if he had disturbed anyone, he slipped into his room, closing the door behind him.

Kate stood still as a sentry for several minutes to see if there was any more movement. Then she slowly and quietly closed her door ensuring the lock was securely in place.

Glancing at her phone by the bed, she saw it read 3:23.

She plopped down as her mind raced. The two men that remained on the property had some peculiarities in the wake of the poor Michelle Goss's murder and the break-ins.

Utterly exhausted, Kate ignored her senses' pleas and buried her head into the pillows shutting off the outside world.

Twenty-Three

Kate awoke to daylight shining into the master bedroom windows.

As she stretched, her pillows fell to the wayside tumbling off the bed and onto the floor. A gentle breeze teased her skin. It felt good as it mixed with the east coast sunrise which was already heating up the day.

She shot up, "Breeze?"

A glance toward the balcony doors showed that they swayed gently with the morning air. Her heart raced. Someone had been in her room while she was sleeping. Eyeing the closet, she saw the piece of clear tape she'd placed between the door and the frame was torn in two.

Jumping out of bed, Kate flung the closet door open.

The safe door was open wide.

She knew Cassie had emptied it to transfer everything to a safe deposit box. At least she hoped that had been the case. Kneeling onto the closet floor, Kate used the light on her phone to peer into the safe. She found the felt floor removed where a little depression, just big enough to hold a few small items was left bare. It too was lined in felt but nothing else was left behind.

Standing up, she held her phone, ready to dial Cassie. She wanted to know if Cassie had potentially forgotten anything in that safe compartment.

Opening the door of the master bedroom, she leapt back as a figure was standing directly in front of the door. Holding her hand to her chest, she gasped, "Gustavo!"

"Ms. Harper. I wanted to see what you wanted for breakfast this morning," the houseman said, his voice calm.

"What? Oh, avocado toast if that is easy enough," Kate said.

"Excellent," Gustavo said, pivoting on his heel.

"Did… did you have a good day off?" Kate asked. Most of her grogginess from lack of sleep had been chased away by her racing heart.

"My day off. Yes, it was very productive. I found a great little surfing spot. Thank you. I hope my absence didn't cause you any issues," Gustavo said.

"No. We were a little worried about you, is all," Kate said.

"We?" Gustavo turned back to Kate.

"Well, yeah, Marco and I. Without your culinary expertise, we went to Café Boulud," Kate said.

"An excellent establishment. I hope it was enjoyable," Gustavo said.

"It was fantastic. Marco was a little heavy handed with the ordering," Kate admitted.

"He was showing off for you. He tends to do that, with whoever he has his eye on at that moment," Gustavo said.

Kate followed Gustavo down the steps, "Where did *you* go yesterday?"

"Oh, just running errands and surfing," Gustavo said.

"We were surprised you weren't back when we got here. I heard you come in around... 3:30?" Kate said.

Gustavo froze and turned on his heel, "I'm sorry to have disturbed you. I tried to be as quiet as I could."

"Yes, with everything that has gone on, I guess I'm a little more sensitive than usual," Kate said.

"Well, I am sorry just the same," Gustavo said, continuing to make his way toward the kitchen.

"What... what errands did you have that kept you out until three-thirty in the morning?" Kate asked.

Gustavo stopped. He turned and faced Kate directly. For the first time since she had met him, he wore an unpleasant, almost menacing expression, "Ms. Harper, I work hard for this estate. I enjoy what I do. But, when I have moments to myself, they are entirely my business."

Kate paled at his response, "Of course, I didn't mean to pry."

"Of course you did. But that's okay. You are an inquisitive woman. Just keep your concerns out of my business if you would," Gustavo said.

"Yes. I'm sorry," Kate conceded.

"Now, would you like a coffee before I set to work on breakfast?" Gustavo asked.

"Yes. I would die for a latte!" Kate said, suddenly horror-struck by her word choice.

"I'll bring it out to you on the patio. It is a lovely morning," Gustavo said.

Kate nodded, "Thank you, Gustavo."

Sheepishly, Kate skulked to the outdoor patio.

Marco sauntered out from the guest house where he had relocated after his room in the main house was slated for demolition.

"Good morning," Marco's Italian voice sang.

"Good morning," Kate said.

Marco cocked his head, seeing right away that Kate was not her usual self. "Is everything okay?" he asked.

"Yes. No," Kate looked at Marco. "Did you hear or see Gustavo come back to the estate last night?"

"No. After drinking both yours and my drams of bourbon, I salted off to sleep pretty well last night," Marco said.

"So, you didn't hear or see *anything* last night?" Kate asked.

"Why? What has you so concerned?" Marco asked.

Kate took a deep breath, "Gustavo came in around 3:30 in the morning. When I asked him about it, he got rather cross with me."

"Well, I suppose the man has a right to his privacy," Marco said.

"Well, *someone* was in my room last night," Kate said.

"Again? Didn't you lock your doors?" Marco asked.

"I did. I am sure of it. Cassie's safe was ransacked," Kate said.

Marco looked confused, "But Cassie took everything out of it."

"Maybe. It is possible she left something behind," Kate said.

"How could that be? I went in and checked with her to see if she needed help," Marco said.

"You did?" Kate scrunched her brows.

"Yeah," Marco stuttered. "When you left with Merilu, I was wrapping up with the foreman. I wanted to make sure Cassie was all right."

"I see," Kate nodded.

"Have you told Cassie about it?" Marco asked.

"Not yet. I was just about to when I found Gustavo standing right outside my bedroom door," Kate said.

Marco cleared his throat and looked over Kate's shoulder.

Kate turned to see Gustavo opening the patio doors with his elbow. He held a pair of coffee mugs in his hands.

For the second time, Kate paled, not sure what Gustavo heard of their conversation.

"I saw you come up from the guest house. I figured you'd be ready for coffee, too," Gustavo said.

"Thank you. That is perfect," Marco said. "I hope you don't take it the wrong way, but Ms. Harper and I were concerned about you. I'm sure we wouldn't have thought of it if it weren't for Ms. Goss's sad ending and the break-ins."

"As you can both see, I am fine. I thank you for your concern. I am making Ms. Harper avocado toast. Would you like something different?" Gustavo said, his entire dialogue said with a steady, indifferent tone.

"That'd be fine. Maybe an over-easy egg to go with it?" Marco asked.

"Of course," Gustavo turned and walked back into the house.

Kate and Marco looked in the wake of the personal chef.

"He is a bit chippy, but as you said, he got in rather late. Probably out with a lady friend," Marco said.

"Probably," Kate murmured between sips of her coveted cup of coffee. Glancing at her phone, she said. "I should call Cassie. Detective Castro as well."

Marco placed his hand on Kate's wrist, "Are you sure you have to do that? He might shut this whole project down for good."

"Marco, Michelle was murdered at the estate. Since then, multiple burglary attempts have riddled the property. Yes, the detective needs to know about this," Kate said, her eyes searching Marco's for a clue to his thoughts.

"No, you're right. I just want to get all of this terrible business behind us," Marco said.

Kate nodded and excused herself from the table. She couldn't help but cast watchful eyes over her shoulder as she walked.

Twenty-Four

Kate expected the knock at the door. She ran down the steps from the master bedroom as Gustavo leaned out from his kitchen duties and Marco stopped conferring with the renovation foreman to spy Detective Castro walking through the front door.

Detective Castro wore a pensive expression as Kate approached, "I thought we might be done with these calls with Ms. VanLangen's items all relocated."

Kate shrugged, "I had hoped so, too."

"Has Ms. VanLangen been notified?" Detective Castro asked.

"She's on her way over right now," Kate said.

"Well, I know the way. Why don't you tell me what happened," the detective began ascending the steps.

"I have been locking all the doors, including the second-floor balcony," Kate said. "I checked everything before bed and woke up to a breeze coming from the veranda."

Detective Castro stopped mid-step, "You were in bed when this occurred?"

"Yeah," Kate's expression showed her horror at the idea. "I was having trouble sleeping. I guess I buried myself in the pillows. Drowned the world out a little too effectively, I guess."

The detective continued up the steps. Reaching the bedroom door, he reached up and plucked a piece of clear tape waving from the door frame. "What's this?"

"I put those on each of the doors, including the closet, to see if the master suite was disturbed while I was gone," Kate said.

Detective Castro seemed to appreciate the notion, "Good idea. Not so useful when you are sleeping right over there, but still a good idea."

Glancing at the tape that was split at the closet door, he proceeded inside the closet. "I thought Ms. VanLangen had taken everything out of the safe."

"I did too. But, there is a little cubby below the floor felt that something could have been hidden in or even fallen into," Kate said.

The detective panned his flashlight along the interior of the safe, "Did you touch anything?"

"No. It is exactly as I found it," Kate said.

After taking a photo, the detective used a gloved hand to move the cocked felt floor layer. "Hmm. Definitely enough space for something to have been removed. But who would have known there was something left behind? Why wouldn't Ms. VanLangen just taken everything?"

"In my rush, I suppose I just forgot," Cassie's voice called from the door to the closet.

"Did you keep anything in there?" Detective Castro asked.

Cassie nodded, "A back-up USB drive."

"What was on that drive?" Detective Castro asked.

"The formula to our upcoming product launch," Cassie said, her voice steely.

"Is that a big deal?" the detective asked.

"Worth millions," Cassie nodded.

Kate frowned, "Even if you get the product to market first?"

"The exact composition can be patented, and we hold the patent to it. But the scent itself is not protected. It wouldn't take much to make a small, inconsequential change and make a near-exact copy," Cassie said, her already weary expression crestfallen.

The detective rose to his feet, "Would anyone else know this?"

"Anyone remotely connected to the industry," Cassie said.

"Like Teresa Lilley and David Hammit," Kate said.

"I'll look into them," the detective said.

"I can't believe I ever trusted him. I don't know how he became what he has," Cassie said.

"I'll get this report filed. I'll have the forensics team out here again. In the meantime, Ms. Harper, I must insist that you relocate," Detective Castro said.

"Yeah, I think someone creeping around while I sleep is a bit too much," Kate said.

"I'll have the concierge at the Breakers expecting you. When you are ready to come over, they'll send a car for you," Cassie said.

"Thank you," Kate said.

"There was one other thing that might have been in that safe," Cassie said, freezing the detective and Kate in their tracks. "A ring. I know it was intended for me from Henrique."

"A valuable ring?" Detective Castro asked.

"It wouldn't be worth what the formula is worth, but it is an easy seven-figure ring," Cassie said. "I know that Henrique has been looking for it."

The detective shot Cassie a look, "You know that he has been looking for it. Why wouldn't you just give it back to him?"

"To be honest, I kind of forgot about it. Until I saw the floor of the safe. It... it was kind of a crazy night when all of that happened. I couldn't remember if I stowed it somewhere. I was... in a bit of a huff. Initially it was thrown out on the lawn. After a desperate search, Gustavo found the box and I put it... somewhere. I might have put it in the safe. I really don't know," Cassie said.

"You don't know?" Detective Castro asked.

Cassie's cheeks reddened in embarrassment, "No. I may have been a touch not myself at that time."

"I see," Detective Castro said, jotting a note in his book.

Cassie snapped her fingers, "Teresa Lilley! My passport missing would disrupt my plans for the launch. Losing the formula would give her time to try and rush a version of her own."

"She was also trying to lure Michelle Goss into a modeling deal, breaking her contract with your company," Kate said.

Detective Castro tapped his book, "There is a lot of motive there. But do you really think Ms. Lilley is scaling second story balconies and breaking into safes? This area isn't a stranger to cat burglaries."

"David Hammit had keys, codes, everything he needed to gain entry to the house, my office and the safes," Cassie said.

"Well, I will bring those two in for questioning. In the meantime, I am glad that Ms. Harper is relocating somewhere that isn't a continual crime scene," Detective Castro said. "You know the drill, don't touch anything."

Cassie and Kate nodded.

As the detective walked away to confer with his forensics team, they looked at each other.

"You really think your main competitor would go to such lengths? She already has an incredibly successful company," Kate questioned.

"It isn't about money any longer. It is about pride. We have been fighting for the top spot for years. I have been able to keep a half step ahead of her. This could change all that in a big way," Cassie said.

"But murder?" Kate asked.

"Wrong place at the wrong time? Threatening to expose Teresa's plans?" Cassie suggested.

"Maybe," Kate shook her head. "Something isn't quite adding up for me with it all."

"Crazy people doing crazy things. I am not sure that adheres to standard math equations," Cassie said.

"I suppose not," Kate agreed, her eyes watching the detective give instructions to his crime scene investigators.

As they disbanded to do their jobs, Kate approached Detective Castro. "Detective?"

Castro slowly panned to face Kate, "Yes?"

"You mentioned this area not being a stranger to cat burglaries."

The detective sighed, "I probably shouldn't have said that."

"I haven't seen anything in the papers about other burglaries," Kate said.

"You probably wouldn't. It isn't the type of thing that gets advertised. In a place like Palm Beach, you don't want to advertise when those who choose this area for security and discretion find their valuables missing. That and you tend to attract a host of would-be copy catters when that happens," the detective said.

"How do you keep reporters from reporting on it?" Kate asked.

"When someone who enjoys that regional discretion owns the local newspaper, it is a bit easier than you might think," Detective Castro said.

"But there *have* been other burglaries," Kate pressed.

"Feel free to file a Freedom of Information Act request and in six to eight weeks you'll get your answer," the detective said.

"I think I already have it. Thank you," Kate said.

Detective Castro grumbled, "Don't go stirring things up. It will only make my job harder." Seeing his team enter the master suite, he left to join them.

Kate paced in her room after everyone left. Subconsciously, she kept a wary eye on Marco as he worked out in the yard.

Replaying the scene of the break in in her head, she tapped a pen on her chin.

Her first puzzle to try and solve was how someone was able to gain entry to the master suite balcony. The scuff on the pillar was one clue, but it didn't tell the whole story.

Starting at that spot, she studied the balcony and the house. One reason balconies are made in the way that they are is that they offer a sense of being safe and inaccessible. Clearly, someone had been defying that sense. The crime scene investigators had not had any luck in finding a method of entry either.

"How could anyone get up there?" she muttered to herself.

Twenty-Five

Kate worked around the house on various projects. She was largely distracted by keeping a watchful eye on the forensics team. Never giving an indication that they discovered anything of note, they left that house after a brief conference with Detective Castro.

The detective cast an unhappy look at Kate, sharing his dissatisfaction with the attention directed at the investigation.

As Castro left to follow his team of investigators, Kate snapped into her own investigation. The first piece of her investigation was the "other" burglaries that the detective had mentioned.

She tapped her lip as she considered how she might get that information. It dawned on her that while the local press might stifle the news, the locals would surely hear about it.

Picking up her phone, she dialed a number, "Cassie, it's Kate. Are you up for lunch?"

Cassie had arranged for a car to pick Kate up. Climbing into the gleaming black Lincoln was like stepping into a refrigerator. Not in a bad way, the moment you were away from direct contact with the ocean and its cooling breezes, the air in Palm Beach was sweltering. The ambient temperature and air-conditioned seats were a blessing though the ride was incredibly brief.

Thanking her driver, Kate climbed out. The Flagler Steakhouse reminded Kate of an old southern plantation house. It had a wide wrap-around porch. Its white rails and balusters stood sentry overlooking the adjacent golf course and the Palm Beach skyline.

Fans and misters along with the porch's natural shade kept the outdoor patio comfortable.

"Is this okay?" Cassie asked.

"This is wonderful, thank you," Kate said. For a moment, she paused and listened.

Cassie scrunched her brow, "What is it?"

"Oh," Kate realized what she was doing. "I was just taking a moment. It is so quiet here."

"Well, you are on a golf course. They are known for their restrictive hushed tones," Cassie said.

"No, the melodic rumble of the ocean is like a living soundtrack. I love it. Add that to the daytime sounds of construction work, I guess I hadn't noticed a true quiet for a while," Kate said.

"Well, you will enjoy spending some time at the Breakers," Cassie said. Her eyes went wide and she leaned across the table, "Did you hear? Of course you have, that's why you asked me to lunch! The police have brought in Teresa and David for official questioning."

"Oh, yes. I did know that was going to happen," Kate said, nodding. "And that is an interesting development in the case. I was curious, if you were aware of other burglaries in the area."

Cassie frowned, "Well, yes. There has been a rumble amongst the estate owners that a series of break-ins have popped up over the past few weeks."

"What's sort of things have been stolen?" Kate asked.

"Oh, I don't know all the details, but I have heard about a family heirloom or two being taken. Now that I think about, they have almost all been jewelry of some sort," Cassie said. Looking at Kate, she asked, "You don't think that has anything to do with our break-ins, do you? What about poor Michelle?"

"It isn't always the answers to the questions, sometimes it is pulling all the questions together and seeing how they fit. That is a long way to say I don't know. But there are a lot of questions and possible connections lining up," Kate said.

"But the detective, he has brought in Teresa and David…" Cassie said.

"For questioning. They are persons of interest. Technically, I am sure we all are," Kate said. "The trick is finding the proof. You might know who committed the crime, you still have to assemble all of the proof to bring about justice," Kate said.

"Merilu said you have a mind for this stuff. I'm not sure whether to call it a blessing or a curse," Cassie said.

"I don't know either," Kate admitted. Squaring her eyes at Cassie, she asked, "Is there anyone you know who might be willing to talk to me?"

Cassie thought for a moment. "The Taylor's and I are fairly close. They were one of the first break-ins. Poor Suzette lost a precious heirloom handed down for generations. She was quite beside herself when she realized it had been taken."

"All of these items are insured, aren't they?" Kate asked.

"Well, sure. Insurance will cover financial loss. It doesn't replace generations of legacy. I know people, even at my end of the spectrum, that would just as soon go bankrupt as lose such a possession," Cassie said.

"That makes sense," Kate said.

"I'll give Suzette a call right now," Cassie said, pulling out her phone and stepping away from the table.

When she returned, Cassie said, "Suzette is expecting your call. I'll send her number to your phone. She lives about a mile south of the estate."

"Thank you, Cassie," Kate said.

"No, thank you. If you can help put Teresa Lilley and David Hammit away for the terrible things they have done, I will be eternally grateful," Cassie said.

Kate started to argue the point that the two suspects had risen highest on the list, but there was still more work to be done. Instead, Kate settled in for lunch, "So, what's good here?"

Suzette Taylor's estate was a step humbler than Cassie's estate, but that still made it the second-most glamorous privately-owned property Kate had ever stepped foot on.

Prototypical palm trees framed a lovely white Italian-architecture home. Curved verandas graced rooms on the upper floors. Kate could imagine a damsel leaning over listening to her betrothed share declared his love through a song down below.

The front doors opened. A stunningly beautiful woman stepped out to greet Kate. A calf-length sarong flowed in the afternoon breeze covering a bathing suit. Her bronzed skin looked as though she had stepped right out of a sunscreen commercial.

"You must be Cassie's friend!" the woman called. "I'm Suzette Taylor. Come, come. Let's get you something cold to drink."

Ushering Kate into the air-conditioned house, the woman led Kate to a long wet bar. A brilliant river of blue curved along the length of the bar. Suzette looked over her shoulder, "I'd invite you out by the pool, but you look dressed more for Sunday brunch."

"Well, thank you. I'm happy you took the time to visit with me," Kate said.

"Oh, I'm happy to. I'm glad to hear someone is looking into the thefts, the police certainly haven't come up with anything," Suzette said.

"I do know it is a priority for them," Kate said.

"Well, right after the murder. What a terrible thing. And to think Robert and I would have been there had we not gotten stuck on the way back from Greece," Suzette said.

Accepting a tall glass of unsweetened iced tea, Kate thanked Suzette. Settling into a remarkably comfortable bar chair, Kate asked, "Would you mind telling me about your burglary?"

"Oh, it is such nonsense. I'm not sure how long it would have taken me to notice, but I happened to be moving items from the old safe to the new one. We had a pearlescent one installed in place of the lower shelves. I never would have thought I would admire a safe, but it is just lovely. Part of the finishing touched on our remodel," Suzette said.

"Remodel?" Kate asked.

"Not as extensive as what Cassie has going on at her place, just the master closet. It is so much more functional now and brighter with new lighting. And the rotating shoe shelves," Suzette clutched her chest. "How would I have survived without those rotating shoe shelves. I can own twice as many now. It is glorious."

"Options are good," Kate said as she nodded. Furrowing her brows, she asked, "Who did the remodel for you?"

"That friend of Cassie's, Marco Di…" Suzette began.

"Marco DiNova," Kate said.

"Yes. That is it. Nice enough man. I learned not to be in a closet alone with him. Just always made me a touch uncomfortable," Suzette said.

"He has a way of warping the personal bubble," Kate said.

"That he does," Suzette said. "So, anyway, I was going through the safe and I almost passed out. That broach had been in my family for generations. It was actually a museum piece in the Louvre for an exhibit for a while."

"Wow, it sounds amazing," Kate said.

"Here, let me show you a photo," Suzette pulled up an article on the Louvre's series on seventeenth century artisan jewelry. Suzette's family piece was a focal point for the exhibit.

"It is lovely," Kate said.

Suzette sighed, "It is worth a lot, too. But I don't care about the money. I would never part with it. I plan on handing it down to my daughter on her wedding day. Or at least, I had planned to."

"Well, I'm sorry. I don't know if there is anything I can do to help, but I am happy to try," Kate said. "Can you show me where this all took place?"

"Sure. Follow me," Suzette sat up from her seat and marched toward one of two slowly curving staircases leading to the upper floor. "I can't for the life of me figure out how they got up here. The patio window was found unlatched. It was the only entry point that had shown sign of being disturbed. We keep it locked for the storms. In fact, it is done automatically every night just in case we forget."

Kate nodded, "Whoever has been involved, certainly seems to know what they are doing."

"Well, here is the room," opening a pair of double doors, Suzette revealed a large walk-in closet.

The scent of freshly laid wood mixed in the air with exquisite perfumes.

"The safe is unusually attractive," Kate said.

"Top of the line, too. But so was the old one," Suzette said. "My husband has always demanded as such."

"Did the contractor, Marco, ever have a need to get into the safe?" Kate asked.

"No. He worked around it. The safe company installed the new one and recently came to haul out the old one. A shelf took its place," Suzette said.

"Can you show me where you think the thief came in from?" Kate asked.

"It is the darndest thing. He can either fly or was trained in the circus," Suzette said.

Opening glass doors to the upstairs balcony, Kate leaned over. It was set up much like Cassie's cantilevering away from the house and suspended without pillars near the edge.

Like Cassie's, there was no foliage or trellis to use to climb up. In this case, there were no pillars at all to aid the climb.

"There was one odd thing. Our gardener found an odd hole in the ground. It was a bit soft following a thunderstorm and it was the same day we realized the broach was missing. He was afraid we had an armadillo or worse trying live under our patio," Suzette said.

"Mind if I go down and take a look?" Kate asked.

"I don't mind, but the gardener has already filled it in and patched the spot it left. It was right on the edge of the concrete work down there. Almost smack dab in the middle of the veranda where we are standing now," Suzette shared.

Kate looked over the edge. The gardener had performed good work because it was impossible to tell a hole had existed there. "About how big was it?" Kate asked.

"Oh, two or three inches is all," Suzette shared.

As Kate began to straighten up from leaning on the rail, she paused. Rubbing her hand across the rail, she felt a subtle depression. Taking a closer look, she didn't think she would have ever noticed had she not happened to swipe at it with her finger.

Turning to Suzette, Kate tapped the rail and asked, "The hole was right about here."

"Seems about right," Suzette asked.

"Hmm," Kate nodded.

"Find something?" Suzette asked.

"Probably nothing, but when was the last time these railings were refinished?" Kate asked.

"Last summer," Suzette said.

Taking a last close look at the near microscopic divot in the rail, Kate thanked Suzette for letting her learn more about her experience.

When Kate arrived back at the estate, she rushed to the back patio. Cassie's backyard near the second-floor verandas was all stone tile and concrete work. There wouldn't be any depressions to make.

Running up through the master suite, she burst through the French doors ignoring her tape trap. Finding the midpoint of the balcony, she ran her fingers along the edge of the rail. Hitting the tiniest depression one that would easily be covered by fresh coat of paint, she looked over the rail at it. It was identical to what she had found at Suzette's.

"Find something?" a voice called from behind Kate making her jump.

Turning away from the rail, Kate looked to find Marco standing between her and the door.

Twenty-Six

"Marco!" Kate gasped. "No, I… I was just admiring the breeze. I swear it is five degrees cooler on this side of the house and the front."

"The beauty, or one of many beauties, of living on the coast," Marco said. "Cassie said you were going over to inspect one of my last jobs."

"She did, did she?" Kate asked. "I had heard about the amazing revolving shoe rack and thought I just had to see it for myself."

"Hmm. Yes, I rather like that. It is a big hit with my clients," Marco said.

"Do you have plans to put that in Cassie's master closet?" Kate asked.

"I could. It would be easy to put that into the designs. Did Cassie mentioning wanting that feature?" Marco asked.

"Not specifically. What I was impressed by is how light and comfortable you made the space," Kate said.

"You can't have too much lighting in your closet. It is the secret to remaining organized and remembering that garment you bought nine months ago that hasn't been worn yet," Marco said.

"Yes, I can see that being the case," Kate said. "It was great work."

"Oh, well, thank you," Marco said, beaming with pride. "Are you here for dinner tonight? Gustavo is making apricot glazed salmon."

"That sounds delicious. How is he doing?" Kate asked.

"He disappeared in his suite for part of the day but came refreshed and back to his own cheery self once again," Marco said. "I haven't seen him like that since the night of the storm."

"The night of the storm?" Kate asked.

"Yes, I came over the next morning to go over plans with Cassie. She mentioned that Gustavo had disappeared for much of the evening prior. He was here in the morning bringing us coffee, but it was not-cheery Gustavo then, too," Marco said.

"The night of the storm," Kate muttered to herself.

"What?" Marco asked.

"Oh, nothing. Sure, please let Gustavo know I will be here for dinner," Kate said.

Marco nodded and jogged down the steps.

Kate stared after him, her head swirling.

Waiting for dinner while watching the setting western sun's rays play colors against the sky as the white-streaked blue of the Atlantic rhythmically splashed ashore was the best part of Kate's day. No matter what atrocity, the ocean would settle her down and make her feel good. It would make her feel as though she could conquer anything.

Tonight, she would be conquering a delicious plate of cedar plank and apricot glazed salmon while making an interrogation seem like friendly dinner conversation.

As they gathered around the table and Gustavo laid out the platter of salmon still resting on the plank of wood-fired cedar, Kate said, "Thank you, Gustavo. As usual, this all looks marvelous."

"My pleasure, Ms. Harper. Sorry if my absence last evening caused you any inconvenience," Gustavo said.

"No, not at all. Like Marco said, we were just worried about you. One of our friends doesn't show up by bedtime, we all get a little nervous right now," Kate said.

"Yes, well. We mustn't live in fear. We must live our lives in a manner that fear sees it did not impact us," Gustavo said.

"Wise words," Marco said, dishing up a slab of salmon onto his plate.

"Do you… is there a group of people in your profession, Gustavo?" Kate asked.

Gustavo studied Kate for a moment, "There are similar roles at other estates. Once in a while we get to interact as hosts, and hostesses overlap events. There's no special club for us, if that is what you mean."

"Are they nice, the other people in your roles?" Kate asked.

"They have to be, or they do not stay employed for long," Gustavo said.

"I suppose that would be the case. It takes an exceptional person to do what you do. Skilled in the kitchen, a profound sommelier, and all wrapped around a great attitude. I don't know how you do it," Kate said.

Gustavo pointed his fork at the grounds and the backdrop of the Atlantic Ocean, "That is how I do it. That and I enjoy working for Ms. VanLangen. It is rewarding, not a chore, to try and delight her and her friends, every chance I get."

"Well, you are excellent at your job, Gustavo," Kate said.

"Kate was over at the Taylors' today," Marco said, giving Gustavo a look.

"The Taylors'? What were you doing there?" Gustavo asked.

"Just getting some ideas for the remodel. Marco had redone their master closet," Kate said.

"A small job. A favor for Cassie, really," Marco said.

"Do you know their executive chef?" Kate asked Gustavo.

"No, not particularly well. I know of her," Gustavo said, his eyes playing with his food. Looking up, he said, "I am glad you are going to be staying at The Breakers. I am worried that staying here, you might get hurt."

Kate looked rattled. Gustavo seemed to pick up on it let out an odd smile, "I just mean, a break-in while you are sleeping. It's just too dangerous."

"Well, part of the remodel is going to be a completely overhauled security system," Marco said.

"You have experience with security systems?" Kate asked.

Marco was flustered, "Well, I know enough. I also know to rely on the experts. Let them do their job."

Kate nodded.

"But I agree with Gustavo. I think it is best you stay at the Breakers as well. For your safety, though I will miss our occasional night cap watching the tide roll in," Marco said.

"Yes, night caps," Kate said.

Gustavo got up from his seat, "Well, stay as long as you like. I am going to start cleaning up the kitchen."

"I should get going too. Thank you for the amazing dinner, Gustavo," Kate said.

Gustavo gave a little wave over his shoulder and disappeared into the house.

Kate excused herself from the table, leaving Marco to finish his freshly poured glass of wine on his own.

Heading up to the master bedroom to gather her things, Kate laid her bags on the bed. Springing open the doors to the veranda, she took one last look at the view from her temporary home. Cassie's bedroom vista was truly awe inspiring. The moon cast a dazzling dance of sparkles on the incoming surf.

A flash in the corner of her eye caught her attention. Moving her view from the ocean to the guest house, Kate swore she saw movement.

Racing down the stairs, she ran through the house and out onto the back patio. Crossing the pool deck, Kate arrived at the guest house, her eyes scarcely leaving the windows where she saw the flash.

Trying the main entrance of the guest house, she found it locked. Circling the house, she tried the bank of French doors that overlooked the lawn and the ocean. The first door was locked. The second door was locked. The third door, almost to Kate's shock, opened.

Pausing, her chest tightened. Kate slowly edged her way into the guest house. Carefully closing the door, she realized she hadn't breathed in nearly a minute. Taking concerted breaths in through her nose and out through her mouth, she tried to calm her nervous system. Her heart continued to pound in her chest but at a rate that didn't make her feel woozy.

Taking cautious step after cautious step, Kate listened intently. She could hear shuffling on the second floor. Sliding her thumb over her phone, she held directly over Detective Castro's number. Creeping to the stairs, she climbed one step at a time. With each setting down of her foot, she paused to listen.

She heard a bang followed by a stifled curse as though someone had banged their shin on a piece of furniture. Just as Kate neared the top step where she could peer around the corner, her phone chimed.

Freezing in place, Kate waited and listened. The entire guest house seemed to freeze along with her. Perspiration beaded on Kate's forehead as she stood rigid and motionless.

Suddenly, a shadow burst past her, knocking her backward and causing her to tumble down the steps. Her arms flailed as she tried to arrest her fall, but momentum won out.

Kate landed in a lump at the foot of the stairs, her phone skidding across the floor. A dark figure stood above her at the bottom of the guest house steps.

The front door burst open, "Kate!" a voice called.

The figure looming over Kate looked down at her, fists balled. Hearing her name called a second time, the figure snapped their head up and raced out the back door of the bungalow as Marco flipped on the hall lights from the front of the house and raced over to see Kate slowly rising from the floor.

"Kate, are you alright?" Marco gasped. "Here take it easy, where are you hurt?"

"I'm… I'm okay. More shaken up than anything. I'll have a few bruises in the morning," Kate said.

"Let me call for help," Marco said.

"No, I just… maybe a drink of water," Kate said, realizing her throat was parched.

Marco helped her to her feet and carefully led to her to a comfortable chair as he went to get water.

Returning with a glass of water and ice wrapped in a towel, he handed them to Kate.

"We should at least call Detective Castro," Marco said.

Kate studied Marco before nodding slowly.

"I can walk you to the main house, let you lay down," Marco said.

"No, I'd rather wait here for the detective. Thank you, Marco," Kate said. Sharing a wary glance, Kate asked, "How did you know to come find me here?"

"I… I happened to be coming down to inspect the guest house. I thought maybe to ramp up our schedule I would consider moving out of the main house instead of playing musical rooms," Marco said.

Kate's woozy mind whirled. Was he coming down to meet the burglar? Was he watching her? Why? He always seemed to appear right after an incident.

Gustavo's voice rang out, "Hello?"

"We're in here, Gustavo!" Marco called.

"What happened?" Gustavo exclaimed.

Marco quickly filled him in.

Kate thought, while Marco always appears right after an incident, Gustavo is always nearby but oblivious.

"Would you mind watching for Detective Castro? He is on his way," Marco said.

"Yes, of course," Gustavo nodded.

Marco sat on the edge of the couch, looking over Kate. For the first time his eyes were softened and kind, not probing as though they were casting a pick-up line.

"Thank you for finding me," Kate said.

"It was only luck that I did. I had stashed a bottle of 2016 Realm Cellars in here and the evening was calling its name," Marco said.

Kate offered a weak smile, "Don't let me stop you."

"No, I do believe that moment has passed," Marco said.

A knock on the guest house door was followed by a familiar voice, "Ms. Harper… Mr. DiNova…"

"We're in here!" Marco called.

Detective Castro walked into the room and saw Kate applying the ice pack to the back of her head. The detective quipped, "I should just move in here myself."

"Why don't the two of you fill me in on what happened here," the detective said.

Kate sat her ice pack aside, "I thought I saw movement in the guest house. I came to check it out. One of the doors around back was unlocked. I stepped inside and heard footsteps upstairs, so I crept my way up. By the time I got to the top, a figure rushed past me, knocking me down."

"I found Kate lying at the foot of the steps," Marco said. "Someone was standing over her. They took off out the back."

Detective Castro rubbed his eyebrows, "All right. So, on the estate of a recent murder investigation, you, Ms. Harper, saw movement in the guest house and decided to check it out. Hearing footsteps upstairs, you proceeded to move through the house? I am sorry you got hurt, but I sincerely hope it knocked some sense into you."

Kate couldn't think of anything to say, instead just bobbing her head.

"What brought you, so fortunately, to check out the guest house at the same time?" the detective asked.

"I saw Kate wander around the house. I came to check on her," Marco shrugged. "As you say, it was just good fortune that I was here."

"And what's your story?" Detective Castro asked Gustavo.

"Routine nighttime check to make sure everything was locked tight. I heard Marco and Kate talking. They filled me in and I called you," Gustavo said.

The detective eyed the three people in front of him. "Okay," he said. "I'm officially locking the estate down, at least from sundown to sunup."

"I have at a place at the Breakers," Kate said, nodding.

Detective Castro looked at Marco and Gustavo.

Both men looked uncomfortable with the idea.

"Does Ms. VanLangen know about this latest incident?" Detective Castro asked.

Gustavo shook his head.

The detective paced as if to contemplate whether he wanted to broach the subject with the cosmetics baroness knowing how it would impact his night.

"Can you get her on the phone? I'd like to speak with her, and I imagine she would want to speak with all of you," Detective Castro said.

Gustavo nodded and called Cassie, putting the phone on video, they huddled around as they filled Cassie in on the latest incident.

Cassie looked pale as she shook, "What is going on?"

"That is what I am going to find out, Ms. VanLangen," Detective Castro said. "You must know, I would like this property locked down between sunset and sunrise."

"I… yes, that is a good idea. I will arrange for accommodations for Gustavo and Marco," Cassie said.

"Very good. If you will allow it, I'd like to have uniformed officers patrol the interior of the property as well as at the front gate," Detective said.

"That would be good, thank you, Detective," Cassie said.

Kate watched as both Gustavo and Marco seemed unsettled by the idea. Cassie just seemed to be done with the drama. She was still clearly heartbroken about Michelle.

"Well, you know the drill, I have to get forensics in here. We'll check for prints and anything else we can find," the detective said. "If it isn't too much trouble, can you all move to the main house while we perform our investigation? Ms. Harper would you like me to call for a medic?"

"No," Kate said as quick as she could. "We'll move to the main house before heading over to the Breakers."

As Detective Castro stepped away to call his team and the crew moved single file toward the front of the guest house, the opposite direction the intruder had gone, Gustavo asked, "Cocktail?"

"Yes, please!" Marco and Kate sang in unison.

Twenty-Seven

As restful as her sleep at the luxurious Breakers resort was, Kate was up at sunlight, making her way back to Cassie's estate.

True to Detective Castro's word, not only was she forced to identify herself and be searched at the front gate, but a pair of uniformed officers also patrolled the front of the house and the backyard.

Trying her own hand at the espresso machine, Kate made a tall coffee and explored the grounds. Her eyes swept across the guest house.

Muttering to herself, she asked, "Why would someone search the guest house?"

As she circled the smaller residence, she continued, "Unless they didn't find what they wanted in the safe. What do they want?"

Peering through the French doors in the back of the guest house, she realized she had never been upstairs. Trying the door handles as she had the previous evening, she found them all locked tight.

"Don't even think about it," a voice called.

Kate jumped. In the sunbathed reflection, she could only see a silhouette standing behind her.

"You really need to stop interfering with my investigation," Detective Castro said.

Kate turned to face the police detective, "I was just looking."

"And how did that turn out for you yesterday?" the detective asked.

Kate scrunched her nose, "Not so well."

Nodding toward her mug of coffee, Detective Castro asked, "Got one of those for me?"

"Maybe," Kate grinned. "I'll trade it for some conversation."

"You know, you are still officially on the suspect list," the detective said.

"Yeah, probably. But how many prowlers take a nosedive down a flight of steps to maintain their innocence?" Kate asked.

"You'd be surprised the lengths people will go through," the detective said.

His words froze Kate where she stood. She turned slowly toward the detective, "They'd go as far as murder…"

"How about that coffee?" Detective Castro urged.

Kate nodded and made her way toward the main house. Her mind was swirling with new ideas. "What if the intruder has been after something other than jewelry in Cassie's safes? It could be something that maybe she wouldn't hide in a safe?"

"Well, if it was important enough, she would," the detective said.

"Maybe," Kate said.

"You like to play what-if games. I get that. As a police detective, I need to follow the clues. Right now, the clues tell me that someone close to Cassie is behind all of this. It is time we get the group back together again," Detective Castro said. "But coffee first, if you don't mind."

"I don't mind," Kate said.

As they made their way to the coffee bar, Marco arrived ahead of the construction crews. Gustavo trailed behind him and made his way to the kitchen.

Kate used her new found skills with the massive Italian machine to make the detective an Americano.

"Thank you," Detective Castro accepted the cup. "You think you can get Ms. VanLangen and Ms. Brenner to join us? I have a few questions for everyone."

"Everyone?" Kate asked.

"Well, I'll visit with Teresa Lilley and David Hammit later," Detective Castro said.

"Any chance I can be a fly on the wall for that?" Kate asked.

"Show me a badge and your master's in criminal justice, then, yes," Castro said.

Kate frowned and asked, "How's your coffee?"

"It's good, but it's not damage the integrity of my investigation good," the detective replied.

"I'll get Merilu and Cassie on the phone and ask them to come over," Kate said.

"What's this? Anything new in the case?" Marco asked after conferring with the project foreman on the day's tasks.

"I just have a few questions for everyone. If you have time now…" Detective Castro said.

Marco waved his hands in the air for the detective to proceed.

"What was your relationship with Ms. Goss?" Detective Castro asked.

Marco's face fell. His eyes landed on Kate before returning to the detective. "On second thought, it might be best if you spoke through my lawyer," Marco said.

"I merely need to understand the nature of your relationship, everyone's relationship with Ms. Goss. How about Ms. VanLangen?" the detective pressed.

"My lawyer. Here is his card," Marco said, retrieving a business card from his jacket pocket. "Excuse me, I have work to do."

Spinning on his heel, Marco disappeared into the throng of construction workers that streamed into the house.

Amongst the work crew, a familiar face tried to mingle.

"There's a suspect for you to question," Kate said nodding toward the person using the work crew for cover.

"Henrique Desperaux!" Detective Castro called out.

Henrique froze. As the construction crew continued on toward their assignments, Henrique stood alone in the entryway. A broad smile took over the surprised look on his face, "Detective, what a pleasure to see you on this fine morning."

"Where were you last night at around 9:00 p.m.?" Detective Castro asked.

Kate leaned in, keen to learn herself.

"I was enjoying sunset atop my penthouse suite with a marvelous Bordeaux," Henrique said in his ever-pleasant tone.

"Can anyone vouch for you?" the detective asked.

"My doorman Raul saw me enter around 5:00. Other than that, no. It was a… quiet evening," Henrique said.

"You ever find what you were looking for here at the estate?" Kate asked.

Henrique's face fell, "I, uh, well, no."

"Any chance you were here last night looking for it?" Detective Castro tried to shoulder Kate out of the conversation.

"As I said, I was at my penthouse," Henrique said.

"With no one to actually corroborate that," Detective Castro said.

"What are you doing here now?" Kate pressed.

Henrique shuffled, his eyes dancing along the tiles at Kate and the detective's feet, "I, I came to check on Cassie, she hasn't been returning my calls."

"I'm right here. And I am fine, Henrique," Cassie's voice snapped from the doorway.

Henrique spun and tried to place his hands on Cassie's shoulders, but she danced away, "I have been worried about you."

"What are you doing here, Henrique?" Cassie's voice was terse.

"Like I said…" Henrique started.

"No, what are you *really* doing here?" Cassie repeated.

"I did want to see how you were," Henrique said, his voice nearly a pout. "Also to see if any, uh, items turned up."

"Maybe you can be more specific?" Detective Castro asked.

Henrique looked at Cassie and then back at the detective, "It's no matter. Without Cassie's hand it means nothing."

The detective looked at Cassie who didn't offer up any clarification herself.

"I have some questions for everyone," Detective Castro said.

"Have your precinct contact my lawyer. I am done with all of this horrible business," Cassie said. Her words took the detective by surprise.

"Ms. VanLangen…" the detective began.

"I'm sorry, Detective. I have grown weary of thieves and murderers. My launch is cancelled, the investor's board is spun up to a frenzy… I am just looking forward to this all being over and escaping," Cassie said.

"I can visit with you and your lawyer at the station or we can have a discussion here," Detective Castro said.

Cassie sighed, "Fine. What do you want to know?"

"Can we go somewhere private?" the detective asked.

"Anything you have to ask can be asked in front of Merilu and Kate. Henrique, you should probably go," Cassie said.

"But not far, I'll be reaching out for a visit with you, too," Detective Castro said. Flagging down an officer, he had Henrique escorted away from the estate.

Turning back to the ladies, he held his hand out for Cassie to lead the way.

As they settled around the patio table, Cassie looked at the detective.

"Mr. Desperaux is persistent," the detective said.

"You have no idea," Cassie said.

"What is he looking for?" Detective Castro asked.

"A ring. An engagement ring," Cassie said.

"Whose?" the detective pressed.

"His. He wanted it to be mine. I rejected it. We, I, somehow lost it," Cassie said.

"Is this ring valuable?" Detective Castro asked.

Cassie shrugged, "It is worth about five million dollars."

Castro squirmed in his seat, "there are a lot of reasons for treasure hunting around your estate. And possibly even murder."

"How did he take the rejection?" Detective Castro asked.

"Not well. He is around all the time, isn't he?" Cassie smirked.

"For the ring or for you?" Castro asked.

"A bit of both, I guess," Cassie said.

"And you, Ms. Brenner... what keeps you around the estate?" Detective Castro asked.

"I'm looking out for my friends. I want to ensure that Cassie and Kate are safe," Merilu said.

"It has nothing to do with a lien placed on your personal property? You are in arrears... what was it?" the detective flipped through his notes. "Five million dollars short?"

Merilu winced. She shot embarrassed looks toward Cassie and Kate. "It is a small hiccup. I had a client pull out of a project that left me in a bit of a bind."

"Who was that client, Ms. Merilu?" Detective Castro asked.

Merilu's head fell to her chest, "Michelle Goss."

"Can anyone verify where you were between nine and ten the night of the party?" Detective Castro asked.

"The entire time? I don't know," Merilu's words fell softly.

"I'm afraid I'm going to have to take you down to the station for formal questioning," the detective said.

"What does this mean? I wouldn't hurt Michelle or anyone!" Merilu gasped.

"What about Henrique... or... or Teresa Lilley or David Hammit?" Cassie shrieked.

"I am weighing all the evidence. I am not charging Ms. Brenner at this time. But I do need her to join me for formal questioning," the detective said, his tone even.

"Then we're going with you!" Cassie said, casting a glance toward Kate.

"I can't stop you from going to the station, but I will be questioning Ms. Brenner alone," Detective Castro said.

"It will be all right. We know Merilu didn't do this," Kate said forcing her voice to sound confident.

Twenty-Eight

"Thank you for driving me," Kate said as Marco pulled his Italian SUV into the Palm Beach Police Station parking lot.

"Of course. We're all friends. I am sure with Cassie being called away and not able to be here, she will appreciate our support," Marco said.

Kate nodded. She was worried about Merilu. She knew the detective was right in that she was a valid suspect. But she knew her friend. She wasn't capable of killing someone.

With a deep breath, Kate sighed to herself, "At least I hope so."

"What?" Marco asked locking the SUV.

"Nothing. I just can't believe Merilu had anything to do with Michelle's death. She certainly wouldn't break into Cassie's house or knock me down a flight of stairs," Kate said.

"I am sure the detective is just being thorough," Marco said.

Kate nodded, "Yes. I'm sure that is it."

Entering the police station, Kate walked up to the desk sergeant. "My friend is being questioned by Detective Castro. I wanted to be able to show my support," Kate said.

The sergeant looked blankly at Kate and said, "Yeah, I don't think that's how it works."

"Can you at least let Detective Castro know I am here? I'm Kate Harper," Kate asked.

"Do you have something to confess, Ms. Harper?" the sergeant quipped.

Kate glared at him.

"I will let him know you are in the lobby. You are welcome to have a seat over there."

Kate turned to a row of seats inside the police station lobby. With slumped shoulders, she consented to sit and wait for her friend to be done.

"It's nice to see how you and your friends all look after each other," Marco said.

"Well, I wished it didn't have to be over such terrible things," Kate said. Her mind seemed to drift. She blurted, "Michelle's murder and the burglaries have to be connected, right? Anyone with access to the house, could access it at any time. Why would they break in? Why would they take such risks?"

"I… I don't know," Marco said. "Well, except for Henrique."

"And David Hammit," Kate added. "How well do you know Gustavo?"

"Gustavo… I mean, he could use his role to try and walk away with a fortune of his own. He seems so nice," Marco said.

"He does. Maybe a little *too* nice?" Kate asked.

"Maybe," Marco said. "But I think everything swirls around Teresa Lilley. Everything was fine until she showed up at the party. She was the big winner. Cassie's launch has completely imploded. Put off indefinitely. That's a big deal."

"Yeah, Cassie certainly got a raw deal. Not as bad as Michelle's fate, though," Kate said.

They leaned back in their chairs to digest their thoughts.

"How about I go run and get us some coffees," Marco suggested.

Kate nodded and said, "That would be nice."

Left in the police station lobby with no one other than desk sergeant to talk to, Kate started to fidget. Shooting up from her seat, she leaned against the front desk, "If it is going to be awhile, do you have a restroom I can use?"

The desk sergeant studied Kate for a minute before sighing, "Yes, come with me. Our lobby is being renovated so the only available restrooms are back here."

The desk sergeant buzzed the lock on the door for Kate to step through. With two fingers, the sergeant waved an officer over. "Would please escort Ms. Harper to the restroom? When she is done, you can bring her back to me."

The officer nodded. With a hand held out for Kate, she said, "Right this way."

Kate's eyes scoured the room for any signs of Merilu or Detective Castro. Not seeing them, she swept the room for anything related to the case.

Peering at the officer's nametag, Kate asked, "So, Officer Hankins, how long have you been a police officer?"

"Two years," Officer Hankins replied.

"Are cases like this common in Palm Beach?" Kate asked.

"Suspicious deaths happen, yes. Murders at one of the beachfront estates? No," Officer Hankins said.

"Where is Detective Castro's office?" Kate asked.

"You know Detective Castro?" the officer asked.

"Well, sort of. He is questioning my friend right now," Kate said.

The officer's eyes grew wide, realizing she shouldn't have been so forthcoming, "Oh!"

Stopping abruptly, the officer stood with crossed arms outside of the women's room.

Kate took one more glance around the station before slipping inside.

Kate slowly pushed the restroom door open hoping to snag a chance to wander. Her hopes were dashed as Officer Hankins remained resolute just outside.

Seeing Kate's wandering eyes, Officer Hankins said, "All right, back to Desk Sergeant Jones."

Kate nodded and followed.

While her eyes didn't catch anything of interest, her ears did. A man in khaki pants, a button-down tropical shirt and a badge hung from a chain across his chest was speaking to a well-dressed woman.

"A cat burglar? Really?" the woman said.

"Four estates have been hit so far, including the VanLangen estate," the man in khakis said.

"My company insures all four of them," the woman said.

Officer Hankins tried to usher Kate along. Kate dropped to a knee to adjust her shoe. She looked up and shrugged, "Sorry, something in my shoe."

As she fiddled with her shoes, Kate listened.

"We are definitely dealing with a professional. In and out. Aside from the VanLangen estate, no one even knew they were hit right away," the man said.

"If that's the case, we'll never recover the items," the woman said.

"I'll print up the reports so you can process the claims," the man in khakis said.

"Thanks, I'll wait out front," the woman said.

Kate shot up and smiled at Officer Hankins, "All set."

The officer escorted Kate back to the desk sergeant, the woman from the insurance company following close on their heels.

As they took their seats, Kate shot a look at the woman and said, "A cat burglar! Here in Palm Beach. That's crazy."

"The checks my company is going to have to write are crazy," the woman said. She shot Kate a curious look, "Who are you?"

"I'm with the VanLangen estate," Kate said. "I'm Kate Harper."

The woman raised her brows, "I'm Carin Brown. I work for the insurance company that secures the estate. I don't even know how to value the loss from there."

"What do you mean?" Kate asked.

"The VanLangen theft wasn't like the others. The other heists were single, very valuable items. Necklaces, pendants, broaches…

The VanLangen theft was items related to VanLangen Cosmetics the insurance adjustor said.

"You cover that, too?" Kate asked.

"Through the corporate umbrella policy. While the disrupted launch lost the company millions in stock, that isn't covered. Only the items themselves. How do you value a formula?" the adjustor shrugged.

"What about the original theft?" Kate asked.

"A black card that was turned off immediately and covered by the issuing bank. A passport which would have temporarily delayed Ms. VanLangen's European departure. A few pieces of miscellaneous jewelry, which is easily worth more than everything in my jewelry box. That's the bulk of the claim from the estate," the adjustor said.

The detective working with the adjustor called from the desk, "Here are the reports."

"That's my cue," the adjustor said and got up to retrieve the papers which had been sealed in an envelope.

Kate watched as the woman thanked the detective and left the police station. Shooting up, Kate followed the woman out to the parking lot.

"Why would a cat burglar stick around and keep stealing?" Kate asked.

The adjustor looked thoughtful for a moment and said, "Because there is a bigger score they are trying to get their hands on."

Kate nodded, her head whirling with this new information.

She began imagining what bigger score a cat burglar might be after.

Rushing after the insurance adjustor, Kate called, "Carin… Ms. Brown…"

The adjustor stopped in the middle of the police station driveway, "Yes?"

"Are you up for a cup of coffee?" Kate asked.

The adjustor looked mildly confused at the offer.

"I was personally attacked by the thief. I'd like to know more about what's been going on. The police haven't been very helpful and the press, well, they don't report on things like this around here," Kate said.

Carin Brown studied Kate as she considered her words, "You're not really part of the jet set world, are you?"

Kate shook her head, "No. I'm not. But my friends are having very real struggles getting over what has happened."

"You mean the death of the model?" Carin asked.

Kate nodded.

"You think they're connected?" Carin asked.

"I think they may be," Kate said.

"The police are handling it…" Carin began.

"Please. I am just trying to help my friends find some answers that no one else is willing to give them," Kate said. Her eyes took an involuntary glance toward the police station where Merilu was being questioned.

"Sure. Coffee. This afternoon? If you don't mind island hopping, there is a great place in Jupiter, the Pumphouse. I'd prefer to talk away from Palm Beach," Carin said.

"That sounds great," Kate said.

"Here's my card. Shoot me a text and I'll send you the address," Carin said. Waving the papers in her hand, she said, "Now I have to try and make sense of all this."

Kate thanked her and began returning to the police station just as Marco arrived with the coffees.

"I brought one for Merilu, in hopes she gets to leave soon," Marco said climbing out of his SUV with a tray of coffees.

"Let's hope so," Kate said accepting a coffee and heading back into the station.

Twenty-Nine

Kate pulled her SUV into the Pumphouse Café. The trip up the A1A was busy as usual, but Kate enjoyed driving through coastal towns. Each dot along Florida's Atlantic shore has its own story to tell.

Known for its golf, beautiful beaches and near-shore scuba adventures, Jupiter was an accessible northern neighbor to Palm Beach. The coffee shop, a shared ventures with an ice creamery, was a small but premium spot nestled between Juno Beach and Jupiter Beach.

Carin Brown was seated at a sidewalk table waiting for Kate.

"Thank you for meeting me," Kate said.

"Busy day, an afternoon iced coffee seemed like a nice break," the insurance adjustor said. "I took the liberty of ordering one of my favorites, a draft latte."

"Thank you," Kate said, accepting the drink.

"So, how can I help you?" Carin asked.

"I'm hoping we can help each other," Kate said. "Finding whoever is behind the break-ins would give my friends a lot of relief and allow our project at the VanLangen estate to move forward without constantly looking over our shoulders or ducking under rolls of crime scene tape."

"I see. And how would you help with that? Are you a detective?" Carin asked.

"No. Not exactly. I have helped police solve a case or two," Kate admitted.

The insurance adjustor looked mildly impressed through a veil of skepticism, "I'm intrigued."

"I am the one who found the, the uh, victim at the party. Since then, we have had several break ins. Nothing is really adding up," Kate said.

"When I was at the station, it seemed like the police had a suspect," Carin said.

"A string of circumstances, but I don't think they have the right person," Kate said.

"The detective thinks the thief got caught, reacted by stabbing the victim and then took off," Carin said.

Kate nodded, "That is a theory. And they might be right. I just think they have the wrong person."

"What makes you think that?" Carin asked, taking a sip of her latte.

"I know the person they were questioning. I get that everyone is a suspect, but she's Cassie's friend. And she's certainly no cat burglar," Kate said.

"My company's investigators think it is the work of a thief they have been tracking for years. The thief blows into town. Hits several high-value heists and moves on," Carin said. "The style of break-ins, specific items stolen and ability to slip through highly secure locations… all without leaving a trace."

Kate leaned back, her mind sorting through the information, "Do they have any clues as to who it might be?"

"No. They have hit eight cities in five years. Each targeting luxury homes or condos. Every time like they were after a singular, high-value item. The last heist is always the biggest," Carin said.

"What sort of thing would that be?" Kate asked.

"A prized gem, a crown, an artifact… something revered and very, very expensive," Carin said.

"Other than expensive, what's the connection between the locations?" Kate asked.

Carin shrugged, "I think expensive is the key word. Gated homes. Seriously wealthy owners. Usually well-connected in the community."

Kate chewed her lip. "I couldn't get a list of locations and items stolen in the Palm Beach thefts, could I?"

Carin laughed, "I shouldn't even be having this conversation with you."

"Obviously the VanLangen estate was hit. And the Taylor's, sweet people…" Kate said.

Carin eyed Kate for a moment, "I will say the other houses hit run in the same circles. In fact one wasn't a house at all. It was yacht parked in Palm Beach Marina, let's just say, you can't miss it. The other was the Taylor's neighbor to the south."

Kate studied the insurance adjustor sensing that was all the information she was going to get.

Carin leaned forward and handed Kate a card, "Listen, if you hear anything, please let me know."

"I will," Kate said, nodding. "Thank you for the coffee."

Kate stepped out of the coffee shop mulling over the conversation. Climbing into her SUV, she began the return trip south down U.S Highway 1. As she crossed the Royal Park Bridge which returned her to Palm Beach, she took a detour toward Lake Worth Lagoon.

Beyond the palm trees, rows of superyachts rose to form their own skyline. As Kate entered the Town of Palm Beach Marina, she gave a wave to the security guard. Her unflinching smile garnered a wave back as she drove through.

The marina itself was dotted with Mediterranean-style structures hosting amenity buildings, private showers and offices. Aside from the secure parking area, Kate found the waterfront spot parklike. A well-manicured lawn hosted a massive banyan tree with its wild system of roots supporting its sprawling limbs.

Finding a parking spot, Kate climbed out and strolled along a paved path to a bench overlooking the marina. It didn't take her long to identify the yacht in question. Maxing out the marina's nearly three-hundred-foot birthing, the gleaming DeBasto Design yacht with its bridge appearing to float above the main deck was a floating art piece. Its size and design made it impossible to miss.

"It's a beauty, right?" a man's voice asked.

Kate snapped her head from the boat to find a man walking his King Charles Spaniel through the park.

"It is… pretty. Not exactly subtle," Kate said.

"No, not subtle. I guess when your life is all about the water and your ports of call include Dubai, Tangier and Genoa, extravagant is the only way to stand apart," the man said.

"Is one of these beauties yours?" Kate asked.

"Oh, no. But I like to dream," the man said.

Kate's eyes returned to the superyacht, "Who owns the big one?"

"The DeMornay family. They are part of the Palm Beach elites. Own a big chunk of Worth Avenue," the man said.

Kate looked thoughtful, "I suppose you have to trade some anonymity for a lifestyle like that. I think I'm content to live a bit more quietly myself."

"I agree with you there. But I wouldn't mind an afternoon or evening aboard that gem," the man said.

Kate took a last look at the glistening yacht. Turning to the man with the dog, she said, "Thank you for the talk."

"My pleasure," the man said. With a gentle tug on the leash, he called, "Come one, Coco, let's find some shade."

Driving away from the yacht, Kate realized she knew nothing about the family that owned it. Because they were also hit by the string of thefts, she wanted to know more. Aside from being wealthy and in Palm Beach, what else connected the dots.

The towers of Palm Beach Atlantic University rose across Lake Worth from the marina. Kate swung her SUV west on the Royal Park Bridge to dig up more information.

After a few laps to find parking, Kate pulled out her phone and followed the university map to the Warren Library. The tan building was framed by majestic palms. Its square-pillared arches and architectural style looked right at home against the Palm Beach backdrop. Flashing a smile at the student librarian, she strode into the building.

Emanating the smells of books and printing, the library invoked a lifetime of memories that made Kate smile. There was something about stacks of books and the particular scent that made her happy. She was happier still when she settled in front of the library's computers.

Stretching her fingers, she wiggled in her seat and prepared to dive into her research. Starting with the Palm Beach burglaries, she found little in local papers and social media to shed any light on the high-end thefts. As she had been advised, those incidents managed to avoid being highlighted by the press.

Searching modern cat burglaries, she learned most modern thefts lack the stealthy antics portrayed in movies and mystery novels. Instead, they revolved around smash and grab theft rings or poaching catalytic converters from cars in people's driveways.

There was one case that got media attention in Canada. A string of thefts centering around Toronto's Bridle Path exclusive neighborhood was plagued by a number of thefts in a two-week period. Royal Canadian Mounted Police found the crime scenes bare of evidence and said that the thefts were so clean, they feared an inside job.

Kate searched for more information on the thefts. Only one additional article was found. A year later, the RCMA still had the case open. They were joined by the FBI who thought the thefts in Canada mirrored high-end homes being burglarized in Beverly Hills. In each incident, only a single, very expensive item was stolen. Like the RCMA, the FBI was at a loss for clues.

A few more articles chronicled the Beverly Hills thefts declaring five homes had been hit, the same number of homes as in Canada. All targets were prominent societal figures who were well-known in their communities.

Kate tapped her lip as she considered the possible connection between those crime sprees and the one taking place in Palm Beach. In both Beverly Hills and Toronto, the thefts were clean. No one was harmed. Something she wished was true of their case.

The one thing that stood out to Kate was that the thief seemed to know what they were looking for in each home. The only thing taken was what was targeted. Kate chewed her lip, Cassie's office safe was emptied. Her master closet safe had two items taken. The case didn't fit.

Mumbling to herself, Kate said, "How did the thief know what to take from where? They had to have a way to target their victims."

Her fingers hovered over the keyboard. She typed in Boolean search parameters for "VanLangen", "DeMornay", and "Taylor", and the computer returned several articles. The most recent was about a benefits gala for foster children. Held at the Flagler Museum, it was a Who's Who of Palm Beach. The lead picture told the story. Captured standing shoulder to shoulder, the main benefactors stood for a photo, each exquisitely dressed for the evening. Their elegant jewelry shone in the photo.

Kate read the caption aloud, "Cassie VanLangen, Virginia DeMornay, Suzette Taylor, Teresa Lilley and Lydia Montgomery."

"Hmm. I wonder if Lydia Montgomery is the other estate the insurance adjustor was speaking of," Kate whispered.

Pulling out her phone, she dialed Cassie.

"Hello?" Cassie's voice called through the phone.

"Hi Cassie, it's Kate."

"Kate! Why are you whispering? Are you okay? Is someone after you?" Cassie asked in a panic.

"No. No. I'm fine. I'm in the library," Kate hissed.

"Oh, thank goodness," Cassie panted.

"Your neighbor to the south of you… is that the Montgomerys?" Kate asked.

"No. They are north of the Breakers. To the south is the Terri and Troy LaRouche. Why?" Cassie asked.

"I met with someone with insight to the jewel thefts. They said the other house hit was to the south of you," Kate said.

The phone was quiet for a moment before Cassie said, "Well, that doesn't make sense. They are in France. Have been since January. If there had been a theft there, I don't think anyone would have even known about it."

"Oh," Kate slumped in her seat. Perking back up, she asked, "South of the LaRouches'?"

Cassie laughed, "That would be Teresa Lilley."

"Hmm," Kate thought out loud. "I wonder… okay. Thanks, Cassie!"

Kate hung up the call and gathered her things. Before she closed out the computer terminal, she hit print on the photo from the gala.

Thirty

Kate followed her GPS instructions to pull in front of a gated drive. In the center of the massive iron gate was an unmistakable logo- TL. Emblazoned in gold, it set the tone for the rest of the estate.

Leaning out her SUV's window, Kate pressed the call button. A video screen popped open and a man's face appeared. "Yes, may I help you?"

"My name is Kate Harper. I am here to see Ms. Lilley," Kate smiled into a camera.

"I do not believe Ms. Lilley has any appointments," the man said.

"I don't have an appointment. I was hoping she might allow me to visit for a few minutes. I am friends with… Cassie VanLangen," Kate said.

The man's expression was unmoved. He said, "Perhaps it would be best if you called ahead or emailed…"

"Can you just let her know I am here and maybe she can make that call?" Kate asked.

The man's face twisted as if he had just bitten into a lemon.

"Please. I think given everything that has gone on in the past week, she might like to meet with me," Kate said.

With a huff, the man agreed, "Fine. I will let her know but I wouldn't expect…"

"Reginald? Who's that?" Teresa's voice could be heard over the speaker. Her head stretched and looked at the screen, "You're Cassie's friend."

"I am. I, uh, I wanted to stop by and see how you were after the party. I know everyone has been shaken up. I'm not sure if anyone has reached out to you," Kate said.

"That is very sweet," Teresa said, her face replacing Reginald's on the screen. "Well, let her in."

"Yes, ma'am," Reginald complied.

Suddenly the gates split open, the T and the L parted in different directions allowing Kate to drive through.

The drive to the house mirrored the entrance. Mediterranean architecture dusted with gold adornments followed guests from the gate to the gold mermaid rising out of the fountain in the center of the driveway.

The perturbed man from the gate video monitor burst through the doors and jogged down to greet Kate.

"Ms. Harper," the man thrust out his arm in an almost indignant manner.

Kate eyed the man and said simply, "I'm good."

Reginald offered a nod, "Very well."

With his hand crooked toward the front doors, he motioned for Kate to move forward.

Kate didn't hesitate to march up the steps and fling open the front door.

Reginald sprinted to catch up with her and stop the door from slamming open. Offering a disgruntled growl, he said, "Ms. Lilley is out by the pool. Would you like anything to drink?"

"I'll have whatever she is and bring her a refreshed whatever it is," Kate said. Spying a bank of French doors leading to the Atlantic Ocean, she strode across the room.

"Yes, ma'am," Reginald said and scurried away.

Kate stepped out onto the back patio. She scanned Teresa Lilley's backyard. Like Cassie's, it had an enormous pool. It featured a sprawling lawn which drew the eyes to a glorious view of the Atlantic Ocean. Unlike Cassie's, it was adorned with a very different aesthetic. Marble obelisks with gold-plated Teresa Lilley logos met every corner of the estate.

Kate laughed to herself but maintained a stoic expression.

Teresa met her with wide-flung arms as if they were long-lost friends. "Kate, it is so good to see you," Teresa said.

"You too, Teresa. I hope you are well," Kate said.

Teresa gasped, clutching her hands to her chest, "We are all so devastated with what happened to poor Michelle. Everyone loved her."

"Yes. She seemed very sweet. She interacted as much with you and your employees as Cassie's," Kate said.

"Isn't that how everyone should be? Forget false lines and barriers and be friends with everyone," Teresa gushed.

"That would be a better world," Kate said. "But it really doesn't work that way, does it?"

Teresa looked wounded, "Are you suggesting my… competition with Cassie had anything to do with Michelle's death?"

"No. Not really. I am just saying that contracts generally require some degree of corporate loyalty," Kate said.

"Of course," Teresa conceded. "It's just in our world, our lines kind of cross sometimes."

"Of course," Kate said. "Did that happen in this case?"

Teresa reeled back looking appalled. "Absolutely not!"

Kate quickly acquiesced, "Right. It had been proposed to the police, though."

"Had it?" Teresa looked aghast.

"I get it. A gain is a gain. A gain from a competitor's loss is a double gain. That is marketing genius," Kate said.

"I mean, it is one of those things that we think about it board rooms, but Cassie and I are… friendly competition," Teresa said.

"And that is healthy for business," Kate pressed.

"Absolutely. Cassie and I are two woman-led businesses at the top of our game. We push each other, we rile each other up. It is good. It keeps us both on our toes. There is nothing wrong with that," Teresa said.

"No there isn't," Kate conceded.

"I just feel terrible for Cassie. I wouldn't wish what she is going through on anyone. And with her big product launch on hold… such a shame," Teresa said. Reginald appeared on the patio with a pair of tall glasses presented on a tray. "Thank you, Reginald."

Turning to Kate, Teresa swooned, "Reginald makes the best mojitos. Second only to Gustavo. Don't tell Reginald that though. If there was ever an employee I'd like to steal away…"

Teresa's eyes wandered against the Atlantic skyline.

Kate broker her daydream, "You recently 'stole' one of her employees."

"David," Teresa nodded. "Sometimes change is good. He needed change, some new opportunities. I had a need for a chief of staff. He is a bit of an odd duck, but David is very good at what he does."

"What does he do?" Kate asked.

"A little bit of everything. He is very knowledgeable about the industry. Knows everyone. It all helps when it comes to product planning, partnerships, managing the industry's ebbs and flows," Teresa said.

"I can understand why you would recruit him," Kate said.

"Oh, I didn't recruit him. He came to me with a proposal. I found it timely and reasonable," Teresa said.

Kate studied Teresa for a moment. "What made it so timely?"

"It is product launch season in our industry. Over the next few months, the beauty and fragrance world will release their newest creations onto the market. For many, it will make or break their year," Teresa said.

"Do you have a launch coming up?" Kate asked.

Teresa's eyes went wide, "We do! Our designers have come up with the most amazing fragrance. I can't wait. In fact, we are fast-tracking it ahead of Milan Fashion Week."

"That's a tight timeline," Kate said.

"Like the saying says, strike when the iron is hot. Our fragrance is summer in a bottle. It's like if you took the palm trees, rolling waves and exclusivity of Palm Beach and made it a scent… Well, we did," Teresa said, beaming.

"That sounds amazing," Kate said, her mind pinning the words to review again when she was back at her room. Her eyes glanced on Teresa, "Odd question, you haven't had a break in recently, have you?"

Teresa looked almost shocked, "Well… I did have something missing. I thought maybe I misplaced it but after hearing about the burglaries… I did file a claim."

"What was it?" Kate leaned forward.

"My tiara. I always place it on a little stand in my bedroom closet safe. I'll be honest, the last time I wore it was a long night. And with the after party, I just felt foolish," Teresa said. "It… wouldn't have been the first time I misplaced something."

"When was the last time you wore it?" Kate asked.

"The Palm Beach Foster Guild Gala," Teresa said. "Nearly everyone who is anyone was there."

Kate could barely contain her excitement. "Where was the after party?"

"The Beach Club. The donors and organizers were invited to a pretty nice soiree. I don't even know who put it together," Teresa said.

"Was Cassie there?" Kate asked.

"Pretty much everyone from the gala was there. I swear, it felt like a competition with no one wanting to be the first to leave. Thankfully, David was there to ensure I got home safely," Teresa admitted. "The next morning, I could barely get an appointment for a recovery infusion. Fortunately, they came to the house. There was no way I was stepping out in public. I was positively ghastly," Teresa said.

"And the tiara?" Kate pressed.

"My hairdresser had it in there pretty good. All I wanted to do was sleep, it took me a good fifteen minutes to free myself. I swore I put it in the safe with the rest of jewelry, but… I don't know," Teresa said.

"No signs of a break in?" Kate asked.

"No. I had no idea. I went into my safe to select earrings for a night out the next weekend and the tiara was gone," Teresa said.

"I hope you get it back," Kate said.

"Me too. Insurance will cover the money, but, I know it is silly, I find the tiara brings me luck. Or at least confidence. I wear it to all of my launches and special events like the gala," Teresa said.

"Thank you for the talk and the mojito," Kate said.

"Anytime. Please give Cassie my best," Teresa said.

Kate paused as if trying to analyze the tone of Teresa's message. Kate had to admit, it sounded genuine.

The shoe finally dropped. Teresa set her glass down and cosmetics mogul Teresa clicked in, "And now, I have a product launch to get ready for."

David Hammit appeared around the corner, a stack of folders tucked under his arm.

Kate seized at the opportunity to grill the enigmatic man who was once in Cassie's employ.

Greeted with a forced curt smile, Hammit whisked by, "Ms. Harper."

"David, I was hoping to…" Kate began.

Tapping the folders, Hammit continued walking, his eyes never landing on Kate, "Much work to be done. Reginald will see you out."

Kate stood watching the back of Hammit's head pause at Teresa's seat. With an arm held out, he escorted Teresa away from the patio. He almost seemed to tug her gently as she looked back with a goodbye glance toward Kate.

Thirty-One

Kate walked into the Breakers almost oblivious to the hotel's beauty. sliding past the vacationers and residents, she pushed her way into her room. Dumping her bag on the bed, she cleared the table that overlooked the ocean and pulled out her laptop and her notes from the university library.

Her fingers worked feverishly pulling up more press coverage of the foster gala held at the Flagler Museum. Quickly reading the article, which was essentially a roster of Palm Beach's Who's Who, she wished she had her printer with her.

Instead, she scribbled furious notes in a pad. Listing each attendee, she put a line under those she had already spoken to or knew had been robbed. Tapping the list, she squinted at the names and asked herself, "I wonder, who on this list was also at Cassie's party?"

One of the articles posted a gallery from the gala event. Kate flipped through them, recognizing many. Her stomach tightened as she saw photos of Michelle captured throughout the event.

"I'm going to find who did this…" Kate muttered.

Continuing to scroll, she saw pictures of Cassie. She looked like her poised and elegant self. Henrique Desperaux could be seen in the photo. He was looking at Cassie, his face appearing genuinely sad and despondent.

Kate almost felt sorry for him. She also knew that somewhere in those emotions, was a potential motive for murder. Desperaux was certainly caught multiple times sneaking through the estate looking for something.

Other photos showed Teresa Lilley and her entourage. For every photo of Cassie was a photo of Teresa straining to emit the same essence of charisma that Cassie naturally wore. David Hammit remained in Teresa's shadow in most of the photos.

Marco DiNova was captured in several shots. In each, he seemed to be cozying up to another gorgeous woman. Kate laughed, stopping short, realizing that Marco's impulsive weakness could be a motive for murder as well.

One picture made her freeze, her finger hovering over the curser. The photo was another angle of the one she had found researching at the library. All of the ladies in their fine jewelry on display smiled for the photographer. In the background, a figure lurked. Kate zoomed in on the subject. It was the man from the party- Neal Roth.

Kate scrolled through her list. She frowned as Roth's name was conspicuously absent from any of the write-ups about the event.

Writing his name down, she circled it several times. With each rotation of the pen, her mind cast out new questions. Placing an asterisk next to the name, she was certain the mystery man had something to do with the case.

Returning to the gala photo of the ladies dressed to the nines, she matched the faces in the photo to the caption. One of them did not show in her notes as a theft victim. Zooming in, the woman wore a dazzling broach. A diamond and sapphire encrusted turtle matched a pendant hanging from her neck.

Kate did a quick search. She was surprised when she found the very set listed as sold from a Worth Avenue jewelry store. The pair was listed at just over one hundred thousand dollars.

Scribbling a note, Kate pulled out the card from the insurance adjustor.

Typing into her phone, her lips instructed her fingers. "Do you cover the Serena Carpenter?"

Her phone popped up a reply, "Yes. Why?"

"Have they been robbed?" Kate asked.

"No…"

"They might be next," Kate said in her text.

Her phone quickly rang.

Detective Castro looked across the table at Kate. Tapping his fingers against his lips, he squinted, "You know who the thief is, and they may be the killer?"

Kate shot a look toward Carin Brown, who shrugged.

"I don't know who it is, but I might know where I can find them," Kate said.

The detective's shoulders slumped at the response, "Ms. Harper… I don't have time for games."

"Hear her out, Detective, I think she might be on to something," Carin said.

Detective Castro shrugged with his hands, "Fine."

"Every victim from the robberies was at the gala. In fact, they were all in this photo," Kate said, handing the detective a copy of the photo she printed at the university library.

Studying the photo, along with the caption, the detective asked, "So, from this, you think the Carpenters might be next."

"I do," Kate nodded.

The detective looked at the insurance adjustor, "Ms. Brown, you agree?"

Carin nodded, "I think someone used the gala as a venue to case their victims. Everyone but the Carpenters suffered a substantial loss."

"Has anyone contacted them to see if they had any break-ins or items gone missing?" Detective Castro asked.

"I did. They reported nothing out of sorts. They did say that their house was being fumigated. They just moved back in yesterday," Carin said.

"I'll make a courtesy call," Detective Castro said.

"That's it?" Kate gasped.

The detective cocked his head to the side, "What is it you would like me to do?"

"I don't know. I thought maybe… you know what? You're right. I just thought you should have the information," Kate said.

"Information received. I appreciate the tip, Ms. Harper," Detective Castro said. "Now, if there is nothing else…"

The detective's face fell as he saw Kate's eyes, "There *is* something else."

"Yes!" Kate gleamed. "While I was waiting for you, I did a little research on Neal Roth."

"He was at the party where… at Ms. VanLangen's party," Detective Castro said.

"He was," Kate said, nodding.

"We haven't caught up to him, yet," the detective said.

"He was at the gala," Kate said. "*And*, he was here at the Breakers."

Detective Castro's eyes lit up, "When?"

"I saw him yesterday when I moved over from the estate. He seemed to recognize me and ran off," Kate said.

Detective Castro sighed, "I would prefer it if you didn't interfere, Ms. Harper."

"I was just having lunch. It was delicious, by the way," Kate said. Snapping her head, she got herself back on track. "He saw that I recognized him. By the time I got up to speak with him, he was gone."

"I certainly hope you didn't spook him," Detective Castro said.

"If he is still around, he may be looking for one more score," Carin said.

"If he has anything to do with the thefts or Ms. Goss's murder," Detective Castro said. "Is there anything else?"

"I looked Neal Roth up in every social media site, none of the profiles match our Neal Roth," Kate said.

"So, you won't find me on social media, either," Detective Castro said.

"He is big into philanthropy. He was at a philanthropic event and there was no mention of him. At all. Anywhere," Kate said.

"There is no law against discretion in your charitable giving," Detective Castro said.

"Maybe he isn't so charitable after all," Kate said.

"I will look into Neal Roth. Okay?" Detective Castro asked, his voice becoming edgy.

"Yes. Thank you," Kate said.

The detective looked hesitant, he asked, "Is there anything *else*?"

"No. That's it. For now," Kate said.

Detective Castro stood up, "I've got this, Ms. Harper."

"Yes, of course," Kate nodded.

The detective nodded to himself, shook the paper in his hands that Kate had given him as if to solidify the promise that he would look into both Neal Roth and the Carpenters.

When Detective Castro was out of earshot, Carin Brown looked at Kate and asked, "What are you going to do now?"

Kate looked thoughtful for a moment. Suddenly a grin split her lips, "Would you give me the Carpenter's address?"

"I mean, I shouldn't, but… okay. At this point, I'll do just about anything to wrap this case up," the insurance adjustor said.

Thirty-Two

Kate was almost giddy as she peered through a set of binoculars she had borrowed from Gustavo. She propped her elbows on the side of the boat to steady her view as it bobbed up and down in the swells.

The evening was almost perfect. She had always wanted to be on a stakeout. The moonlit sky, only slightly disrupted by wispy clouds carried along with the coastal breeze set up a nearly perfect evening.

Marco DiNova ginned from behind the wheel of their borrowed boat. Holding a bottle of Bordeaux he had liberated from Cassie's bar, his eyebrows lifted.

"Well, almost perfect," Kate muttered to herself. It was only then that she recalled his wife disappeared while boating. Shaking her head, she whispered, "No. We need to be on our game out here! I'll take snacks if you brought them."

"Right," Marco nodded putting the bottle away. "See anything?"

"It is a great vantage. Thank you for arranging for the boat," Kate said.

"Ah, my friend was eager to help," Marco said. Maneuvering so that he could sit on the same bench as Kate, the boat listed slightly in their direction.

Pulling cellophane off a charcuterie tray, he placed it between them.

"Ooh, Coppa…" Kate picked up a slice of marbled meat and placed it on a cracker.

"Coppa Piacentina, Prosciutto di San Daniele, and Pancetta Basilicata," Marco said.

"This is a lovely stake out spread, I must say," Kate said making another cracker, meat and cheese sandwich.

"Try it with the fig spread. Delicious," Marco said.

Kate returned her eyes to the rear of the Carpenter's house. She struggled to focus as she wished to keep an eye on Marco as well.

"Really think we'll see anything?" Marco asked, his eyes glancing at the empty wine glasses.

"I don't know. It adds up. But the thief might have moved on already," Kate said.

"What makes you think they haven't?" Marco asked.

"If it is the same cat burglar that hit the other cities, there is a pattern. Criminals tend to fall into patterns. There are five hits. Generally escalating," Kate said.

"And the Carpenters have the high value piece?" Marco asked.

Kate pulled the binoculars away from her eyes and pursed her lips, "No. Not exactly."

"But…"

"I don't know. Maybe the thief was forced to go out of order because of the Carpenter's house being fumigated. I'm not sure," Kate said.

"And you're sure it will be the Carpenters?" Marco asked.

"It adds up from the photos and the other households in the photo. They were all hit, except for here," Kate said.

"Well, I'm not going to argue. It is a beautiful night. We're out on the water. We have a magnificent charcuterie… are you sure you don't want any wine?" Marco asked.

"We probably shouldn't," Kate said.

"Fine. How about some Pellegrino?" Marco asked.

"That would be lovely," Kate nodded, her eyes once again sweeping the Carpenter property.

Occasionally, as the breeze pushed the palm fronds, shadows would dance across the lawn. Kate would bristle with excitement only slump as she realized it was foliage and not an international jewel thief.

Maintaining vigil on the sides of the house, Kate looked for any sign of movement. She tried to imagine how a thief would attempt entry. For that, she had to divorce herself of her own physical and skill set limitations. Still, looking at the high second-story balcony, she couldn't imagine how anyone without a ladder would gain access.

The boat rocked as Marco opened and poured a sparkling water for Kate.

"Thank you," Kate said, never taking her eyes from the binoculars.

"Didn't you tell the police?" Marco asked.

"I spoke to the detective," Kate said.

"And?" Marco pressed.

"It was just a hunch. He apparently doesn't operate on hunches and theories," Kate said.

"Hmm," Marco said as he prepared a cracker with meat and cheese for himself.

Kate spied through the binoculars. It took her eyes a moment to accept what they were seeing. In the glow of the pool lights, a figure stood. It seemed to pause for a long moment before slipping back into the shadows.

"He's here!" Kate hissed. "He's here!"

Marco looked stunned. Holding the cracker sandwich, he didn't seem to know what to do with himself.

"We need to go! Now!" Kate said.

Marco nodded as he reluctantly set his would-be snack down.

Hitting the start button, the boat's motor growled to life. Easing into the throttle, Marco brought the boat streaming toward the shore.

As they neared the beach, Marco looked confused with Kate's plan. "Now what?" he asked.

"We catch a thief!" Kate said.

In a single movement, she leapt off the boat and dove into the ocean.

"I, uh, I'll wait here. In the boat…" Marco called.

Kate used the power of the Atlantic to propel her toward the beach in front of the Carpenter's estate. Reaching the sand, she shook herself off and jogged up the steps that led to their lawn.

Kate's eyes were on high alert, sweeping the patio in front of the house searching for the figure she saw. Nothing caught her attention other than the palm swaying lightly in the breeze.

Crouching, Kate stole across the velvety grass and scampered along the travertine tiles of the patio. Kneeling alongside a planter, her eyes worked overtime to pick up any kind of movement.

Not detecting any, she crept forward. As she moved, her heart pounded in her chest. She knew at any moment, she could be face to face with a cat burglar or murderer or both.

Step by step, Kate danced lightly along the stone patio toward the house. As she was framed in herself in the blue glow of the pool's lights, a figure emerged.

Cloaked in the shadows of the palms and tropical foliage lining the side yard, the figure stepped out. Merely a gray human-shape amidst the blackness of the night, the figure seemed to stare back at Kate.

Kate's body was frozen in place. Only her heart fluttering wildly in her chest seemed to still function. Even her lungs ceased to draw in air.

Fighting to move forward, Kate wanted to confront the figure. Her limbs and lips wouldn't cooperate. Fear overtook Kate. Inability to function left her vulnerable to the whims of the intruder. She knew at any moment, she might be the next victim.

Suddenly, the figure melted back into the shadows.

Kate looked bewildered. Her muscles regained their movement. She leapt forward. Fumbling with the waterproof case her phone was in, she turned on her phone flashlight only to find herself alone in the side yard.

Floodlights snapped on and frantic dogs barked as the house doors opened.

Kate whirled. Freezing in place, she was penned in by two dogs as she was bathed in light. Two people emerged from the house. "What is going on out here?" an unhappy voice called.

"I, uh…" Kate began. Her shoulders slumped, "I was trying to catch a thief!"

Thirty-Three

"You were trying to catch a thief!" Detective Castro fumed.

"I was on a stakeout," Kate said. Her voice was meek as if she were being confronted by her parents.

The detective let out a deep sigh. He leaned on the interrogation room table and glowered at Kate, "What part of don't get involved in my investigation did you not get?"

Kate winced, leaning away from the detective, "All of it?"

The detective looked irate, "I should arrest you for obstruction. I should arrest you for trespassing, but the Carpenters seem to believe you and won't press charges. You frightened them, especially after I called on them and let them know about the recent thefts."

"But the thief *was* there!" Kate said leaning forward.

"Were they? The Palm Beach officers didn't find anyone but you there. And Marco DiNova floating offshore," Detective Castro said.

"You have Marco, too?" Kate asked.

"He's in the other room. Undoubtedly singing your praises. He is not your biggest fan at the moment and with his reputation, that is quite the indictment," the detective said.

Kate nodded, "You're right. I'm sorry. I just thought…"

"You'd interfere with an ongoing murder investigation. *My* investigation!" Detective Castro snapped.

"I just wanted to help," Kate said, her chin bobbing to her chest.

"You can help by letting me run my investigation," the detective snapped.

"But there *was* someone there. Just like I said there would be," Kate said.

"Who was it, Ms. Harper?" Castro asked.

"I don't know. I couldn't make them out. By *someone* was there," Kate said.

"Were they male? Female? What, if anything, can you share with me?" Detective Castro asked.

"I couldn't tell," Kate said.

"You couldn't tell," the detective repeated.

"They *were* there. It was dark. It was almost like…" Kate's eyes widened. "They were waiting for me. I was trying to draw them out. They were drawing *me* out!"

"You think a lot of your detective abilities, don't you, Ms. Harper?" Detective Castro asked.

"I think a lot of my abilities to help out my friends, Detective," Kate said.

"We scanned the Carpenters' security cameras, and we didn't find any evidence of anyone being there other than you," Detective Castro said.

"We are dealing with a professional cat burglar," Kate said. "They would know how to avoid cameras and not leave a trace of themselves being there."

Detective Castro leaned back in his chair. After staring at Kate and taking a deep sigh, he leaned forward, "There was a trace. A man's shoe, roughly size eleven. It was indistinct as though they were wearing protective booties."

"Well, we can rule out me because I was barefoot and apparently in full view of the Carpenter's security system," Kate said. After a moment of thought, she said, "We can rule out Marco DiNova, too. He was offshore in a motorboat waiting for me to return."

"That is where the Coast Guard found him," Detective Castro nodded.

"He's not the thief… but it doesn't rule him out for the killer," Kate said in a breathy, thoughtful voice.

Detective Castro shook his head and said, "You don't give up, do you?"

Kate looked the detective in the eye and said, "No, sir. I do not."

"You know, his wife disappeared on a boating trip with him. She was never found," Detective Castro said.

Kate nodded. "Yes. I admit that ran through my head, but... I had to know."

Slapping his hands on the interrogation room table that Kate was handcuffed to, the detective laughed, "If you weren't interfering in my investigation, I would almost like you, Ms. Harper."

Kate lowered her head like a turtle and sulked.

"What are we going to do with you, Ms. Harper?" Detective Castro asked.

Kate's eyes gazed past the detective's shoulders. Her mind was reeling. "Bring me the photos from the gala. Both of the ones with the Palm Beach ladies all gathered together."

The detective looked surprised at the request. After a moment of contemplation, he rose from seat, and said, "All right. I want to see where this goes."

Kate stared at the interrogation door as she waited for the detective to return. Her mind was back at the Carpenter estate. She definitively felt like the shadow figure was there for her, waiting for her to show up. Why?

"They wanted to know who was on their trail!" Kate gasped. "They were there for me, not the Carpenter's jewels!"

The door pushed open, and the detective entered with a raised eyebrow, "You okay, Ms. Harper?"

Kate blushed being caught talking to herself, "I definitely didn't interrupt a burglary tonight. I was being outed by a burglar wanting to know who was on their trail."

"And a likely murderer, Ms. Harper," Detective Castro said.

"Let me see those photos," Kate demanded.

The detective spun the photos down on the table to face Kate.

Kate leaned forward, studying the photos. At first, she furrowed her brows in frustration, then her brows lifted. "I had the right idea, but the wrong house!"

Detective Castro scowled, "What do you mean?"

"The Carpenters' jewelry, while expensive to normal people, is pretty modest by Palm Beach gala standards. There was someone else in the photos…. here," Kate said as she stabbed her finger at a woman in the photo just offset the group of Palm Beach socialites.

Detective Castro winced, "That is the mayor."

Kate sat up in her seat, "Her house might be next!"

The detective fell back in his seat.

Looking at Kate, he said, "I have to make a call."

Streaking out of the room, the detective disappeared with his phone to his ear.

Kate desperately wanted to hear the conversation, but the door closed abruptly behind Detective Castro.

She didn't have to wait long. The door to the interrogation room was flung open and the detective took his seat again. His eyes flashed on Kate's, "Mayor Williams wasn't wearing *her* jewelry. It was necklace on loan from Ionic Jewelers on Worth Avenue."

Kate pondered the news. Her head shot up, "Is it valuable?"

"Worth seven and a half million dollars," the detective said.

"That would be the most valuable item in the photo from the gala. That is what the thief is waiting for. It is their last score before they disappear!" Kate said.

"It is in a secure vault built to keep would-be jewel thieves at bay," Detective Castro said. His eyes widened, "Why don't we draw them out again? This time with the necklace!"

"Excuse me?" Kate gasped.

"We'll draw them out with the necklace," the detective repeated.

"How would we do that?" Kate asked.

"We'll create an event where the jewels can be worn by… I don't know, a female officer. And we will catch them in the act!" Detective Castro said.

"Someone, who seems keenly aware of the Palm Beach elite will fall for a sudden, random event?" Kate asked.

The detective's eyes narrowed, "We will see what is scheduled."

"The thief, if they are smart at all, are on the clock," Kate said. "And if they have evaded the police and federal authorities in multiple countries, then they are going to be wary."

"All right, what do you suggest?" Detective Castro snapped.

"Something more organic. Something more spur of the moment, but believable," Kate said.

The detective looked thoughtful for a moment. He snapped his fingers and said, "That Marco in the next room seems to have a thing for you. He has a swagger like he's loaded. What say he 'purchases' the necklace as a gift for you. It leaks out into the Palm Beach echelon, whom it seems our culprit has their pulse on. And we nab 'em!"

"You want me to be bait for a jewel thief and possible murderer?" Kate asked, her eyes in a frown. Relaxing, she shrugged, "All right. I'm in!"

Thirty-Four

Kate pushed into her room at the Breakers ready for a shower and change of clothes. Tossing her phone and keys on the bed, she froze.

Her pile of notes and printouts from her research at the library was torn to shreds. In the middle of the pile was a note card sitting like a tent on top.

Instinctively scanning the room for intruders, Kate picked up the card. Flipping it open, the words "Stop or you'll be next!" were scrawled in red ink.

A chill ran down her spine. Kate dropped the card like it burnt her fingers. She cast a second look around the room and checked the doors and windows were locked.

With a sudden rush of resolve, Kate picked up the card and smiled as she flicked it with her fingers, "I guess we're getting close."

Despite her optimistic outlook, Kate knew she needed sleep and the prospect of a late-night visitor did not sit well with her. She couldn't imagine showering without feeling secure.

Taking one of her belts, she wrapped it around the handles on the sliding glass door of her balcony room and secured it in place tight. Removing a hanger from the closet, Kate used the curved hook and poked it between the door and the fame. When she was certain the hook was around the latch, she pulled the hanger tight making the locking mechanism freeze in place until she removed it in the morning.

For a bit of extra security, Kate dragged the hotel suite's desk and slid it in front of the door. Satisfied that the only way in was either breaking glass or breaking down the door, Kate allowed herself to relax.

Subconsciously locking the bathroom door, Kate started the shower. The roar of water pouring through the shower head made her uneasy as her sense of hearing was impaired. Sliding into the shower made her even more uneasy.

She felt so vulnerable. Limited hearing, limited vision and trapped in a corner, Kate took one of the fastest showers of her life.

Climbing out, she toweled off and slipped into her sleepwear. Taking a final tour around the hotel suite to ensure all entrances were covered, Kate flopped into bed.

Her ears worked overtime as she wrestled with sleep. Exhausted, she accepted her fate. Her heavy eyes slammed shut.

Kate shot up out of bed, her heart racing. Kicking her feet into the mattress, she pushed herself to the headrest. Her weary eyes scanning the room in panic. Kate a took a deep breath when she realized she didn't have to fight the darkness. A slit of sunrise streamed through the crack in the curtains.

Rubbing her head, Kate sighed, "Just a dream."

Rolling out of bed, Kate spread the curtains wide allowing the morning sunshine to pour in. Somehow, she'd managed to sleep through the night.

Looking out onto the beach, Kate felt a warm breeze gently blow her hair. Her eyes shot to the door. Her belt was still in place, yet something was off. Inspecting the door, she realized the entire panel had been pulled from its track.

Her heart seized. Rushing to her phone, to call Detective Castro, she froze. An unsent text message filled the screen. "Hello, Kate".

Kate dropped the phone and spun around the room. Sliding the desk out of the way, she wriggled the coat hanger jamming the door latch out of position. The thought of hands reaching out behind her plagued her mind as she worked to free her own security device.

Releasing the handle, she raced out into the hallway. Turning both directions, she sprinted for Cassie's room.

Detective Castro wasted no time arriving at the Breakers following Kate's anxious phone call. Greeting her, he was taken aback as the usually confident woman collided into his arms for a comforting hug.

"All right, let's see what you found," Castro said.

Kate released her grip on the detective and nodded.

Castro followed Kate to her room. Navigating past the desk and the discarded coat hanger on the floor, Kate pointed to the phone on her bed. With a cloth, Detective Castro picked up the phone. Using Kate's face recognition, he opened it and read the message.

"We'll dust it for prints, but I doubt we'll find any. I'm sure whoever came in had gloves," the detective said. Moving toward the balcony door, Castro asked, "You think they came through here?"

Studying the door, he nodded. Glancing at Kate's belt still held in place, he said, "I like the extra security, but it didn't work in this case. Unless a security screw is placed in the upper track, someone with the right skills can easily lift these sliding doors out of place. We see it all the time."

Kate's eyes told the detective all they needed to know about her concerns.

"I'll speak to hotel security. They run a tight ship here. With a couple of tweaks, we'll make sure you're safe. I'll ask they move you to a more centralized location as well," Castro said.

"Thank you, Detective," Kate said. With the police detective's presence, her fears began to wash away and were replaced with anger. "Have you put together the pieces for the plan? I want to end this."

Detective Castro looked surprised, "Oh, no. Not after this…"

"*Especially* after this," Kate growled.

When forensics was finished in her guest room and her cellphone, they found Kate in her new, enhanced security suite. Located on a top floor and centrally located to other guests, it gave Kate an increased sense of safety.

Thanking the crime scene tech, she took the phone out of the plastic bag it was in. A quick glance saw several messages from Nick.

Kate wandered to her new view looking over the beach and the Atlantic Ocean and dialed his number.

"Kate, it's good to hear your voice. How is everything down there?" Nick asked.

"Sorry if I left you hanging. I just got my phone back from forensics," Kate said.

"What?" Nick gasped.

"It was kind of evidence," Kate admitted, her sheepish voice clear over the phone.

"What do you mean your phone was evidence?" Nick asked.

"Someone left a message on it, to scare me," Kate said.

"Like they snatched it off your table at a café? Or picked your pocket?" Nick asked.

"No, nothing like that. It was in my hotel room. On my bedstand," Kate said

"While you weren't there…." Nick's voice trailed off awaiting her confirmation.

"While I was sleeping," Kate said. She winced imagining Nick's reaction.

"That's it, Kate. No more of this," Nick said, his voice dripping with worry.

"I'm fine. The detective is taking care of things. He had hotel security install a few upgrades on my room, moved me to a higher floor," Kate said. "He thinks the note was left in response to the stake out last night."

"Stake out. What stake out? With this detective?" Nick asked, his voice incredulous.

"No. With Marco. He got a boat, and we watched the house from the shore. Sure enough, someone was there. But they got away," Kate said. "It was probably the same person who left the note."

"And probably the murderer. Even after his wife disappeared on a boat trip with him. You are insane. I think I regret being your friend. It is too hard on the nerves," Nick complained.

"Well, the detective is warming up to me. Sort of. Ooh, he is even using me in a sting to catch the bad guy once and for all," Kate said.

"Bait. The police are using you as bait," Nick said in a long sigh.

"Well, yeah. See, we'll have the bad guy caught in no time," Kate said, her voice cheery.

"No, Kate. You are taking too many gambles with this one," Nick said.

"Oh, the detective is calling me now. We need to set up for the sting," Kate said.

"Kate…"

"I promise I'll call you when we're done. I'm sorry, Nick. I have to go. They're waiting for me at the police station," Kate said.

Kate felt bad for cutting the conversation off with Nick. She could imagine how frustrating it must be for him to be so far from the action and to worry. Her lips creased into a slight smile when she thought of him worrying about her.

She grabbed her things, ensured the room was locked up and left to meet Detective Castro.

The Palm Beach Police Station was buzzing with excitement. Palm Beach Police Chief Cindy Huff greeted Kate. The woman wore a sour expression on her face, "Ms. Harper, I appreciate your willingness to help the department. I need to be clear: You do not have to do this."

"Thank you, Chief Huff. I'm all in. I am tired of losing sleep over whoever is doing this. And, while I didn't know Michelle very well, she deserves justice," Kate said.

"That's admirable. Detective Castro is in the briefing room getting the team ready. I'll take you back there," Chief Huff said.

Kate followed the police chief. As they walked by, officers sitting at their desks looked up and watched. The experience made Kate feel uneasy. She couldn't tell if they were impressed, horrified, or just curious.

Police Chief Huff poked her head into the briefing room. Catching a nod from Detective Castro, Kate was led in front of a group of officers. Some were plain clothed, others in uniform.

"This is Ms. Kate Harper. Her safety is the number one priority. Catching the bad guy is secondary to keeping her safe tonight," Detective Castro said.

The officers nodded.

"Our tech will get you wired up. We will have a tracker on you, and we will have a tracker on the jewels. Not that we'll need them. You'll never be out of our sight," Detective Castro said offering Kate a reassuring smile.

Kate nodded. A wireless transmitter was pinned to the strap of Kate's sundress . After a quick test, the tech escorted her back to Detective Castro.

"Mr. DiNova is already on location at Ms. VanLangen's estate. We have several officers in place. You will arrive. Mr. DiNova will have a spread for you on the back patio. He will give you the gift of the jewels out in the open. Try them on. Make a show of them. Put them back in the box, leave them poolside. You and Mr. DiNova will go for a walk on the beach. That will leave an opening for the perpetrator to make their move. We'll rush in and nab them. Case closed" the detective shared.

"It sounds like a plan," Kate said. "But how will the thief know I have the jewels?"

"There was a pretty public display of Mr. DiNova purchasing them this afternoon completely with armed security escorting Mr. DiNova down Worth Avenue to his car. A very large policy was written to Ms. Brown's agency. Prior to picking up the jewels, Mr. DiNova shared his intentions over a cocktail laden lunch with many of Palm Beach's power players in ear shot," Detective Castro said.

"Does Gustavo know of the plan?" Kate asked.

"Ms. VanLangen's houseman knows that Mr. DiNova was bringing guests on site and to prep a dining experience for the two of you," the detective said.

Kate simply nodded.

"You ready for this?" Detective Castro asked, a calming hand on her shoulder.

"I'm ready," Kate said, wiping her palms on the sides of her sundress.

"All right," Castro clapped his hands together. "Let's roll!"

Police Chief Huff shot her detective a clear look, "Don't mess this one up!"

Detective Castro offered a quick nod of assurance.

In a smooth procession, the team left the station. Kate shot Detective Castro a glance.

"You'll drive your own car like any other night. You won't see us behind. You won't see us pull up to the estate, but we'll be there," the detective said to Kate.

Slipping behind the wheel, Kate took a deep breath and started her SUV.

The VanLangen estate was eerily quiet as the gates opened and Kate navigated her SUV down the drive. Gustavo's little Italian car was conspicuously missing. Marco's sports car was parked up front. If there were police officers onsite, you wouldn't know it from the front of the stately house.

Strolling through the house, Kate felt like she was stepping onto a Hollywood set. Everything there was just a prop for the big scene. While she tried to act normal, focused on the patio doors, her peripheral vision worked overtime searching for a set of eyes looking back at her from the shadows.

As she sprung open the French doors leading to the patio, the effect didn't change. Seeing the lavish spread set up on one of the patio tables, the romantic overtones with candles and flowers in the center of the table felt farcical.

"Kate, it is so good to see you. Please," Marco waved his hand toward a seat as he rose to greet her.

Kate smirked. The Italian architect was clearly enjoying his role for the evening.

Sliding her seat in for her, Marco offered, "Wine? I have selected a fantastic Montepulciano d'Abruzzo. It should pair perfectly with Gustavo's truffle and fig balsamic tenderloin."

"That sounds great, thank you," Kate said. "He really went all out."

"It is a special occasion. Two souls entwined by fate," Marco said, his Italian accent ringing across the pool.

"Two souls on a common mission," Kate said in her low voice.

Marco smiled, "We can have a little fun with it, can't we? Help sell the experience."

"I'm certainly going to enjoy Gustavo's meal," Kate said straightening in her seat. Her eyes glanced on a silver box sat on the corner of the table. A robin's egg blue ribbon tied in an elegant bow was wrapped around it.

"Shall we?" Marco motioned his hands toward the cloches on the table.

"Yes, please!" Kate said.

The cloches revealed beef medallions drizzled with a rich sauce reduction. Alongside were Harissa and honey carrots.

"A step up from stake out charcuterie," Marco said as he dished up the plates.

"No complaints. I think as stake out food goes, it probably ranks up there," Kate said.

"To stake outs and memorable evenings!" Marco raised his glass in a toast.

Kate carried her glass to his. Her eyes scanned the estate. Other than the soft evening breeze rustling through the palms, the property was quiet.

Giving in, Kate thoroughly enjoyed Gustavo's meal. Purposefully sipping her wine slowly, she shook off Marco's heavy-handed attempts to top her glass off.

When the meal was complete, Marco grabbed the box. Swiveling his chair so that he could lean towards Kate, he presented the gift.

"Meeting you has been the bright spot in all the chaos," Marco said, a twinkle in his eye.

Kate fought hard not to smirk in the event they were being watched more closely than she thought.

In a grand spectacle, Kate pulled on the bow, freeing it from the box. Lifting the lid, she revealed the million-dollar necklace. Pulling it out of the box, she lifted it to her chest and displayed it for Marco and anyone else who might be present.

"Marco, it's too much," Kate gasped in a loud voice.

"It, my dear, is just the beginning!" Marco said.

Leaning in, his lips targeted hers. Kate dodged to the side just in time for her cheek to absorb the targeted affection. Instead, she enveloped Marco in a showy hug.

As they separated, Kate held up the necklace once more in admiration. As per the plan orchestrated with Detective Castro, she placed the valuable necklace in the box.

Marco scooped up their wine glasses and grabbed the bottle of wine. Kate hooked her arm in his and they walked toward the beach.

Kate's ears burned listening for any sound that might hint at an intruder. She had to fight to not turn back toward the table and the loaned jewels.

Heading for the moonlit beach, they descended the steps. Thinking they were out of view, they relaxed.

"Well, a good a time as any for a glass of wine," Marco suggested.

"It may be the perfect occasion," Kate said, trying to maintain her composure.

As Marco handed her a glass, she almost dropped it. From the shadows near the seawall, a figure stepped out, the gleam of a gun barrel shining in the moonlight.

Glass in hand, Kate froze. She realized not only were they out of view from an intruder on the estate grounds, they were also out of view of the police.

Shrouded in a hoody and a handkerchief wrapped around their face, the figure waved Marco and Kate to take a step further toward the water and further into the moonlight.

In what was clearly a contrived raspy voice, the figure growled, "I warned you!"

"What happens now?" Kate asked, taking a voluntary step closer to the water's edge.

"You die!" the figure snarled, moving the pistol in Kate's direction.

In a single motion, Kate flung her wine glass at the intruder's eyes. An explosion of red wine and shattered glass pulled the intruder off target, a shot ringing through the night. Grasping Marco's collar, Kate pulled him into the water. Diving under the wave, she knifed deep into the water as another shot was fired harmlessly into the surf.

Still holding onto Marco's shirt, Kate lifted her head for one deep breath and swam to the ocean floor. She kicked her feet and stroked with one arm while propelling Marco with her other until they were around the little jetty that separated Cassie's property from the Breakers.

Using the waves, they made their way to shore. Kate dragged a choking Marco up to the beach. Collapsing on the sand to catch her breath, Marco stumbled nearly landing on top of her. His knees straddled her hips and his outstretched hands dug into the soft sand on either side of her head.

For a moment, they froze, trying to catch their breaths.

A jet ski roared around the jetty making a beeline for the beach firing shots recklessly toward the shore.

A figure loomed over them, shining a bright light at the jet skier. The handkerchief and hoody-less jet skier, fearing being recognized, gunned the engine and cranked the steering hard, veering away from the beach and vanishing into the night.

Kate's eyes grew as they recognized the face peering on them.

"Hello, Kate," the figure said.

Her back still planted on the sand, Kate looked up.

"Nick!"

Holding his hand out, he asked, "Marco, I presume?"

Marco accepted his hand. Nick's muscular pull yanked the wide-eyed, disheveled architect to his feet.

Kate rolled to her feet and stood, dusting sand off her dress. "What are you doing here?" she asked.

"Saving you, as usual," Nick said.

"I didn't need saving. Okay, maybe a little. But I told you I was fine," Kate said looking out at the water where the jet ski vanished.

"Seems so," Nick said, his tone declaring his discontent.

Before either of them could say another word, they were surrounded by Palm Beach police officers. Freezing in place, they waited for the officers to sort out the scene.

Detective Castro strode up as the sea of officers parted.

With a wary look, the detective asked, "Who's this?"

"Detective Castro, this is Nick Mason. He's my… friend," Kate said. "He saved us from who I believe is the killer."

"The killer was waiting for you down by the bulkhead," the detective sighed. Shaking his head, "Our attention was on the jewels and the jewel thief."

"While using Kate as bait. You nearly got her killed," Nick said. Taking a menacing step toward the detective, his fists clenched..

"I am here on my own accord. The detective's plan was solid except for one thing," Kate said, stepping between Nick and the detective.

"What's that?" Detective Castro asked.

"The thief and the murderer are clearly *not* one and the same," Kate said.

Thirty-Five

Kate was allowed to dry off and change before making her way to a hotel conference room to debrief with Detective Castro and his team.

As she got off the elevator, Nick was waiting across the hall. His arms folded, his feet crossed as he leaned against the wall.

"Nick!" Kate danced across the hall. "I am so glad you're here."

Nick studied Kate for a moment, "I should have been here from the beginning."

"It's *great* to have you here. It is unnecessary. They are two different things," Kate said.

"It looked pretty necessary from my perspective on the beach," Nick said.

It was Kate's turn to study Nick. She struggled to interpret whether the comment was in regard to the shooter on the jet ski or Marco's awkward position with her on the beach.

Kate slipped her arm in his and bounced, "Well, you're here now. Escort me to what I am sure will be a scathing debrief?"

Nick laughed and shook his head, "You do make friends with police departments, don't you?"

Finding their way to the conference room the hotel set aside for them, the pair found Police Chief Huff pacing in front of the group. Her frustration and anger at a boiling point, she appeared to take a calming breath before addressing her audience.

Her eyes landed on Kate with a mix of relief, condolence and annoyance at being in the situation at all.

"Thank you for coming, Ms. Harper. And, Mr. Mason, I take it?" Chief Huff asked.

"I'm Nick Mason," Nick said.

"Where's the Italian guy?" Chief Huff asked.

"Marco is cleaning up after his night swim around the jetty," Kate said.

"Well, time is wasting," the chief said. "After we found you and Mr. Mason on the beach at the Breakers, we sent our shore patrol and the Coast Guard out looking for the jet ski, but they weren't able to find it. They are quick, easy to hide, easy to park."

"Were you able to see whether it was a man or woman?" Detective Castro asked.

Kate shook her head, "They were covered except for their eyes, and they disguised their voice in sort of a growl. I… really couldn't say."

"How about size?" the detective pressed.

"A short to medium-sized man or a taller woman. They were… thin?" Kate scrunched her nose, disappointed with her own account of the shooter.

"The gun report sounded like a nine-millimeter. It was lucky you weren't hit," Detective Castro said.

"In the water, I wasn't worried. On the beach, we were in trouble," Kate said. "If Nick wasn't there…"

"It was *my* responsibility," Detective Castro said looking grim.

"It was," Nick nodded.

"In that, we agree, Mr. Mason," Chief Huff said, her eyes in a scowl.

"I was a willing participant. Who knew Marco and I would be the target and not the jewels? Where are they by the way?" Kate asked.

"Police-escorted courier back to the jeweler," Detective Castro said.

"We might have lost our window to the jewel thief," Kate said.

"That is what you're worried about, Kate? You could have been killed tonight!" Nick snapped.

"Well…" Kate winced.

"We are more concerned about your safety and catching the killer," Detective Castro said.

"How did the murderer know to find you?" Nick asked.

All of the heads in the room turned to Nick.

Detective Castro stammered, "We planted enough seeds around town. We thought we were dealing with an individual motivated by the jewels."

"But your jewel thief and murderer are two different people," Nick said.

"It appears so. And you are the second person with that theory," the detective admitted.

Nick cast a glance at Kate who shrugged.

"We do know there is a killer loose on Palm Beach who is increasingly agitated. They do not appear amused by Ms. Harper's antics," Chief Huff said.

"It also means we are getting closer to the truth," Kate said.

"That may be. But I will tell you, your involvement in or anywhere near this case is over," Chief Huff said.

Seeing the defiant look on Kate's face, the chief added, "I would rather see you in one of my jails than in a body bag, Ms. Harper."

Kate's shoulders slumped.

"Where does this leave the investigation?" one of the officers asked.

"We narrow our focus on those that would have been tipped off by the grapevine that we fed. That would include…" Detective Castro's eyes floated up to the ceiling as his thoughts came together. "That would include the staff at the Palm Beach estates. The families and their guests. Anyone with a connection to the galas."

Kate reeled at the thought.

"Where was Mr. Silvestri this evening?" the detective asked.

"Gustavo? As per the plan, he left, I guess. His car wasn't parked where it usually is," Kate said. "I never saw him."

Detective Castro pondered for a moment, "Based on the size of your attacker on the beach, could it have been Mr. Silvestri?"

Kate shook her head as she didn't want to believe but shrugged, "It could have been."

"He had opportunity. He certainly would have seen through the ruse we had planned. He is the only one outside of this department that would have known the plan for you and Mr. DiNova to be on that beach," Detective Castro said.

With a nod from Chief Huff, the detective ordered a pair of his officers, "Put out an APB on Gustavo Silvestri. Bring him in for questioning."

The officers immediately left the room to follow their orders.

"Ms. Harper, I am going to assign an officer to you for the remainder of the investigation," Chief Huff said.

Kate hugged Nick's arm, "Is it necessary?"

The chief considered Kate's position. "If you stay on property, no. I will have officers here at the Breakers and at the VanLangen estate. If you wish to leave either, I want you to have clearance from either myself or Detective Castro. My number one priority is to prevent any additional harm to the people of Palm Beach. Catching the murderer and the thief fall after that," Chief Huff said.

Kate looked hesitant but nodded.

Chief Huff looked at Detective Castro, "Have sea patrols out in front of both the Breakers and the VanLangen estate. And see what is holding up Mr. DiNova."

"Yes, Chief," Detective Castro said. His head dropped his head like a loyal puppy that had been scolded.

"Ms. Harper, I trust you can make your way back to your room without incident? Officers are already positioned around the resort," Chief Huff said.

"Yes," Kate said, nodding. "I'll be fine."

The chief studied Kate as though she were highly skeptical in her answer.

Kate looked up at Nick, "If he's up for it, I'll have Nick by my side."

Nick offered a nonchalant nod.

"Thank you both for your effort. I don't hold Detective Castro accountable. I was a willing participant," Kate said on her way out of the conference room.

Electing to not walk through the hotel's corridors, Kate led Nick outside to the rear patio. Part of the breakwater seawall, waves splashed against the stone patio serenading them as they walked.

"So, you've had quite the adventure in Palm Beach," Nick said. He shuffled his feat a bit as he walked.

"It has been a wild ride," Kate admitted.

"What are your theories? Who's the cat burglar? Who's the murderer? Are you sure they aren't one and the same?" Nick asked.

Kate stopped and lit up as Nick knew just what buttons to press.

"Well, if you were a cat burglar, even if you had committed a murder and were afraid someone was close to figuring out it was you, taking the chance to grab the jewels and disappear would make the most sense. Why worry about the nosey amateur sleuth at all? Grab the necklace and go," Kate said.

"Only a murderer with roots here in Palm Beach would stick around and risk going after you… and Marco," Nick said.

"Right!" Kate said.

"Unless, they were tipped off," Nick suggested. "What if they are still one and the same, but they knew it was a trap?"

"Hmm," Kate pondered. "That would align with Detective Castro's theory. Avoid the trap. Hope to catch me off guard on the beach. But why bother?"

"You're either getting close or you're just ruffling the wrong feathers," Nick said.

Kate shimmied close to Nick and batted her eyelashes, "Do you want to help me find out who it is?"

"I wouldn't want to step on any toes…" Nick drawled.

Kate put her hands on her hips and looked Nick in the eyes. She said, "Marco may have his intentions, but I shared none of them. My heart and mind are… preoccupied with another."

"Hmm," Nick shoved his hands in his pockets and gave a sheepish look. "That Gustavo fella?"

"You're ridiculous, Nick Mason," Kate circled to stand directly in front of Nick. "I *told* you I was happy to see you. Besides, you're my best sleuthing partner."

Thirty-Six

Nick and Kate eyed each other over their cups of coffee in the Breakers' hot brunch and evening lounge spot the Circle.

The familiar face of Detective Castro floated through the crowd. Spying the two, he made a beeline over to them.

"Mr. Mason, I hope you are settling in," the detective said.

"This is a beautiful place," Nick said, eyeing the surroundings.

"It is," the detective agreed, though his tone was indifferent. "Ms. Harper, I came to once more extend my apologies. Putting you in danger was never part of the plan."

"Except it *was* the plan," Nick said.

Kate waved him off, "No one could have predicted how it went down. I sure didn't."

"I hope you accept my apology nonetheless," Detective Castro said.

"Accepted, though unwarranted," Kate said. "I feel like we were close. It was just the wrong target. We were close to catching a murderer, not a cat burglar."

The detective nodded, "We need to rethink all of this. I was sure Ms. Goss was killed as a witness to a robbery. If we caught the thief, we would bring her killer to justice."

"There may still be a connection, yet" Kate said over her cup of coffee.

"How so?" the detective asked.

"Honestly, I don't know. Just a string I keep tugging at," Kate said with a shrug.

"Before you do anything, you call me first," Castro said, his voice firm.

"Of course," Kate said.

Nick snickered. Both Detective Castro and Kate swung their gazes to him. Nick smiled and shrugged.

"Well, be careful," Detective Castro said. "Mr. Silvestri, he has, it seems, been seeing someone on the sly. Teresa Lilley."

Kate's eyes went wide before a sliver of recognition came to light, "That makes a bit of sense."

"Any thoughts on how that fits our case?" Detective Castro asked.

Kate shook her head.

"Well, if you think of anything, please let me know," the detective said.

"I will," Kate nodded.

As the detective left the restaurant, Nick asked, "What now?"

"We need to look at the murder and theft as two separate cases. Then, we can see if they intersect," Kate said.

"Sounds difficult and dangerous, as always," Nick said. "Chase a murderer who tried to kill you last night and an international cat burglar who has evaded law enforcement in several cities."

"We've got this. Especially with you here," Kate smiled. Her face fell to a frown. "I was so sure…"

Pulling out her phone, she flipped through photos she had saved. Finding the one she had in mind, she used her fingers to zoom it open. Tapping it, her eyes grew wide. "There *has* to be a connection, just not the one we were thinking of," Kate said.

Nick looked past his coffee at Kate.

"We need to build a crime board!" Kate said, shooting up from her seat.

"Oh, okay," Nick said at the abrupt interruption and followed her out of the restaurant.

Making their way to Cassie's guest house, Kate set up her computer and connected it to a printer.

Using tape and the massive glass windows overlooking the ocean, she began arranging clues and suspects from each of the crimes. The murder of Michelle Goss on one side, the jewel thefts on the right.

Kate placed a photo right at the top of the murder section.

"Who's that?" Nick asked.

"Teresa Lilley. Cassie's main cosmetics and fragrance rival who happens to also live not far from here. They were jockeying for Michelle Goss' spokesmodel contract. Her death disrupted Cassie's next big launch. The theft of her formula along with the delay in launch may have fallen into Teresa's lap as she is now fast-tracking a launch with a remarkably similar profile," Kate said.

"She doesn't look much like a murderer. Or a thief," Nick said.

"She had plenty of motive and opportunity. She also had this guy," Kate slapped a photo of David Hammit just under Teresa's. "He used to work for Cassie and is now Teresa's right hand. While not physically imposing, he is devious and was caught sneaking into Cassie's office the night of the party. He was also courting Michelle for her services on behalf of Teresa."

"Sounds like a good candidate," Nick said. "What about your buddy Marco?"

"Marco?" Kate asked. She looked thoughtful, "He didn't have a lot to gain, but he might have had a lot to lose. Say Michelle caught him being up to something…"

Kate's eyes went wide and she snapped her fingers, "Like helping a jewel thief."

"Or dumping his wife in the ocean," Nick said.

"He would lose his good standing with the power players in Palm Beach overnight," Kate said.

"Losing is as good a motive as gaining, if not better," Nick said. "How about Gustavo? It sounds like he is always around."

"He had been present for pretty much all of the events, except for last night," Kate said.

"Because he was waiting for you on the beach?" Nick suggested.

"I hope not. He seems like a really nice guy," Kate said. "Besides, he alibied out."

"Who else?" Nick prodded.

"There is Cassie's new boyfriend Donovan, but I haven't seen him around much and I don't see a motive," Kate said. "Old boyfriend Henrique Desperaux on the other hand, he could have had motive. Especially if Michelle had dirt on him that would further soil his relationship with Cassie that he seemed desperate to reignite. It was their affair that ended it in the first place. He was caught breaking into the house several times claiming he was looking for something that he lost."

"Solid option," Nick nodded. "I hate to say it, but you have to add Cassie and Merilu in to the mix."

"Might as well add myself, too," Kate said.

"You? I trust you with my life," Nick asked.

"You are here because you didn't trust me to be able to handle myself," Kate said.

"I trust you with *my* life. Not necessarily your own. You aren't afraid to throw yourself in harm's way. Admirable, but terrifying for those that… care about you," Nick said.

Kate froze and stared at Nick. Her shoulders relaxed and she nodded, "Thank you, for coming."

"We're partners in crime- solving. Besides, I saw the workmanship on the new gazebo, figured I might need to lend a hand with a hammer while I'm here," Nick said.

Kate laughed, "All right, mister. Back to the crime solving."

Turning to the board, she said, "Michelle's death cost Cassie a small fortune and Merilu had nothing really to gain."

"But there is this guy," Kate said, slapping a final picture to the wall.

Nick leaned into study the photo, "Who's this?"

"I'm not sure. I am told his name is Neal Roth. He was at the party. He was at the gala where the photo of all the jewels that have stolen was taken. All but the necklace we used for bait," Kate said.

"But its locked up in a high security location, now," Nick said.

"If it's the same thief as the one from the other cities, it would be way out of their M.O. to steal it from there," Kate said. Taping the photo from the gala event to the glass, her eyes scanned it. "Wait! We had the wrong target!"

Nick leaned close to Kate and studied the photo.

Kate's finger stabbed at a figure in the back of the photo glancing up at the women.

"Henrique Desperaux! He had something in his possession that night that the jewel thief wanted," Kate said. "And I think I know what it is."

"Do we ask him about it?" Nick asked.

Kate grinned, "We find it."

Thirty-Seven

Kate led Nick to the patio that wrapped around the pool, all the while, recounting the stories she heard about the party where Desperaux tried to propose to Cassie, but instead, they broke up.

"According to Cassie, she and Henrique got into a fight out on the patio. It was late. There were… abundant libations. Henrique tried to propose. They had an argument and Cassie declined. In a show of anger, I guess she threw the ring," Kate said.

Kate walked around the patio. She imagined where Henrique Desperaux might want to propose in the aftermath of a party. "Come here!" Kate called.

Nick walked dutifully over.

Grasping his forearms, Kate positioned him. She grinned, "Stand here and propose to me."

"What?" Nick's eyes grew wide.

"As if you were Henrique Desperaux proposing to Cassie," Kate said.

Nick nodded. Looking around, he positioned Kate so that she could view the ocean. "The pool lights would be shining through the water bathing them in a hint of blue. The moon somewhere overhead illuminating the white froth of the rolling waves…" he started.

"You're good at this," Kate giggled.

Nick's cheeks grew red.

"Come on," Kate coaxed him to continue.

"K… Cassie…" Nick dropped to a knee in front of Kate.

Handing her a pretend ring, Kate took it. For a moment, she appeared to admire it. Then she became cross. She rocked back and forth. Nick stood up. He tried to take Kate by her forearms but she twisted away.

"No!" Kate yelled. In a slash of her arm, she threw the pretend ring into the pretend night.

Kate and Nick followed her arm motion.

"I know where to find the ring," Kate said.

Nick's eyes remained fixed on the end of Kate's simulated throw, "Yep."

Kate was off in a rush toward the main house. Nick followed not exactly knowing where she was heading.

Flinging open the French doors, Kate led Nick to Gustavo's room. She rapped her knuckles excitedly and called, "Gustavo?"

The door flung open and Gustavo looked out. Seeing Kate, he asked, "Is everything okay, Ms. Kate?"

"Yes, but we need your help. Gustavo, Nick. Nick Gustavo," Kate said.

"Pleasure," Gustavo said.

"Likewise. I have heard great things about you and your food," Nick said.

Gustavo studied Nick for a moment before breaking into a smile and said, "All exaggerations, I assure you."

"Until you taste his cooking. He's a genius. He's a surfer, like you, too," Kate said.

"Multitalented," Nick said.

"So, Gustavo… where do you keep your pool vacuum?" Kate asked.

"Is there something wrong with the pool?" Gustavo asked, his voice concerned.

"Oh, no. But it may have the answer to some of what is going on around here," Kate said.

"Well, if we can put an end to that, I'm happy to help," Gustavo said. Casting a look over his shoulder, he said, "Let me show you."

With a nod, Gustavo stepped through the doorway and into the main house living space.

"Follow me," Gustavo said. "What is it you are hoping to find?"

"I'll know when I see it," Kate said.

"All right…" Gustavo shrugged.

The houseman led Kate and Nick to a stucco shed flanked by small palms just a few feet off of the poolside patio.

"Here we go. Not sure what you're looking for. I clean the pool twice a week, but the pool is typically clean. Probably dump the vac once a month," Gustavo said.

"That might be the miracle we need," Kate said.

"Here," Gustavo grabbed an old screen and placed it over a pair of sawhorses. Sliding a blue tarp underneath, he shrugged, "There you go."

Unlatching the filter basket from the pool vacuum, Gustavo dumped it on the screen. All eyes fell on the sludge that oozed out. Gustavo looked around for a tool to stir the slurry. Grabbing the pool filter wrench, Gustavo pushed the contents of the filter around. Turning on a garden hose, he maneuvered a light spray of water to help the process.

Nick shined a light on the effluence in an attempt to highlight any shine from a stray object.

"There it is!" Kate squealed. Pinching her fingers in the midst of the slurry, she plucked out a diamond ring. "Believe it or not, this is five million reasons for theft and murder."

Gustavo was speechless as he studied the ring in Kate's hand. "Is that…?"

He stepped toward Kate, hands twitching as if he wanted to hold it himself.

"Cassie must have flung it in the pool when she had her fight with Henrique," Gustavo said.

"Did you see the argument?" Kate asked.

"Not really. I was cleaning up. The night had gone on a little long at that point. I heard them on the patio. Their voices were already elevated from hours of music and wine. Cassie was very animated that night," Gustavo said.

"She said she threw the ring," Kate said. "I guess, right into the pool."

"So… the box in Cassie's safe was found empty," Gustavo said, his eyes drifting to the ceiling as he mulled the situation. "I remember finding it and giving it to her, but I never opened it to check."

"This ring is why the spokeswoman was killed in the gazebo?" Nick said, his face scrunching into a frown.

"I don't know," Kate said, her voice trailing.

"Well, if that polished rock is worth killing for, we should get it to that detective," Nick said.

"Yeah," Kate said, her mind still clearly grinding gears.

Nick shook his head. He knew the look, and it likely meant Kate was hatching a plan.

Thanking Gustavo, they began their walk back toward the house with the police escort and prize in hand.

"What are you plotting? We *are* going to give it to the police detective, aren't we?" Nick asked when they were in the safety of Kate's guarded room at the Breakers.

Holding it up to the natural sunlight streaming through the oceanfront windows, Kate said, "We let it leak out that it was found. And we see who takes the bait."

"Sound like a familiar theme with a potentially bad ending," Nick said.

"I think it all depends on who receives the message," Kate said.

"And you can put some very specific, directed message in the sky somehow?" Nick asked.

Kate grinned, "Somehow."

Thirty-Eight

With Gustavo's help and against Nick's pleas to let the police take over, Kate strategically shared with the Palm Beach community that something valuable was found at Cassie's estate. Kate asked Cassie to host an impromptu dinner in honor of Michelle.

Despite her resistance to the idea and the emotions that stabbed at her from the night of her friend's death, Cassie agreed.

"If it helps end all of this, then… fine," Cassie conceded.

Kate assured her the dinner would be an opportunity to begin the healing process over the loss of her friend. She admitted she hoped it would also be a beginning to the end of the threats that had descended on her estate. Cassie showed the slightest glimmer of hope in her eyes.

Working with Gustavo, Cassie and Kate invited the guests and assembled a crew to assist in the kitchen.

Nick and Marco hovered in the background, each offering their help while they jockeyed for Kate's attention. The two men were more than willing to roll up their sleeves and take on any of the tasks Kate tossed their way to prepare for the dinner party. Construction equipment was stowed, sawdust was swept up, and boards were placed in neat stacks.

Merilu giggled, a spectator to the suitors' battle. Each man looked at the other, ensuring the stack of wood in their arms was larger than the others. Marco had to admit defeat when he lost grip of his armful, nearly spilling the lumber into the pool.

By the time the hostess arrived at her own estate, twilight had fallen. Cassie looked nervous and hopeful at the same time.

Kate and Merilu book ended her sides, each sliding a comforting arm around her back.

Offering a weak grin, Cassie said, "I get to finally meet the mysterious Nick Mason."

Kate blushed, "He was very helpful in getting everything together for tonight."

"I'm sure he was," Cassie said, her eyes sweeping her home. She frowned slightly, "You can hardly tell this place is under a remodel."

"We did some tidying up. You can thank Nick and Marco for that," Kate said.

"Oh, and how are those two getting along?" Cassie asked.

Kate started to answer but Merilu beat her to the punch and blurted, "It has been like watching the opening to a Jane Austen story!"

"I'm sorry to have missed that," Cassie said, giggling.

"It's not like that!" Kate insisted, her face scrunched in a scowl.

"Then you won't mind if I arrange the seating chart. Nick one side, Marco on the other?" Merilu teased.

Kate's scowl deepened. Her voice was firm as she said, "The seating is fine how it is set."

As they turned the corner, Kate stumbled as her feet nearly froze in place. Nick stood with his hands crossed in front of him. His neatly pressed linen suit highlighted his deepened tan from working on his friend's sailboat.

Kate's change in posture told Cassie everything she needed to know. The cosmetics mogul whispered to Merilu, "The battle is already won."

Kate shook herself after shooting a Nick an admiring smile, she said, "Nick Mason, Ms. Cassie Van Langen."

"Ms. Van Langen, it is a pleasure. Thank you for welcoming me to your beautiful home," Nick said.

Cassie beamed, "I'm glad to have you. And if you will, Cassie is fine if you don't mind me calling you Nick."

"Cassie it is," Nick said.

His eyes swept Kate in her white sundress. With his hand held toward the patio doors, he offered, "May I?"

Kate smiled and nodded.

Accepting Nick's escort, they stepped out onto the patio.

A table with three large candelabras set in even intervals illuminated neatly placed settings. Bouquets of beach sunflowers and asters sprang from vases like firework displays. Cassie clamped her hands to her chest and gasped, "Michelle's favorites!"

"The local florist was helpful," Kate said.

"Thank you," Cassie said, giving Kate a thin smile.

"Cassie, darling," Marco called. Striding into the light, the Italian wore a fine white suit. A pink shirt with a white tie accentuated his natural olive skin tone.

"Marco, I assume you had a hand in pulling all of this together," Cassie said.

"We all did," Kate said, her eyes shifting to Nick.

"Well, thank you. All of you," Cassie said.

On cue, Gustavo backed his way onto the patio, a large, covered dish in hand.

"No way we could have a dinner party without you, Gustavo," Cassie smiled at her houseman.

"My pleasure, Cassie," Gustavo said as he placed the dish near the center of the table.

Marco seemed to almost shake with anxiety, "May I poor some wine for everyone?"

"That would be great, Marco," Cassie said.

The normally thick Florida air seemed even thicker. Marco's eyes flitted to Nick. He was joined by Gustavo's wary eyes, trying to determine whether he trusted the newcomer.

"Pour me a glass, if you would, Marco," a voice called from the French doors of the main house.

Cassie spun to see Donovan stepping out onto the porch, "Donovan, what a surprise!"

Giving the actor a hug, Cassie pulled back and gave her boyfriend a look over. His silk shirt unbuttoned to his sternum stood in sharp contrast to the well-dressed men, including Nick's rare dressy attire. Somehow, the actor managed to pull the look off.

"Since you're pouring, I'll have a glass," another voice said joining the group on the patio.

Donovan's eyes narrowed.

"Henrique! What are you doing here?" Cassie shrieked.

"It's okay. I invited him," Kate said quickly, hoping to diffuse a scene.

Cassie gave the debonair man a stern look, "Behave this evening, Henrique."

Henrique Desperaux grinned. He patted down his exquisite suit jacket. Looking as if he just walked off a megayacht, he said, "I will be on my utmost behavior, darling."

Donovan slipped a steady arm around Cassie, "Come on, let's get you a glass of wine. I know I could use one."

Nick leaned next to Kate. Able to place the players she had described to him in person, he sized them up, realizing any one of them could be a thief, a murderer or both.

With a grin, he whispered, "This *is* going to be a fun night!"

Cassie glanced at Kate as Marco poured her a glass of garnet-colored wine, "Any more surprises?"

Kate shuffled, "I can't promise there won't be any. But I can tell you these are all the people on the official invite."

Cassie nodded. Her eyes drifted to the flowers Kate had selected on Michelle's behalf.

Addressing the well-attired, yet somehow still motley crew, Cassie raised her glass and said, "Tonight is a night to cut through the sadness of the loss of our dear friend. We come together to celebrate a wonderful woman who touched our lives in many ways. We take a break from tears to remember. Remember the moments we shared with her. She brightened every room. She is missed."

The group joined Cassie in a toast.

With wine sipped, Kate began orchestrating seating. She and Nick took the opposite end of Cassie and Donovan. The seating allowed her to have a view of the entire table and the main house. Merilu and Marco settled in on one side of the table while Henrique and Gustavo took the other. Gustavo slipped between Henrique and Donovan.

"What do you have for us this evening, Gustavo?" Cassie asked.

The personal chef placed his hand on the massive cloche, "Another of Ms. Michelle's favorites. Chicken marsala."

Gustavo revealed a heaping pan of golden pan-fried chicken and mushrooms bathed in a rich Marsala wine sauce.

"It looks delicious, Gustavo. Thank you for putting this together on such a short notice," Kate said.

"My pleasure, Ms. Kate," Gustavo said. Standing, he helped dish the guests' plates.

As they settled into their meals, eyes began glancing around the table. While most of them had had meals together, this one seemed different.

Marco gave Kate occasional smiles while his lips curled slightly as they crossed past Nick. Gustavo, while also concerned with the new face, seemed to give scrutiny to Marco, Donovan and Henrique.

Merilu giggled at the new tension that Nick brought to the table.

"So, Henrique. I didn't know you would be here. Did you use the front door this time?" Donovan lobbed the first sortie across the table.

Henrique smiled, undaunted. He looked Donovan in the eyes as he spoke, "Where there is a will, there is a way. I handed Cassie my key. I do recommend she mix her passcodes and things up a bit."

Turning his attention to Cassie, he said, "I know you well enough, Cassie. You like your codes to be something memorable.

Once you rule out birthdays and such mundane options, you explore markers in your life. It took me a couple of tries the last time but the introduction of your Spiagga line launched you onto the national stage. The scent of affluent beachgoers wafts in the air and into your front door code."

Cassie looked surprised. She almost smirked before frowning, "Henrique! I will need to really put some thought into my next series. Maybe move to a different type of security."

"I could offer some ideas," Nick said.

"Yes, that's right, you are a… handyman?" Marco asks, his voice ringing with condescension.

"Among other things," Nick smiled evenly. Glancing at the gazebo, he started, "I was meaning to talk to you about…"

Kate kicked Nick's shin under the table.

"I mean, I'd be happy to look over your plans tomorrow," Nick offered.

"Charming, but I think we have the remodel well in hand," Marco said.

"I, for one, am happy to have another capable man around," Merilu said. "Especially one who wasn't here during… all of this nonsense."

"I think it is best to keep things more intimate right now," Marco said.

Donovan shot a look toward Henrique, "We really should."

Reaching across Gustavo, Henrique asked, "More wine anyone?"

Trying to grab a bottle of wine, he knocked it over instead, a stream of red liquid splashing off the table and onto Donovan's shirt.

Pushing quickly from the table, Donovan rose.

Henrique stood waving his cloth napkin toward Donovan as a feeble attempt at aid.

Donovan ripped his wine-soaked shirt off.

Merilu grinned at the well-sculpted actor.

"This *is* fun!" Nick leaned in and whispered to Kate.

"You did that on purpose!" Donovan growled.

Instead of accepting Henrique's feeble attempt at assistance, he tossed the remaining wine from his own glass on Henrique's white shirt. Henrique tried to dodge the wine, as he did so, his jacket flowed open, revealing the handle of a revolver gleaming in the candlelight.

"You have a gun!" Donovan exclaimed.

Henrique flustered and then a soft smile creased his lips, "A gentleman is always prepared. Isn't it an American thing?"

"In mentally sound hands, perhaps," Merilu quipped.

"There is a murderer afoot," Henrique protested.

"You are a suspect!" everyone at the table declared in unison.

"One thing I can say, he *isn't* the cat burglar," Kate said glancing at her phone.

All eyes swiveled to Kate.

"I said I couldn't promise there wouldn't be any unofficial guests. Our jewel thief is upstairs as we speak," Kate said standing up from the table.

Her eyes glanced up at the dark master bedroom balcony. Cassie looked confused.

"Nick and I set a trap this afternoon. It won't hold them long, but it shouldn't have to," Kate said.

Eyes from the table maintained their puzzlement.

"Come on, let's catch a cat burglar!" Kate said, leading the charge into the house.

Running up the stairs, they could hear banging from inside the master bedroom closet. As they streamed through the doorway, a wall of sheetrock exploded, and a figure leapt between the wall studs.

Hoping to dash away, the figure was instead caught in Nick's grasp, his fists clutching the intruder's dark clothing. Flailing, the intruder tried to slip free. As Nick gave him a shove toward the back of the room, further away from the possible exits, a trio of flashlights snapped on, each clamped to a service pistol.

Detective Castro stepped forward, "Neal Roth, if that is your real name, you are under arrest for burglary and the murder of Michelle Goss."

Kate held up a finger and strode toward the detective as one of his officers placed Neal Roth in handcuffs. "Multiple accounts of burglaries, around the world, really… but not murder," she said.

"We'll talk about that later," Detective Castro said, his voice firm but his eyes belying his curiosity.

Neal Roth glared at Kate, "How did you know?"

"You tipped your hand," Kate said. "And you overstayed your welcome trying to get the missing piece to your score. The piece that seemed to evade everyone until… well, the detective can fill you in on all that."

Detective Castro instructed his team, "Book him. I will be at the station shortly."

His eyes landing on Kate, the detective said, "Good work, Ms. Harper."

"I had help," Kate smiled, her eyes draping over Nick.

The detective nodded, his own eyes finally taking a moment to look over the dinner party. The shirtless actor, the intrepid Henrique with his red-stained shirt and Nick the newcomer. His eyes squinted, "Do I want to know?"

Kate shook her head. "Not really, Detective. Thank you for being here."

"Staking out a trap set for an international cat burglar is certainly a first. Please come by the station first thing in the morning for official statements. I'll leave you all to… whatever it is you were doing," Detective Castro said and disappeared down the master bedroom steps.

Cassie looked at Kate, "You trapped a cat burglar in my bedroom closet. How?"

"Well, if a cat burglar can get through a safe, a closet door would be no match. I had Nick swap out the regular door with a heavier steel door," Kate said.

"I added non-removable pin hinges and a top locking bolt which automatically engaged when the door was closed all the way. Kate's right, while it would be a prison for a regular person, for an experienced cat burglar, it would be a nuisance and a delay," Nick said.

"He must have sensed something was wrong and discarded his usual elegant methods for a quick exit through the closet's weakest point, the drywall," Kate said.

Cassie looked impressed, "Well, handyman. I may take you up on your security consult after all."

Marco and Donovan winced.

Thirty-Nine

Detective Castro was waiting for Kate and Nick at the front desk of the Palm Beach Police Station.

Kate thrust a box of donuts from Main Street by the Breakers. Nick followed with a tray of coffees.

The detective studied the two for a moment, deciding whether to accept the offerings or decline them, especially with Kate technically a potential suspect in a murder case.

"I'm sure the officers will appreciate the donuts. I, uh, I'll take a coffee," Detective Castro said. Grabbing a coffee from the tray Nick was holding, he nodded his head toward the door, "Follow me."

After he pressed a button from behind the desk, the door separating the lobby from the rest of the police station clicked open. Backing into the door to protect their breakfast items, Kate and Nick followed the detective into the station.

"You can set the stuff over there on the table. Don't worry, it won't take the crew any time to find them. They can smell donuts and coffee not brewed through a machine built in the 70s from a mile away," Detective Castro said as he stood in the doorway of his office.

Kate and Nick stepped into the office as the detective closed the door and waved his hand for them to take seats across from his chair as he slid behind desk.

"Thank you for coming down and your assistance yesterday. I will say it isn't customary for us to work an operation like that with civilians," Detective Castro said.

"It was our pleasure to help, Detective," Kate said.

"I do have some questions for you," the detective tapped his pencil down his notepad until he got to the line he wanted to ask. "How did you know the thief was Neal Roth?"

"I didn't," Kate admitted. "I had a suspicion. A strong suspicion. He was at a gala that all the victims had attended. Each was wearing the item that was stolen in a subsequent heist."

"There were lots of people there," the detective pressed.

"I started combing through the photos from similar thefts in Canada and in Beverly Hills. Digging long enough, someone who looked a lot like Neal Roth was at similar events in those cities," Kate said.

"I don't understand why a thief of that caliber would take the risk at Cassie's estate after missing on previous occasions," Nick said.

Detective Castro nodded, "I have the same question."

"I believe there are a couple of reasons. First, he is very sure of himself and his skills. I think his cockiness caught up to him," Kate said.

"He ran into you," Nick grinned.

The detective appeared to stifle a response, "And the other?"

"The ring isn't just any ring. It once belonged to a Spanish princess. While also being stunning and possessing a large, rare blue diamond. That is why it is worth so much. For a jewel thief with an ego, it would be a once-in-a-lifetime opportunity," Kate said.

The detective frowned, "How do you know all of this?"

Kate grinned, "I researched the Henrique Desperaux's background. I found the connection between him and the princess deep in his family's history. When I saw the ring, I remembered seeing it in an article."

"It is so special there was an article about it?" Nick asked.

Kate nodded, "I guess so. I had to go back to my hotel and look it up on my computer. Sure enough, that is the ring."

"You are… quite the researcher," Detective Castro said.

"She's an incredible investigator," Nick said.

"Hmm," the detective coughed. "If the ring is so special, why didn't the owner come forwards about it?"

"I think Desperaux wanted to find it without any more attention drawn to it. From Cassie or from anyone learning its real value," Kate said.

"Except for Neal Roth, because he is an expert in rare jewelry," Castro said.

Kate nodded. "Exactly. With the ring lost, it wasn't in the safe for him to find."

"What was in the safe that was stolen?" the detective asked.

"The box for the ring, which only served to confirm to Neal Roth that the ring was still around. He just needed to hear the good news that it was found," Kate said.

"That was a nifty trap you set for him," Detective Castro said.

"I knew it wouldn't hold a cat burglar for long. I'm glad you agreed to be there once it was sprung," Nick said.

The detective looked across the desk at Kate, "Well, Ms. Harper has proven to have some good instincts. But it doesn't answer the question of who killed Michelle Goss."

"So, you believe me that Roth isn't the killer?" Kate asked.

"It was a good tool to elicit a confession from him," Detective Roth said.

"He confessed?" Kate gasped.

"Well, you did catch him red-handed," the detective said. "The prospect of being pegged for a murder he didn't commit got him talking pretty good. He wouldn't admit to the thefts in the other cities, but when forensics came back with the rest of the jewels found in an airtight container in his hotel room toilet, he decided to be cooperative regarding the robberies here in Palm Beach."

"That's good. You brought down an international jewel thief!" Kate said.

"We'll forward our information to the other investigation teams, see if there is anything that supports them in their cases," the detective said.

"But there is still a murderer loose in Palm Beach," Nick said.

"I don't suppose you have any information to share on that front?" Detective Castro looked at Kate.

"Nothing more than you likely already know," Kate said. "Unless you'll let me take a peek at your crime board. We can compare notes."

"That's not going to happen," the detective said.

Kate slumped. Suddenly she pushed out to the edge of her seat. With a finger in the air, she announced, "But Teresa Lilley is throwing a launch party for a new product. I would bet my bottom dollar that the killer will be there."

"You aren't suggesting another trap?" Detective Castro asked.

"Kate, this is a murderer we are talking about," Nick protested.

"I am only saying we should go. Who doesn't love a good Palm Beach party?" Kate asked.

Nick cocked his head, "I can think of one person, Kate."

Kate's face fell, "Right. I didn't mean to be insensitive."

Detective Castro scratched his chin, "No. You're right. Her attendee list likely mirrors Cassie VanLangen's."

"All of us staying at Cassie's are invited," Kate said.

"I can see if I can get a warrant and have you wired, if you'd be willing," Detective Castro said.

"No. Kate has stuck herself out there enough," Nick said. "*I'll* wear the wire."

Kate grinned and batted her eyes at Nick, "Then you'll have to stick close by my side all night!"

"You can count on it," Nick said. The look on his face displayed his concern.

"We'll be right outside the estate with cars on you at all times," the detective assured.

"Fine. If it helps put an end to all of this. Let's do it," Nick said.

"Good. I'll let you know as soon as I can get the judge to sign off on the warrant," Detective Castro said.

"In the meantime, I have a little sleuthing I can do," Kate said.

Nick winced.

"So, what happens to the ring?" Kate asked.

"As soon as all of the evidence has been processed, we can return it to its rightful owner," Detective Castro said.

"Good," Kate nodded.

"Thank you, Detective," Nick said standing up from his chair.

"Thank you, Mr. Mason… Ms. Harper," Detective Castro said.

As Kate and Nick walked out of his office, the detective called out, "Be careful, Ms. Harper. Try and keep her out of trouble, Mr. Mason."

Nick shook his head and scoffed, "If I had a dollar for every police detective that has told met that."

Detective Castro laughed. Whispering to himself he said, "I bet!"

Forty

Kate and Nick arrived at the VanLangen estate weaving in and out of busy construction workers. Marco DiNova was flipping pages of the work orders for the day.

"And now we have a wall to fix in the master bedroom. We'll have to factor that in when we get to the master suite," Marco said to the foreman.

"I can fix it. I was planning on resetting the closet door anyway. Cassie doesn't need to worry about being trapped in her own closet. Though as closets go, if you had to get stuck, it is a pretty nice one," Nick offered.

Marco turned and looked at Nick and Kate. "I appreciate your offer, Mr. Mason. But I can only work with qualified, licensed crews," Marco said.

"I'm licensed," Nick said.

"I have all of his credentials on my laptop. I'll forward them to you," Kate said.

"We already have a lot of catch-up work, boss. Every little bit helps," the foreman said.

"Fine, I mean, we're talking some drywall, right?" Marco said, his hands fluttering in the air in a dismissive gesture.

"Right. Dry wall. And some studs, insulation, beadboard. I can grab supplies…" Nick started.

"Give me a list of what you need, and I'll have it ready for you in an hour," the foreman said. "We have more material than we'll likely need for the interior projects."

"We'll whip up a cup of coffee in the meantime. Would you like one?" Kate asked the foreman.

The foreman's eyes widened, "I would love that. Thank you, Ms. Harper."

"We'll leave you two to it. I'll track you down when the coffee is ready," Kate said.

When they walked away, Nick whispered, "I don't think Marco likes me."

"He doesn't like how much *I* like you," Kate said. The words rolled out before she could weigh them. Already said, she just shrugged and smiled.

"How much is that?" Nick pressed, bumping her shoulder gently with his.

"Well, of all the eligible bachelors around here, you are the only one who isn't a murder suspect. And I find that *very* attractive," Kate teased.

"One of my more admirable qualities," Nick stood straight and snapped his linen shirt proudly.

Kate laughed and tugged at him, "Come on! You can help me figure out this infernal machine!"

Kate and Nick handed out trays of freshly brewed coffee drinks. All the while, Nick caught Marco keeping a close eye on him.

Showing the contractor that he knew he was being watched, Nick flashed a direct smile at the man. Receiving a perturbed scowl, Nick chuckled.

Not oblivious to the exchange, Kate corralled Nick away from the construction work and the overzealous Marco.

In the foyer, they found Cassie deep in conversation with Gustavo.

"I know, Gustavo. David did connect me with Marco. It doesn't mean he's untrustworthy. If that was the case, we'd have to include Donovan as well. It was David who set up the dinner before the awards banquet in L.A. He was the primary handler for…" Cassie said before her voice trailed off.

"Yeah," Gustavo bobbed his head. "I'm just saying, with everything going on around here, Hammit… Marco… we don't know who we can trust anymore."

Cassie sighed heavily, her chest falling.

"I'm just trying to look out for you, that's all," Gustavo said.

Placing a hand on the executive chef's forearm, Cassie said, "I know. I appreciate it."

Looking up, the pair saw Kate and Nick paused in the hallway.

Kate blushed, "I'm sorry. We didn't want to interrupt. We were just running up to plan fixing the closet."

"I have a few ideas I wanted to share while I'm at it," Nick said.

"Sure," Cassie nodded. "That would be great."

Turning to follow Kate and Nick up the stairs, Cassie looked back at Gustavo, "We'll catch up in a bit, okay?"

Gustavo nodded.

"Your ex-employee connected you with Marco?" Kate asked as they ascended the steps.

"Well, yeah. David was my right hand. He managed a lot of the miscellaneous details. Marco came highly recommended," Cassie said.

"And he connected you with Donovan," Kate added, her voice ringing.

"He did. David had a knack for connecting people. His abrupt departure aside, he was quite an asset," Cassie said.

Entering the master bedroom, seeing the mess from the cat burglar's exit, the weight of the last week fell on Cassie.

Noticing the cosmetic mogul's fallen affect, Nick said, "So, looking at the house blueprints, I saw some dead space behind the closet wall."

Cassie looked at Nick, waiting for the explanation.

"I had an idea. We can imbed your safe behind a rotating shoe rack. Only you will know it is there. A push of a button and I can make the wall and shoe rack move, revealing the safe. Almost as easy to access, but safe from prying eyes and jewel thieves," Nick said.

Cassie nodded and offered a thin, weary smile. "That would be great. Thank you."

"And if you like," Nick said excitedly, "I can revamp your security system. Plug some holes, add some modern tech like thermal cameras and digital tripwires…"

Cassie looked at Nick. Her eyes swept the ruggedly attractive man's face and said, "I have no idea what you just said. But, if it will make the estate safer, then, please. Have at it. Just have Marco order the items and add it to the remodel bill. I'll compensate you separately, if you like."

Nick looked taken aback, "Oh, I'll just do it. You're a friend of Kate's."

"I met Kate a week ago and a friend of hers is already offering to do me favors," Cassie said in a laugh.

Kate and Nick frowned.

Seeing their expressions, Cassie added, "I am so used to people looking for an angle. You two are something else. He's a keeper, Kate. So are you."

"I can see how all of this has affected you. No one should feel uncomfortable in their own home," Nick said. His words brought a smile to Kate's face.

"Thank you, Nick. You and Kate both have been far more concerned about me than those who are supposed to be closer, maybe save Merilu," Cassie said, her eyes instantly looking like they'd prefer to take back the sentiment.

Kate cocked her head and asked, "What about Donovan? And Marco? Gustavo and even Henrique?"

"I don't know," Cassie said, her head drooping. "The downside of being exceptionally wealthy, it becomes exceedingly difficult to know who your friends are."

"That's sounds rough," Kate said, her voice soft.

"You and Merilu are different. Not once have either of you asked anything of me. Gustavo as well. He has been there for me, without question," Cassie said.

Kate squinted. Her lips quivered as though she were afraid to ask, "What about Henrique?"

"Henrique?" Cassie winced. With a laugh, she said, "He may have asked the most. Forgiveness and forgetfulness."

Kate bobbed her head, her eyes sweeping her feet.

"He seems… interesting," Nick said, his voice ringing positive.

"He is a nice guy. He just never grew up," Cassie said.

Nick bristled at the comment.

"He is definitely charming. To maintain a relationship, you need to be dependable and faithful," Kate said.

"If you find one of those, keep them," Cassie quipped, her eyes moving to the back wall as if to visualize Nick's suggestions.

Nick shuffled uncomfortably. Pursing his lips, he asked, "How was Marco vetted?"

Cassie's eyes moved to Nick's, "David vouched for him. He had done jobs for other Palm Beach estates."

Nick nodded.

Cassie's phone buzzed. She glanced at it and sighed. Pointing toward the master suite veranda, she said, "I should take this."

Kate and Nick nodded, descending the stairs to give Cassie her privacy.

"You have my credentials. Do you have Marco's?" Nick asked.

Kate frowned, "I never asked."

"Hmm," Nick grunted.

Kate's eyes narrowed, but she refrained from commenting.

"My head is swirling. I am going to duck into the guest house to try and sort some things out," Kate said.

Nick nodded, his fingers already dancing along his phone's keyboard.

Kate stood back, her eyes sweeping across the board she had set up in Cassie VanLangen's guest house. Each column was titled with initials. A series of bullet points lined up underneath the title. Red arrows streaked across the board showing connections to one name circled at the bottom- Michelle.

Everyone seemed to have at least a cursory connection to the late spokesmodel. Cassie was at the top as Michelle was integral to her marketing campaigns, including the product that was postponed due to the model's death.

Teresa Lilley, Cassie's archrival was courting the model to work for her cosmetics company, a charge that seemed to be led by David Hammit.

Kate circled Hammit's initials.

Scratching her chin, she drew more arrows. Cassie's former right-hand man Hammit, now Teresa Lilley's confidant, seemed to be connected to everyone. He was the one who connected Cassie to Marco for the renovations. His role overlapped with Gustavo's when he was employed by Cassie. He seemed to lobby on behalf of Henrique, even though he set Cassie up with Donovan.

Kate's eyes narrowed as she subconsciously stared at Hammit's initials. What likely made him a strong business asset also put him uniquely in the middle of everything. He was courting Michelle to work for Teresa Lilley, but perhaps he was courting her for himself. Unrequited love was a strong motive.

Kate jumped as the guest house door flung open. Footsteps sounded throughout the house as they scampered from room to room. Suddenly Nick's head poked through the doorway.

"There you are!" Nick called, a broad smile splashed across his face.

"Here I am…" Kate repeated as she eyed the seemingly excited man.

"Murder board, of course," Nick said.

Kate winced, "I had to get my thoughts out."

Shaking his phone, Nick said, "I have news to add to it. And I have *my* number one suspect."

"Do you now?" Kate asked. Before Nick could speak, she blurted, "Let me guess. Marco DiNova."

Nick's face fell, "Yes."

"Aside from being a bit wandering with his eyes, he isn't the architect he purports to be," Kate said.

"Yes. Exactly," Nick said. "How did you…?"

Kate laughed, "I know enough about remodeling to see the construction foreman had to correct some of Marco's design work, like keeping him from trying to knock down a load bearing wall."

Nick cocked his head, "You knew?"

"I wasn't sure, but something tells me you have the proof," Kate said.

"Marco DiNova was a set builder, not an architect," Nick said.

"Set builder?" Kate frowned.

Nick nodded, "Yeah, you know, Hollywood type stuff. He designed movie sets and even some theme park facades. He knows aesthetic design, but not actual building construction."

"That starts to make some sense," Kate said. "So, why was he brought in for work around Palm Beach?"

"He had a stunning portfolio that showed off work of his in Naples, Malibu, Monaco… none of them real properties, though," Nick said. "Las Vegas hotels, movie sets and a storefront and restaurant at Florida's favorite theme park."

"When Cassie introduced us, she said he was highly regarded," Kate said.

"Regarded by who?" Nick asked.

"I guess David Hammit. He seemed to have his hand in most of Cassie's connections," Kate said.

"Maybe Marco bribed Hammit. Sounds like the bribable type," Nick said.

"Probably. We need to find out," Kate said.

"Maybe Marco killed Michelle to keep his secret?" Nick suggested.

"I don't know, that sounds like a stretch," Kate said.

"To move from a six-figure income to seven? That is a lot of reasons for murder," Nick said. "*And* he's a bit on the creepy side."

Kate's moved to the board. Picking up the pen, she placed an asterisk next to Marco's initials.

Forty-One

Kate and Nick abandoned their crime board discussion to head back to their rooms at the Breakers to change and get ready for Teresa Lilley's launch party.

Invited to the post-launch celebration, they met in the lobby of the hotel.

Nick pulled the cuff of his shirt cuff through the arms of his jacket as Kate turned the corner. For a moment, he stood frozen as he watched Kate stride toward him. Her stormy blue dress swished around her as she walked. The full-length gown tapered just below her knees. White filigree swirled around her shoulder straps and bodice.

Stopping, Kate frowned, "Is something wrong?"

"No," Nick said. His eyes swept over Kate. "You look… stunning."

Kate blushed and stepped beside him. Giving Nick a once over, she smiled, "You clean up pretty good, yourself."

Nick shuffled. Spreading the lapels of his jacket wide, he displayed a piece of silk protruding from his breast pocket, "I brought a tie, just in case."

With a laugh, Kate flopped her hand at him, "You just be you."

Nick's eyes went wide, "I can put shorts on?"

"Well, maybe *this* version of you. You look snappy," Kate said. Holding her arm out, she asked, "Shall we?"

Nick scooped her arm in his and with a nod, they strode out of the hotel lobby.

Arriving at Teresa Lilley's estate was a scene fit for the Met Gala. An actual red carpet was flanked with photographers and reporters. As cars came to a stop alongside the walkway to the house, all eyes turned to see who would climb out.

Kate looked sheepish at cameras flashed in front of her. Nick hesitated to get out of the car, but an insistent valet waited for him.

Joining Kate, he once more took her arm and escorted her up the red carpet toward Teresa's house. Just outside the door, they found Teresa receiving the guests.

A line had formed. To Kate it looked like the who's who of her crime board.

Teresa herself was closely flanked by David Hammit. Waiting in line to make their entrance were Marco DiNova, Gustavo and Merilu. A few guests in line behind them were Cassie and Donovan. Awkwardly gawking behind them was Henrique Desperaux.

"You always invite me to the best parties," Nick whispered in Kate's ear.

"Murder mystery parties are in vogue," Kate said.

"This one comes with a *real* murderer," Nick said.

"Let's make sure there aren't any more victims," Kate hissed receiving a hearty nod from Nick.

Teresa Lilley seemed to be having the time of her life. A broad smile was permanently etched across her face. Her arms reached out wide to give hugs as though everyone in line was a long-lost friend.

When she got to Marco, Gustavo and Merilu, her eyes went wide and shot into the line to find Cassie.

"I'm so glad you could all make it. It is such an honor. Thank you for coming," Teresa said even as Merilu dodged a hug and offered a flat smile as she lunged to slip past the door and into the house.

"Cassie VanLangen, Donovan Drake. I'm glad you are here. You have been through so much!" Teresa's wide arms didn't allow Cassie to slip by unaccosted.

Cassie gracefully accepted a brief hug. Her eyes landed on David Hammit who danced nervously behind his new boss. "It sounds like I can add corporate espionage to the list. Your fragrance is oddly familiar," Cassie said.

Teresa grinned, "Great minds, right? I mean, someone told me your pending line is similar."

"Eerily," Cassie said.

"Well, enjoy your evening, Cassie," Teresa said, looking past her rival to the next guest.

When Kate and Nick arrived at the front of the line, Teresa eyed them, "Cassie's friends. How wonderful you could make it."

Give each a quick side hug, the hostess quickly focused on the rest of the line.

David Hammit eyed the pair as they entered the house.

Nick leaned toward Kate, "You might be right about Hammit. Though I wouldn't put it past that lady."

Kate laughed, "I think she'd do just about anything to upstage Cassie. But her dutiful little soldier gives me the creeps. I can easily see him committing murder."

"We have a lot of people to keep an eye on this evening," Nick said.

"Marco, Hammit, Teresa…" Kate said.

"What about Cassie's new guy, Donovan?" Nick asked.

"Everyone is fair game," Kate said. "Including her former beau Henrique Desperaux."

"Right," Nick nodded. His eyes found a server dancing through the crows with a canape. "Ooh, those look good!"

Knifing through the crowd, Nick caught up to the server. Draping his hand over her silver platter, he cupped a Gouda filled tart. Eyeing his prize, he started to take a bite. Hearing a pair of familiar voices, he paused to listen.

"This isn't the time or place!" Cassie hissed at Donovan.

"I mean, why is he here?" Donovan asked.

"I didn't invite him," Cassie said.

"Why am *I* here?" Donovan pressed.

"Don't be like that. I don't really want to be here, but I am not going to let a lesser opponent intimidate me," Cassie said, full well knowing her words had a double meaning. Her message seemed to work as her new beau fell in line.

Making his way back to Kate, brushing canape off his jacket lapel, Nick reported, "I don't think Cassie's boyfriend is very happy to be here."

"I don't blame him. Attending the party of Cassie's rival to celebrate a product launch that was stolen from her," Kate said.

"I think he is not thrilled with that Henrique guy being here," Nick said.

Stifling a chuckle, Kate said, "Yeah, I could imagine. Desperaux is a handful."

"You don't strike me as the jealous type," Nick said. Instantly regretting his timing of words, Marco DiNova stepped up. His tailored tuxedo gave him an air of austerity.

"Ms. Kate… and Mick. How nice to see you here," Marco said.

"Nick," Kate corrected.

"Right. Nick," Marco nodded. "Could I get you a glass of champagne? I'm on my way."

"I…" Nick started.

Kate offered a steady smile, "Thank you. Nick and I were just about to head over."

"Don't bother. I'd be happy to get it for you. Both of you. Champagne and… an American light beer?" Marco asked.

Nick bristled.

"I think two bourbons on the rocks," Kate said.

Marco studied Kate for a moment. A smile snaked across his lips, "Very well. I'll be right back."

As the Italian faux designer walked away, Nick snapped, "*He's* the guy. *Please* let it be him."

"Him who?" a voice asked from behind them.

"Merilu," Kate said, giving her friend a hug.

Merilu smiled at the couple

"Nick, it's nice to see you again," Merilu said. "You clean up rather nicely.

"It's good to see you, too, Merilu. You look lovely," Nick said.

"You really think there is a murderer among us tonight?" Merilu asked as she leaned in close to the pair. "Is it that little rat, David Hammit?"

"He seems to be the architect for trouble. He could have got his nose in a bit too deep," Kate suggested.

"Michelle barely gave him the time of day. Yet, he was all over her like a nervous teenager," Merilu said.

"Infatuation is not an uncommon motive for murder," Kate said.

"My money is on Marco," Nick said.

Merilu looked up, "Marco? I mean, he is a bit of a schmoozer, but I think he's harmless."

"Did you know he wasn't a real architect? Or contractor? He was a Hollywood set designer," Nick said.

Merilu scrunched her nose and shrugged, "Could be similar skill sets."

"I don't know," Nick said, his eyes watching Marco wade through the crowd with drinks in hand.

"Bourbon on the rocks," Marco said, handing highball glasses to Kate and Nick. "Merilu, can I get you something?"

"You can walk me to the bar," Merilu said, holding her arm out.

Marco looked at Kate for a moment before accepting. Merilu cast a sly glance over her shoulder as she let Marco lead her away from the pair.

"I like her," Nick said, his voice thoughtful.

"She is a good person," Kate said.

"Capable of murder?" Nick asked.

Kate watched as they disappeared into the crowd, "They say anyone can be in the wrong situation. But I don't believe it. Murder suggests it is unjust. I think the vast majority of people would never cross the line."

"What makes someone do something like that? Just to get ahead?" Nick asked.

"No," Kate shook her head and looked thoughtful. "To not lose what they already have."

"Like Marco and his new Palm Beach lifestyle?" Nick asked.

"It's not him," Kate said, an air of confidence in her voice.

Nick studied Kate. His eyes widened, "You know who killed Michelle Goss."

Kate's eyes glazed for a moment as she decided what to do.

"Care to share?" Nick asked.

"You figured it out a while ago. Who at Cassie's party had the most to lose?" Kate asked.

Nick shook his head and shrugged.

"I can't believe I didn't put it together before," Kate fumed.

"Put what together, Ms. Harper?" a stern voice snapped behind them.

Nick and Kate turned to see Detective Castro. His head cocked to the side as if to compel Kate to share.

"The Palm Beach lifestyle is nearly unattainable for most people," Kate said.

"It isn't easy," Detective Castro said, his eyes sweeping the crowd. Glancing at Teresa, he said, "Some people cheat."

Nick looked at Marco, "Some people lie."

They all looked at David Hammit and said simultaneously, "And some people steal it."

Forty-Two

The detective made a beeline for David Hammit.

Kate and Nick followed in tow. Kate reached out and touched Detective Castro's shoulder. "It's not him," she said.

The detective stopped and spun on his heel. Looking at Kate, his eyes narrowed, "What do you mean?"

"He's a weasel, who likely committed a number of crimes against Cassie and her company. But he didn't kill Michelle Goss," Kate said.

"Who did?" Castro snapped. His voice told he wasn't in the mood for a guessing game.

"Someone who had a lot to lose. Someone who ironically found something but was caught. By Michelle Goss. Michelle confronted them at Cassie's party. In desperation to not lose everything, they struck out and killed Michelle in the gazebo," Kate said.

"The ring!" Nick gasped.

"The ring?" Detective Castro frowned.

"The ring was lost. It was found- a fortune for most people. In the palm of their hands. But Michelle saw them. When confronted, they must have snapped and killed Michelle," Kate said.

"But you found the ring. Nearly a week after the murder," Detective Castro said. His voice tinged with irritation.

"We did. Because the person who found it realized what they already had was worth a whole lot more. They tried to put the ring back– where it got lost in the first place. They tossed the ring just like Cassie did. They washed their hands of it and returned to their very comfortable life," Kate said. "With Michelle gone, no one would know. Their secret would be buried with her. A betrayal that never actually happened."

The detective's hands fell to his hips, "Are you going to get to the who?"

Kate nodded. Her eyes drifted across the crowd. Waiting in line at the bar, were Marco, Merilu, Gustavo, and Donovan. Not far from them was David Hammit having a terse conversation with his former boss.

"Let's go catch us a murderer, Detective," Kate said, leading Nick and Detective Castro. through the crowd.

The detective looked at Nick, "You know what she's talking about?"

"I do now," Nick said. "Got your cuffs handy?"

Detective Castro patted his pocket.

As they neared the group, the detective hung back, a keen eye fixed on Kate.

"Can I talk to you for a moment?" Kate asked.

Everyone's eyes turned toward Kate. One set of eyes looked uncomfortable as they landed on the detective who trailed close behind her.

With a nod, Gustavo shot his drink down his throat and left the bar. Snaking through the crowd, they found their way to a sitting room near the foyer.

"What… what's this about?" Gustavo asked. "Is everything okay?"

"No, Gustavo. I'm afraid everything isn't okay," Kate said. "You killed Michelle Goss."

Gustavo leaned back, his eyes wide in shock, "What? Why would I…?"

"Because she knew you found the ring. You started to bring it to Cassie, but you had a change of heart, and you pocketed it. You held more money in the palm of your hand than you had in your entire lifetime. Unfortunately, Michelle Goss saw you. She confronted you at the party. You panicked. Cassie values loyalty and honesty. You were afraid that if were caught stealing from her, or technically Henrique- but that doesn't really matter- she might lose faith in you," Kate said.

Gustavo swallowed hard.

"You have a good life at the estate. You'll never acquire the wealth of the people that you serve, but you live in Palm Beach. On a grand estate right by the ocean. You get to surf anytime you want. When Cassie is away, you have your own multi-million-dollar oceanfront resort. That moment of right or wrong tested you," Kate said.

"You don't… you don't have any proof," Gustavo said.

"Actually, I do. And you gave it to us. When we were looking for the ring in the pool filter, you said the diamond in the water would have been nearly invisible, but the platinum would shine. Henrique tried to give the ring to Cassie at night. She immediately tossed it. The only way you would have known what the ring was made of is if you had seen it yourself," Kate said.

"That's… I…," Gustavo looked at detective, searching for a way out.

Nick instinctively moved to block the door.

"I didn't mean to. I didn't mean to kill her. She was drunk and raising her voice. I just wanted her to be quiet. I was going to give the ring back, but then everything got weird. I threw the ring in the pool. I left her lying there. It was terrible," Gustavo said, his head drooping.

"Gustavo Silvestri, you are under arrest for the murder of Michelle Goss," Detective Castro said, leading Cassie's houseman out of the Lilley estate as he read him his rights.

"Gustavo…" Nick whistled. "I liked him. He was nice."

"He was… as murderers go," Kate said.

Nick cocked his head at Kate's words.

Word around the party spread quickly. Soon, those connected to Cassie and her estate had gathered around the front steps of the house. Gustavo was placed in the rear of a squad car as Detective Castro supervised.

Looking up and seeing the audience, the detective bristled.

Seeing one partygoer in particular, he walked over.

"I have something that belongs to you. The District Attorney said we didn't need to hold on to it anymore," Detective Castro said placing a box firmly in Henrique Desperaux's hand. "Take care of it. It tends to be trouble."

"You have no idea," Henrique said curling his fingers around the box.

Spinning, his cheeks glowed as he found himself staring at a small crowd. The ring had been trouble. It embarrassed him.

Clearing his throat, he announced, "The detective is right. This ring is troubling. It represents my biggest failure. It is a reminder that love is special and needs to be paramount. Love is worth everything and the love of your life should be cherished. This ring represents a bond that should have been. I broke it. I am so, so sorry."

Taking strides up the steps and the onlooking crowd, Henrique brushed past Donovan Drake and stood in front of Cassie.

Dropping to a knee, Desperaux held his hand out in front of him. His head bowed, he said, "I don't deserve a second chance. I am not sure I deserve you. But I do know that I love you more than anything. And if you do give me chance, I will devote my life to celebrating you and my love for you. Every… single… day!"

With his thumbs, Desperaux carefully presented the gleaming ring to Cassie.

"Cassie VanLangen, I humbly beg you to give this foolish man a chance. Just one chance to be your husband. To make you my priority today and every day," Desperaux pleaded.

Looking up and into Cassie's eyes, he plucked the ring from the box. Squeezed between this thumb and finger, he held it up.

Cassie looked at Desperaux. She looked at the ring. Her eyes danced around the crowd for a split second before narrowing. Snatching the ring from Desperaux's fingers, he winced, ready for her to once more throw the ring into the landscape with peeved abandon.

Instead, she held the ring up and studied it. "It is a beautiful ring. Are you sure it isn't cursed?" Cassie asked.

Desperaux swallowed hard, "I… I don't know. We can have it blessed?"

Cassie smiled, "Well. Are you going to put it on me or do I have to do it myself?"

Desperaux leapt to his feet and slid the ring onto Cassie's finger.

Her arms snaked around Desperaux's neck, and she pulled him into a kiss.

Donovan's cheeks paled as he looked around. "Does this mean…?"

Merilu placed a hand on his shoulder and nodded.

"I'm going back to the bar," Donovan said, his lips in a pout.

Everyone who remained on Teresa Lilley's front steps applauded.

"What do you say you take me away from here?" Cassie asked.

"I was hoping you would ask," Desperaux said. With a gallant bow to the crowd, he slipped his arm around Cassie and pulled her tight as he escorted her to the awaiting valets.

The paparazzi were lost in the moment, taking it in. Suddenly aware, they took rapid fire shots of the couple.

"Well, I didn't see that coming," Nick said.

"I kind of did," Kate said.

"Of course you did," Nick grinned.

"Take me away from here?" Kate asked, her eyes locking on his.

"I was hoping you'd ask," Nick said. With a wave toward the valet to retrieve his car, he looked over his shoulder. "What about your friends?"

Marco slid up to Merilu. Holding his hand out, he offered to escort her back inside.

"He may not be a real architect, but he isn't a murderer," Kate said. Looking up at Nick, she smiled, "They'll be fine!"

Forty-Three

The VanLangen estate was a mix of relief, exhaustion and, for the first time in over a week, hope.

Kate and Merilu worked together to craft brunch for the bedraggled group of friends. Nick worked the bar pouring mimosas and bellinis. Cassie sat next to a permanently smiling Henrique Desperaux, her hand slipped into his. The five-million-dollar engagement ring caught the morning sun and sent out brilliant beams of light, turning the patio into a kaleidoscope.

Marco, accepting defeat against Nick, turned his Italian charm on Merilu while he worked the espresso machine. While wary, Merilu didn't seem to mind the attention.

When they had gathered around the patio table, Cassie stood and addressed the group. Her mimosa glass held in the air, she took a long, deep breath before she spoke, "To friends. Over the past week, you have all become like family to me. I will be forever heartbroken with loss of Michelle. I am deeply saddened by the wicked turn of our friend Gustavo. The fact that keeping a secret from me was worth the taking of an innocent life. I will never wash that from my heart and mind."

Cassie's eyes fell on Marco and then swung toward Desperaux, "No more lies. No more secrets. No more wondering whether our words are true. I can't handle anymore. What I do need, are real friends. Life partners. People I can trust, blemishes and all."

Henrique Desperaux gave a nod.

Marco twisted in his seat, almost spilling his drink. "I, uh, I have something to say."

"You aren't a real architect or contractor. I know. But you do have an amazing eye and finishing touch. You tell a story through your work. Just, hire an actual contractor, please," Cassie said.

Marco's cheeks reddened, "I'm sorry to have deceived you."

"Don't do it again," Cassie said, her words pointed.

"I promise. It is a new leaf for Marco DiNova," Marco said.

Cassie's eyes cast on Desperaux.

"I pledge my life to you. Sincerely, I give you my love for all my days," Desperaux said.

Cassie's phone buzzed and a video image appeared. Hitting a button, she looked at the group. Once more holding her glass high, she said, "To friends, to family, to Michelle, may she look down on us knowing that even in her death, we had her back!"

"Hear, hear!" the group cheered and took a sip of their breakfast drinks.

"Excuse me," Cassie said and walked into the house.

In moments, she reappeared with Detective Castro in tow behind her.

"Excuse the interruption. I thought you all might like an update," the detective said. Scanning the group around the patio table, he said, "Gustavo Silvestri confessed to everything. He told me in our interview that he snapped. He felt horrible for what he had done but panicked. Not knowing what to do, he tried to pretend he was nowhere near Michelle Goss and the gazebo that night. He said he owed Ms. VanLangen a lot. The thought of stealing from her was a cross too much to bear. He seems genuinely remorseful for deceiving Ms. VanLangen and for Michelle Goss. The District Attorney will decide if that has any impact on his case."

Letting his words sink in, the detective continued, "I thank you all for the patience throughout the investigation and in some instances, your assistance."

His eyes landed on Kate and Nick.

"I'm glad justice was served, Detective," Kate said.

Castro nodded.

"Would you like to join us, Detective?" Cassie asked.

"I need to get back to the station. I'm meeting with the District Attorney before closing out the case from my end. But, thank you. Enjoy your breakfast. And… enjoy each other. I'll let myself out, Ms. VanLangen," the detective said and left the group to their brunch.

As they settled in and dished up crepes with berries and lemon curd along with thick strips of applewood bacon, Cassie's phone chimed again.

With a glance, her brows furrowed. With a sigh, she hit a button on her phone. Rising out of her seat, the rest of the group watched as Cassie strode toward the house. In moments, she returned to the patio with Teresa Lilley on her heels.

The competing cosmetic moguls stood beside the breakfast table. Teresa Lilley cleared her throat, "I, uh, Cassie thought you all might want to hear what I have to say, too."

The breakfast silver was laid down and all eyes were on the cosmetic queens.

"Sometimes in our world, we seize on opportunities that seem like a good idea at the time. In retrospect, they are the opposite of the elegance and grace that our brands strive to embody. In a fit of guilt, David Hammit shared that he had broken into Ms. VanLangen's office safe and stolen the formula which he gave to us. It was pretty clear where it came from, but I didn't ask for it. It was just given to me. I used the disruption in Cassie's launch to take advantage and launch a product of my own. *Her* product. Furthermore, it was taking advantage of poor Michelle's death. I cannot live with that. I came to tell you that I'm sorry. I'm sorry and I am donating all profits from the new product to a charity in Michelle's name. If you prefer, Cassie, I can give those profits back to you," Teresa said.

Cassie shook her head, "No. I love the fact that Michelle's legacy can live on."

"May we borrow her likeness? You technically still own the rights," Teresa said.

"I'll check with her family. It is their call. But I think they'll like it, too," Cassie said.

Teresa pivoted so that she was squarely in front of Cassie. "I am so sorry. I'm sorry for all this and I'm sorry for the way I acted."

Cassie studied Teresa for a moment.

Teresa asked, "Can you forgive me?"

With a nod, Cassie tossed her arms around her rival and gave her a hug. "I forgive you."

Teresa's face looked genuinely relieved.

"Good luck with David. Watch your back," Cassie said.

"Oh, I fired him last night," Teresa said.

Cassie chuckled, "That explains the six calls this morning. Stay for breakfast?"

Teresa looked at the table and panned across the guests, "It looks lovely, but I have some things that need to be taken care of. Rain check?"

"Rain check," Cassie agreed. "I'll see you out."

As the two rivals disappeared into the house, the group around the table swapped glances.

Kate broke the silence, "You have a good one, there, Desperaux."

"Don't mess it up," Merilu warned.

"I do have an amazing one and I have no intention of messing it up," Desperaux said.

As Cassie stepped back out on the patio, Merilu raised her glass, "To Cassie and Henrique. May their days be sweet, prosperous and drama free."

"Here, here!" Cassie chimed enthusiastically.

Forty-Four

The waves of the Atlantic smashed against the rocks dividing the Breakers and the VanLangen estate, sending water shooting high into the air. An offshore storm delivered stronger than usual swells to Palm Beach.

The couple walking along the beach paused to enjoy the spectacle.

Kate pressed into Nick, a hand on his stomach and on his back, "This is spectacular."

"It's gorgeous," Nick said.

"I'm glad you're here," Kate said.

Nick looked down into Kate's eyes, "You sure? You seemed to try pretty hard to keep me in Cape May."

Kate's eyes drifted from Nick to the churning sea. "I want to know that I can take care of myself," she said softly.

Nick chuckled, "You can most assuredly take care of yourself. But just because you can handle something alone, doesn't mean you have to."

"We do make a good team," Kate said, looking back at Nick.

"I like to think so. Isn't it a bit more fun to work together?" Nick asked.

"It is," Kate said, nodding.

Nick's feet shuffled in the sand, "I *know* you can take care of yourself. You are one of the strongest women that I know. You are one of the strongest people that I know."

"I don't know about that..." Kate demurred.

"I do. You are. But it doesn't mean that I don't worry about you. You may not need me when you push your nose into a murder investigation, but I sure like being there in the end to look at you. To hold you and to know that you're okay," Nick said.

Kate looked up at Nick. Annoyed at her own watery eyes, she pressed up and pushed her lips against his.

Wrapping her hand around the back of his head, she held him close until they could barely breathe. In a breathy whisper, she said, "I like you being here to hold me when it's all over too."

"Then let me," the words escaped Nick's lips before he could filter them.

Studying his eyes for a moment, Kate's eyes narrowed before she nodded, "All right. Offer accepted."

Nick had to shake his head. He looked wary, "You mean it?"

"I do," Kate said, her arms extended to keep her hands secure on his neck.

"So... where to next?" Nick asked.

Kate let out a grin, "Oh, I think you are going to like this next one..."

About the Author

 Seth Sjostrom is a serial entrepreneur, adventurer and author. His novels include the thrillers *Blood in the Snow*, *Blood in the Water*, *Blood in the Sand*, *Penance*, *Penance: Unredeemable*, *Penance: Absolution*, *Patriot X*, *Patriot X: Insurrection*, *Dark Chase*, *Dark Chase: Dead Run* and *Dark Chase: Beast* as well as the romances *Back to Carolina*, *Finding Christmas*, *The Tree Farm*, *Letters from Santa*, *The Nativity*, *The Toy Store*, *The Christmas Café*, *Love at the Christmas Con* and *A Southern Charm Christmas*. Seth is also the author of the popular Beach House Mysteries series which include *Trouble on Treasure Island*, *A Caper on Carolina Beach* and *Peril in Palm Beach*.

Seth has also partnered with Hire Heroes USA, Special Operations Warrior Foundation, Jen Lilley's Christmas is Not Canceled and Jill Wagner's the Patriotic Pick as well as the Mel Greene Institute to Stop Human Trafficking.

www.SethSjostrom.com
Twitter: @SethSjostrom
Facebook: @authorSethSjostrom
Instagram: @SethSjostrom

More Books by Seth

Christmas Titles
Finding Christmas
The Tree Farm
The Nativity
The Toy Store
The Christmas Café
Love at The Christmas Con
A Southern Charm Christmas

Beach House Mysteries
Trouble on Treasure Island
A Caper on Carolina Beach
Peril on Palm Beach

Other Titles
Back to Carolina
Penance
Penance: Unredeemable
Penance: Absolution
Penance: Awakening
Dark Chase
Dark Chase: Dead Run
Dark Chase: Beast
Patriot X
Patriot X: Insurrection
Blood in the Snow
Blood in the Water
Blood in the Sand

Children's Books
Letters from Santa
The Hollow
Cryptid Rangers: The Secret of the Skunk Ape
Cryptid Rangers: The Beast of Bladenboro
The Heart of a Reindeer
The (Too) Helpful Little Angel
Hurricane Channing and the Puppy Christmas
Hurricane Channing and the Lost Flamingo
Hurricane Channing and the Mommy Manatee
Hurricane Channing and the Daily Dolphin